What did you say to a husband you hadn't seen for ten years and couldn't remember?
The husband you would never remember...

"Hi," she said. "Thanks for calling."

"Yeah. You, too." He laughed, but not with humor. "I understand you've had a head injury. Memory loss."

"Fortunately, I escaped a lot of the problems that usually go with that kind of injury. In fact, I'm a midwife—"

His sharp intake of breath stopped her. "Go on."

"But I lost my entire personality. My earliest memory is from ten years ago, in a hospital in Boulder. Someone found me down by the creek and brought me in." It was then that she'd walked into her own life in the second act, with no idea what had happened before. "I understand we have a daughter."

"Yes. Gabriela. She's twelve."

The sheriff had said her parents and grandparents were dead, that Cullen and Gabriela were her only known family. "And...have you remarried?"

She had time to untangle the phone cord halfway before he said, "No." After a pause, he asked, "What about you? Involved with anyone else?"

"No."

He cleared his throat, away from the phone. "Then I'd like to see you."

To see me?

"I want you to come home."

ABOUT THE AUTHOR

Margot Early's first Superromance novel, *The Third Christmas*, was published in 1994 and was a RITA Award finalist for Best First Book. *The Keeper*, her second novel, was a finalist for the 1996 Janet Dailey Award. She is profiled in the *Romance Writer's Sourcebook*, published by Writer's Digest Books, and has been quoted in the *Wall Street Journal* and in newspaper articles across the country. *You Were on My Mind* is Margot's eighth Superromance title; watch for the other two books in her Midwives series, coming next year.

Margot's novella, *Soul Kitchen*, appeared in an anthology, *For My Daughter*, published this past spring.

When not wandering the fictional realms of her stories, Margot lives in Colorado with her husband and son.

Books by Margot Early

HARLEQUIN SUPERROMANCE

Don't miss any of our special offers. Write to us at the following address for information on our newest releases.

Harlequin Reader Service
U.S.: 3010 Walden Ave., P.O. Box 1325, Buffalo, NY 14269
Canadian: P.O. Box 609, Fort Erie, Ont. L2A 5X3

YOU WERE ON MY MIND
Margot Early

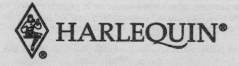

TORONTO • NEW YORK • LONDON
AMSTERDAM • PARIS • SYDNEY • HAMBURG
STOCKHOLM • ATHENS • TOKYO • MILAN • MADRID
PRAGUE • WARSAW • BUDAPEST • AUCKLAND

ISBN 0-373-70802-5

YOU WERE ON MY MIND

YOU WERE ON
MY MIND

PROLOGUE

Jenny Hix, Tennessee
November

"PEOPLE MUST BE GETTING their Christmas packages in the mail early."

"Before Thanksgiving?" Tara laughed. "I doubt it, Mom." The line was creeping, but Tara recognized several faces from the midwifery conference she and her mother and her sister, Ivy, had just attended. The conference, hosted by a local midwifery school, must have doubled the size of the small town of Jenny Hix. And sure, they'd be in this line for twenty minutes, but "You know, I'm so high from the conference that not even this line can get me down."

Her mother sighed.

"You don't have to wait, Mom. Why don't you go find Ivy, and I'll meet you guys at the deli?"

"No." Francesca sighed again. "Let's stick to our plan. If I try to find Ivy, she'll probably come back here, and I'll miss her. You know how it is."

If she sighs one more time, I'm going to lose it. The sighs asked more plainly than words why Tara needed to mail a check to the phone company right now, today. Tara saw no reason to share that particular war story with her mother, though she'd told Ivy; there was nothing you couldn't tell Ivy. She'd realized that soon after meeting Ivy seven years ago. Ivy was special, which was most of why Tara had suggested to her mother that they adopt her, make Ivy part of their family. It wasn't a legal adoption, but they'd had a ceremony, and Ivy had taken Francesca's last name as her own.

Anyhow, if she tried to explain to Francesca about the last time her phone was cut off, her mother would suggest she quit working at Maternity House—the birth clinic on the border paid very little—go to nursing school, get certified as a nurse-midwife....

That conversation just wasn't going to happen. No way was she going to bow to the political pressure to become a certified nurse-midwife. She'd attended over two thousand births in three countries, with just one stillbirth and one Down's baby—unavoidable outcomes in each case. If anything, the midwifery conference had strengthened her conviction to remain a direct-entry midwife, whatever the legal and financial ramifications, whatever the personal cost.

The post office line moved again. Francesca was rubbing her temples. Irritated, Tara faced the posters on the corkboard above the desk. Wanted posters, missing persons. It looked like no one ever changed the posters; one of them was for a man who'd disappeared in 1984.

Tara studied the faces of two missing girls. She wished she knew them, had seen them alive and well. She wished she could reassure their families. But the faces were unfamiliar, and she moved on to another poster, showing a woman who had disappeared from Guyandotte, West Virginia, a decade ago.

Gasping, she grabbed Francesca and spun her around. "Look. *Look.*"

"Oh, God. Now what?"

"Keep my place." Tara climbed over the cable and crowded up against a trash can to scrutinize the poster. The woman was blond and blue-eyed, born 9-13-66. Her suntan brought out a light smattering of freckles. Tara studied the small, straight nose, the wide smile and even white teeth. Only the hair was different—shoulder length and turned up at the ends in the picture, long and straight now.

She took a deep breath and read the instructions, what sheriff's office to contact. She should write down the number. Oh, hell…

"Tara!" her mother hissed as Tara tore down the poster. "I think that's illegal."

Tara had been in jail so many times she'd lost count. Student demonstrations, practicing medicine without a license, standing up against oppression in Chile—and plain old bad luck in Mexico. Ignoring her mother's protest, she climbed back over the cable and handed her the flyer. When she spoke, her voice cracked. "It's *Ivy.*"

CHAPTER ONE

Guyandotte, West Virginia

SOMETHING HAD HAPPENED. Cullen knew it.

To Gabriela?

Or to Daddy...?

The sheriff of Guyandotte County, West Virginia, had not come into Mountain Photography for a new campaign photo. He was wearing his got-news-for-you face.

"Hi, Orrin." Cullen waited for bad news the way he had ten years ago, for news that Gina's body had been found.

"Cully." Orrin Pratt had known him since he was five years old and licking an ice-cream cone in his daddy's chambers at the courthouse. The sheriff arranged his bulk in one of the customer chairs in front of the reception desk. "How's business?"

"Good." He'd just finished up school photos and he had four weddings booked before Christmas. *Say it, Orrin. Whatever it is, you're making me nervous.*

The sheriff flipped open the album on the desk, skimmed the graduation photos and baby pictures. Then he shut the book with a bang.

He wouldn't be acting this way if someone was hurt.

Or dead.

"Found your wife, Cully. And she's alive."

THE STUDIO HAD NEVER seemed so quiet. The name, phone number and address the sheriff had left stared up at Cullen from the counter. *She figured you might have remarried. She wanted you to have the chance to contact her when you felt ready. But count on it, if you don't, she'll contact you. We had to tell her the basics, Cully.*

The basics were a husband.

And a daughter. Gabriela.

Cullen massaged the bridge of his nose and reread the slip of paper.

Ivy Walcott, P. O. Box 39, Precipice, Colorado.

She'd changed her name.

She's had a head injury, Cully. Has no recollection of her life as Gina Till. Or Gina Naggy, before she'd married him.

How would he tell Gabriela? Not just Gabriela, either. He shut his eyes and pictured the faces in his life. His daughter, his parents, his sister and her husband, his sister-in-law...

Matthew.

And one more face, the face he really didn't want to see, especially after he shared this news.

Tracy would recover fast and say how wonderful for Gabriela. She would back off from him and respect the bonds of his marriage to a woman the sheriff had assured him would be a perfect stranger—and would consider him a stranger, too.

As he reached for the phone, an idea occurred to him, casting a new slant on his ambivalence, on all his confused feelings.

If Gina didn't remember him, had *she* found someone else?

Precipice, Colorado

"IT'S FOR YOU." Blue eyes somber, Francesca handed the phone to her daughter, the daughter she'd adopted as an adult when Ivy had admitted to Tara and Francesca that she had no family of her own—and no past she could remember. Now, seven years later, Ivy's unremembered past was on the phone. Covering the receiver, Francesca said, "It's him."

"Thanks, Mom." Ivy tried to make her smile reassuring.

Tara, who had decided to stay in Precipice until Ivy's husband contacted her, left the living room of the Victorian house Ivy and Francesca rented. Her mother followed. Ivy knew they'd done this to give her privacy.

But it felt like desertion.

She forced herself to speak. "Hello?"

"Hi. This is Cullen Till." The unfamiliar voice was deeper than she'd imagined, his slight drawl interesting, almost musical.

What did you say to the husband you hadn't seen for ten years and couldn't remember? The husband you would never remember. "Hi," she replied. "Thanks for calling."

"Yeah. You, too." He laughed, but not with humor. "I understand you've had brain damage."

"A temporal lobe lesion. Fortunately, I escaped a lot of the problems that usually go with a head injury. In fact, I'm a midwife—"

His sharp intake of breath stopped her. "Go on."

"But I lost my entire personality. My earliest memory is from ten years ago, in a hospital in Boulder. Someone found me down by the creek and brought me in." It was then that she'd walked into her own life in the second act, with no idea what had happened before.

And this man... She told him, "I'm so sorry. It must have been bad for you." The Colorado police had tried to learn her identity a decade ago, with no success. She'd known that someone, somewhere, must be worrying. "My sister... Sorry, that'll confuse you. My friends saw the flyer in a post office in Tennessee. We'd been at a midwifery conference. We called the sheriff right away."

"He told me." In his studio, Cullen held his head in his hand. She was a midwife. *You didn't lose as much of your personality as you think, Gina.*

Ivy settled on the nineteenth-century couch that Tara hated and Francesca treasured. It was a couch that made you sit on the edge of your seat, and there was no way she could do anything else. There was no other way she could ask the questions she must.

"I understand we have a daughter."

"Yes. Gabriela. She's twelve."

The sheriff had said her parents and grandparents were dead, that Cullen and Gabriela were her only known family. "And...have you remarried?"

She had time to untangle the phone cord halfway before he said, "No."

"I hope you didn't suffer much. Worrying."

After a pause he asked, "What about you? Involved with anyone else?"

"No."

He cleared his throat, away from the phone. "Then I'd like to see you."

To see me?

"I want you to come home."

Eight, nine, ten years ago, she would have donated an organ to hear someone say those words. Then, while she was in nursing school, she'd met Tara and Francesca at a midwifery conference. For the first time in her new existence, she'd found friends; it had been Tara's idea to invite her into their family. Now, Tara was her sister and Francesca her mother—the only family she had.

No. She had a family she couldn't recall in Guyandotte, West Virginia. A family who wanted Gina Till to come home.

But Gina Till was as dead as her husband must have feared.

"I want to see Gabriela. I definitely want to know my daughter. But I'm not the woman you remember. I won't know your face. I'll never share your memories."

"Unless I share them with you."

It sounded intimate, a man who'd loved the woman she used to be, carefully filling her in on her missing past.

A man and his daughter were waiting for her to come home. They'd waited ten years. She shivered. The man was a stranger to her; so was their daughter. A daughter she'd given birth to, and held and nursed and loved.

She said, "Do you mean...come there to stay?"

A long breath from the other end of the phone.

"I'm telling you, Cullen, I'm not the same."

"Nobody is after ten years. But I married you for the long haul. You have a home here with us if you want it."

He was brave or honorable or crazy—she didn't know which. She whispered, "The man who sets his sights firmly on the outcome will avoid the entanglements that befall people in relationships."

"What's that?"

"The *I Ching*, I think." She'd made him promises, too, in her former life. For richer for poorer, for better for worse, in sickness and in health.

This was the worse part.

Was it right to try to keep those vows? She wished the issue was black and white; instead it was foggy, obscured by mist and mountains. How many times during those first hours in Tennessee had she gazed northeast? They could have driven on to West Virginia, but she and Francesca had had pregnant clients waiting at home in Colorado.

Maybe Cullen still loved Gina Till. Maybe he was simply honoring his promise. In any case, he wanted her "home."

Who was this man? What did he look like? What did he believe? What did he eat for dinner? Was there any chance at all that they could be compatible? Given her usual disagreements with the men she dated, she didn't think so.

But they had a daughter.

She stalled. She asked him about himself and Gabriela.

They lived on her—Gina's—family property in a hundred-year-old cabin. She heard the satisfaction in his voice as he described the additions he'd made, how he'd tried to modernize without compromising the integrity of the building. He told her about his work, portrait and freelance photography. He drank little and didn't smoke. His parents and siblings lived fifteen minutes away from him and Gabriela. Gabriela took ballet. Gradually, he filled in some of the blanks in her life, as well as the years they'd spent apart.

Ivy remembered how she'd arrived at the Boulder hospital. The unanswered questions were all relevant.

"What kind of marriage did we have?"

Just a brief hesitation. "Loving. We were friends first. Like…the pillars of the temple."

"What do you mean?"

"The pillars of the temple must stand apart. Kahlil Gibran on marriage."

"That's beautiful."

In his studio, Cullen clutched an arm around himself. Gina had picked that reading for their wedding.

Ivy Walcott had never heard it.

Ivy said, "You never answered my question. If you're hoping I'll come to stay."

It seemed to her that his next pause wasn't hesitation. It was something else. "Yes."

"Because of Gabriela."

"Partly."

He has reason to want me back. For him, there were more than promises. There were memories. *But I have none of him.* She had only this conversation and the way the sheriff had spoken of him—with respect and familiarity. But Cullen Till held the keys to her past.

And they had a child.

"All right. I'll come…home." *This* was her home. With Francesca, in Colorado's San Juan Mountains. "I just want to request one thing."

"What's that?"

"That you please call me Ivy. It'll help you remember—that I'm not Gina anymore."

Silence on the line. "Sure. Ivy. Anything else?"

She couldn't think. "No. No."

A thousand miles away, Cullen wondered how much brain damage she really had. Because if he were a woman going to a strange town to move in with a perfect stranger, there was one more request he would have made.

GABRIELA HAD BALLET after school, and as Cullen walked to Tracy Kennedy's dance studio to meet his daughter, he wondered what to say. To both of them.

This is insane. Only two or three years had passed since he'd stopped hoping Gina would return, since he'd made a deliberate decision to let go. He and Tracy had been seeing each other for the past year. Now he didn't know what to feel.

Class was over, and students were leaving as he hurried through the glass door and the small foyer and past the dressing-room doors to the arch that led onto the polished oak dance floor. There was Gabriela, her hair in a loose ponytail as Gina used to wear hers. She swung her backpack onto her shoulders over layers of dancing clothes and joined her teacher, who was saying goodbye to a parent.

Tracy had gathered her frothy brown curls in a chignon at the base of her neck. She'd danced with the New York City Ballet before coming home to Guyandotte to open a studio. Cullen had known her younger sister in high school. Within a week of Tracy's return, Cullen had noticed her—but Gabriela had been her student for three years before he'd decided to ask her out. At first, it had seemed awkward, because she was four years older than him. That had faded on their first date.

She spotted him and waved, her smile accentuating her high cheekbones.

He returned the wave and waited for her and Gabriela to come to the door. No hiking boots allowed on the floor.

"Daddy, can we go to Tracy's for dinner?"

"Not tonight. School night."

Gabriela snapped her fingers in an "Oh, darn" gesture and made a face at Tracy.

Tracy's arm was already around his waist. "How was your day?"

An unanswerable question. His mind saw Gina's soft hair, her Joni Mitchell smile. "Interesting."

She released him, still keeping her hand on his back. The touch he'd once enjoyed suddenly irritated him, and he had to resist stepping away.

"Anything wrong?"

He opened his mouth. Hesitated. "I'll come by while Gabriela's doing her homework."

His daughter's mouth fell open. "That's not fair!"

"Of course it is. I don't have school tomorrow. Been there, done that."

"Oh, shut up." She elbowed him good-naturedly.

What is this going to do to her?

"If I hurry with my homework, can I come with you?"

"I don't know yet." He wasn't sure how he'd feel leaving Gabriela alone after delivering this news, but he didn't want her present when he told Tracy. If he owed Tracy anything, it was sensitivity. Especially now.

And already her dark eyes were searching his face, trying to read his feelings, guess what he had to say.

He wanted to tell her that he'd cared about her, that he'd always respected her. He would leave those things unspoken. There was little he could say beyond *I'm sorry.*

"DO YOU THINK YOU MIGHT marry Tracy?"

Cullen nearly drove the Camaro into the oak tree with three trunks at the end of Missing Girl Hollow, at the start of their road. Naggy's road. It had been Gina's grandmother's place, and Gina had put his name on the deed when she married him. *I'm grateful, Cullen. I want to give you something.*

Gabriela's question was the perfect lead-in.

"No." As he steered over the rutted dirt road and the cabin finally came into view through the dense trees, he formulated his words.

"Oh, I didn't want to be pushy, Dad. You know I'm happy with just the two of us. It's just…"

He parked the Camaro, the same car he'd driven in high school. Gina had ridden in this car. She wouldn't remember.

Ivy wouldn't remember.

"…if you were going to marry someone, I think it would be pretty cool if it was Tracy."

He switched off the ignition, unfastened his seat belt and turned in his seat. "Gabby, I don't know how to tell you this. I had a big shock today, and it's going to be a big shock for you, too."

Her face dropped. "Did Grandpa die?"

"No. No." He shook his head. "He'll probably live for years." Another problem pricked him. *One thing at a time.* "What happened is…I learned that your mother's alive. I talked to her on the phone, and…she's coming home. At least for a while."

Gabriela looked like she might throw up.

Quickly, trying to make everything clear, he filled

her in, sharing everything he knew. Especially the incomprehensible horror of Gina's lost memory. ''She wants me to call her Ivy. And she doesn't seem like the kind of lady to insist that you call her Mom.'' He paused. ''It's going to be hard for all of us.''

''Hard? Some perfect stranger is coming to live with us? And what? You're just going to dump Tracy? Tracy's cool, and this other person sounds weird.''

It was the last reaction he would have expected from Gabriela. In grade school, she'd tortured him with questions about Gina and made up amazing fantasies about her mother that she'd described to him. He'd always nodded solemnly as she went through those scenarios and said, ''Could be.'' Could be she'd been kidnapped by a circus and taken behind the Iron Curtain. Could be she'd hit her head and gotten *amnesia....*

Oh, Gabby.

Hero worship for Tracy Kennedy was behind her rejection of Gina—Ivy.

''This other person,'' he said, ''is your mother. And my wife. That's why she's coming home. However bad things have been for you and me, you can bet they've been just as hard for Ivy Walcott. Harder, even. Imagine waking up one day with no idea who you are and no one to take care of you. Imagine suspecting that people are worried about you, but you don't know who—or how to reassure them.''

Her blue eyes, eyes like Gina's, stared hard and angry at the dash. ''I'm really sorry for her.''

He'd had about two years to get sick of that smart-ass tone of voice, what he thought of as her Alanis Morissette act. This time, he let it go. "Gabby, I loved your mom. I still love her, in my heart." He touched his heart.

"Could have sworn you loved Tracy yesterday."

"Enough, Gabriela. Ivy is your mother. I'm not going to let anyone hurt you. But you need to respect her."

"How can you call her my mother? She's not even the same person you married!"

"She carried you inside her for nine months."

"I'm honored. I bet we'll make a really happy family." She overenunciated each syllable in "family."

"Gabriela. Start being honored. Start now."

"ON YOUR WAY TO MAKE Tracy's night?"

He zipped his parka. "Gabby. Would you please clean the bathroom before I get home?"

"Oh, that's *such* punishment." She lay on the couch that had been Ivy's grandmother's, reading Gelsey Kirkland's *Dancing on My Grave*. With her hair twisted up in a knot, she was a dead ringer for Gina at seventeen or eighteen. Already, boys were calling. Boys whose voices had changed. Cullen wanted to put her under lock and key.

Instead, each day she slipped further away from him.

He touched the knotty maple door frame, noted a place where the chinking was coming away from the logs. When he and Gina were married, he'd built on the loft upstairs and the sunroom addition in the back. Since then, he'd added onto the sides of the cabin, with a room for Gabriela and a place for her to practice ballet.

What would Ivy Walcott think of this place, the place where she'd grown up as Gina Naggy? Where she'd lost her mother when she was two—the same age at which Gabriela had lost hers.

Gabriela was reading again—or deliberately ignoring him.

"Why do you talk to me that way?"

"What way?"

"Put down that book and look at me."

She did. Almost.

"I asked you a question. Does it pain you that I pay for your ballet lessons and give you a clothing allowance? That I spent last December driving you to Charleston four times a week so you could be Clara in *The Nutcracker?*"

She blushed.

Her eyes sneaked a look at him. "I'm sorry, Daddy."

Only an ogre wouldn't forgive that expression, that voice.

"Thank you," he said. "Enjoy your night. And please clean the bathroom."

NOEL NATHAN WAS fourteen years old to Gabriela's twelve and a half. She lived next door to Grandpa and Grandma's house, Coalgood, and she was Gabriela's best friend, the only person with whom she could possibly share this abysmal news.

"So, it's like this *stranger* is coming to live with us. A brain-damaged stranger. Bet she's lively." Holding the phone against her ear with her shoulder, Gabriela painted her toenails black. She would put white moons and stars on them next. Her cheek pushed the button on the phone, interrupting Noel's reply with a loud beep. "Sorry, sorry. I'm painting my toenails."

"I said, she's your mother. Aren't you excited to meet her?"

"If you hadn't seen your mother since you were two and in the meantime she hit her head and forgot you existed, would *you* be excited?"

"You've got a point." Noel wasn't stupid. "But is your dad excited? I've seen her picture. She's totally beautiful, and you look just like her."

"Thanks. I guess he's excited. He gave me all this 'Honor thy father and mother' crap today. At least, that's what it felt like."

"What's Tracy going to do?" Noel was in Gabriela's ballet class, and everyone knew the ballet mistress was going out with Gabriela's dad.

"Get over it, I guess."

"Your dad's a hunk. Gosh, Gabs, you could drive your mother away like the twins did to the icky fiancée in *The Parent Trap*."

Gabriela snorted. "Excuse me? We are talking about my mother."

"Sorry," answered her friend. "Sorry, sorry. Well, I hope she's cool."

"Yeah. Me, too." Drive her away... *Real funny, Noel.* But at least her friend hadn't brought up all the speculation. It was crazy to grow up never knowing what had happened to your mother. Some people thought she'd walked out on her husband and daughter. Others thought she'd been murdered.

Dad had always said, "You know, Gabby, anything could have happened. There's no way of knowing, but I'll tell you one thing. Your mother loved you." And that had pretty much kept Gabriela from losing her mind thinking about her mother walking out on her family.

She *had* thought about her being murdered, though.

When Noel had to get off the phone, the cabin was suddenly horribly quiet, and Gabriela wished she hadn't been a jerk to her dad. She loved him more than anybody in the world.

And what frightened her most, in a list of about a hundred things, was that Ivy Walcott—her *mother*—would steal him away from her.

CULLEN'S PARENTS' neighborhood was isolated, a circular street separated from the town of Guyandotte by a highway and a steel trestle bridge over the river. Beyond the bridge, the cloudy moon shone on tall roofs with many gables, brick palaces, stucco-and-beam mansions built by coal barons when coal was still king. Cullen's father, the district judge—retired—was the grandson of such a baron. His home was called Coalgood.

The half-timbered and masonry Tudor perched on its own hill of velvety blue grass, crowning two acres, the largest plot on Ore Circle. Leafless maples sprawled on either side of the recessed entry, high above road level. From the attic windows, Cullen and his sister, Zeya, used to peer down at the houses on the island that was the center of the circle. They still, occasionally, sledded down Coalgood's hill with Gabriela and with Zeya and Tom's five-year-old daughter, Scout. Tonight looked perfect for sledding; all was smooth and white with snow, the roof eaves glowing softly with tastefully placed holiday lights.

Cullen drove past the house, noticing cars. Shelby's VW bug was in the driveway with Zeya and Tom's ancient Volvo. Matthew's XKE, Mother's Oldsmobile and Daddy's Lincoln would be in the garage. The judge didn't drive anymore—unless he forgot and no one stopped him.

The lights were burning downstairs, behind the steel casements and the leaded glass. Maybe he'd stop by after he talked to Tracy, tell everyone about Gina—Ivy.

Maybe he wouldn't.

Tracy lived on the other side of the island in a brick house with cast-iron lacework everywhere. She'd grown up in that house and bought it from her parents when they moved to Logan. Cullen had spent the night there twice, while Gabriela was at slumber parties. Tracy had never slept in his bed.

Now he wished he'd never so much as kissed her.

Her porch light was on, and she opened the door as he climbed the steps. She shut it behind him when he entered the foyer, and he saw she'd changed into jeans and a sweater.

Her living room was ivory, with a black baby grand piano in the corner. Sitting on the kind of furniture that always made him want to check his clothes for mud, he told her his wife was alive and returning to Guyandotte.

He told her everything, as he'd told Gabriela.

"What are you going to do?"

He went still, then told himself it was a reasonable question. "She's my wife. And Gabriela's mother."

Her mouth trembled some, then steadied. "That's the right thing to do, Cullen. I'll miss what you and I have shared. But I know Gabriela will be happy."

There was nothing left to say. He wouldn't tell her his reasons for making the choice he had. He would never say to Tracy, the other woman, *She was hurt. I have to be there for her if she needs me.*

No point in saying that the promises he'd made thirteen years ago still mattered to him. He could never explain why they mattered so much.

"I'm sorry, Tracy. I really thought she was dead."

Tracy sat tall and straight, her hands folded in her lap. "It would be easier if you weren't sorry, Cullen. But I know you are. And I want you to believe that I wish you the best. All three of you. Of course, I'll still see Gabriela in class."

"Yes." Contemplating his hands, Cullen thought,

Wedding ring. It was in the top drawer of his dresser with a picture of Gina, the picture they'd put on the missing-person poster. What had happened to her rings?

In a restless movement, Tracy rose. "What can I get you to drink?"

He got up, too. "Actually, Gabriela's home alone. And I wanted to stop and see my dad."

Excuses for parting. *I'm sorry, Tracy. I'm sorry.* He was sorry for hurting her.

But after the last few minutes, he was sorry most of all that they'd ever become involved.

OUTSIDE COALGOOD, Cullen leaned on the steering wheel. He didn't think he could tell the story again.

And he wasn't ready to tell it to at least one person inside that house.

Numb and half-crazy, he lingered, undecided, till the front door, way up the hill, opened wide. He unfastened his seat belt then, and when he stepped from the Camaro, his father's voice called down, "Cully, that you?"

Someone else warbled a call from inside. The tone was fear. "Sam? Sam?"

Sam Till came down the flagstone steps cut into the hillside of glittering white. *Watch out for the ice, Daddy.* The judge skidded but didn't fall, and Cullen started up the walk to meet him.

"Sam?"

The porch light snapped on. A head of smooth blond hair, recently colored, peered out. The woman vanished then returned, her red sweater and green plaid pants bright as the holidays. She carried his father's wraps.

Cullen waved to his mother.

"Sam, you need your coat." Mouth tight, she picked her way down the walk after her husband. She clapped his wool driving cap over his head, wound his muffler round his neck. Helping her husband into his coat, she cast Cullen a look that said, *You won't let him go anywhere, will you?*

Later, if she was alone with Cullen or with Cullen and Zeya, she would say, "He's almost the same as always, don't you think?"

The judge did seem sharp tonight. Blue-gray slacks creased. Fresh red polo shirt under a cashmere sweater. His small round glasses winked back the starlight, and below the sides of his cap, his bald head gave off a satin sheen. He walked tall. Tall and handsome, smart and good.

Fitting on his gloves, the judge made it down to the sidewalk. "You've been a stranger."

"Busy."

The lights in a neighboring white Colonial flashed on. Big front room with a grand piano. A young girl sat down to play, her ponytail waving over her straight spine.

"Let's take a walk," said the judge.

They walked together in the empty street, on the fresh snow, avoiding the narrow sidewalks. "You all right, Cully?"

"Yes." Sure. Fine. No. Lousy. "Gina's been found. She has total amnesia."

His father's look was blank, either over Gina or amnesia. It was a funny word to forget, but there it was. That was how they'd begun to notice he was sick. That—and forgetting other things.

Cullen straightened his insides. Daddy was sick. He couldn't expect any advice, any intelligent comment. As far as he could tell, his father hadn't even recognized Gina's name.

The judge said, "I'm sorry about this. About the way I am."

It wasn't the first time he'd mentioned his illness to Cullen. Cullen hoped the conversation wouldn't take its usual course.

"I guess it happens," he said, "when we get old." It could happen to him. The odds were good.

His father's arm settled across Cullen's shoulders. A shaky surprise. "This is just between you and me. I've always loved you best."

His father's gift had a history. *Your Honor, why couldn't you have loved one of your other children best? Matthew, for instance. I don't deserve the favor, thank you.*

"And that's why I'm asking you this," the judge said.

Cullen braced himself. The judge had asked him for this thing twice before; he probably didn't remember.

Cullen wished he could forget, too.

"Should have done it…earlier. But I thought about

it right from the start. No impaired judgment. No guilt, Cully.'' A breath. "I want you to help me die."

Shit.

"You're the only one with the integrity. Matthew's got the guts, but he wouldn't trouble to keep the secret from your mother."

Matthew was better at keeping secrets than the judge knew. And Cullen already had more secrets than he wanted.

"Someday I'll wander off. You could help me into the river—down a mine shaft. Promise me, Cully. It's for your mother."

Not hardly. His mother would hate the idea.

But his father wanted it, and she might go along with it for him. She'd surprised Cullen most of his life.

"Daddy, you need to talk about it with Mother."

"Your mother will never agree, and it's my life."

And if she did agree and if the judge died in an "accident," there would be life insurance fraud, which was a crime in spirit and in law. Whereas assisted suicide… There was enough here for a university ethics class. Cullen changed the subject. "Daddy, do you remember Gina?"

The judge walked with him, their bodies linked by that arm across the son's shoulders.

His profile showed nothing. Blank.

Suddenly, he seemed to come back to himself. He glanced at the house. "We'd better get in for dinner."

Cullen didn't bother to tell him that it was almost ten and that the judge had already eaten.

CHAPTER TWO

"WE REALLY HAVE TO GO to Coalgood for dinner tonight?"

"It's Grandma's birthday."

"I'm totally traumatized by the concept of meeting my mother for the first time. I don't want to go."

Twenty-four hours had passed since he'd told Gabriela about Ivy. That morning, Ivy had called him at the studio to say she was on her way and should arrive the following afternoon, Wednesday, the day before Thanksgiving.

Gabriela had blanched at the news.

"We're going."

"Have you told them?"

About Gina. "No. I will tonight."

Dragging her feet toward her room, she muttered, "I bet *they'll* be thrilled."

His antenna went up. "Why do you say that?"

She acted like she hadn't heard.

"Gabby. Why did you say that?"

In slow motion, she turned and leaned against the doorjamb. After four years of ballet, she could still slouch. "You think I'm stupid? Grandma and Grandpa don't like my mother in a big way. You got married too young. I've only heard *that* about fifty times. If only you'd gone to college like Matthew and Zeya." She shook her head sadly in a dead-on imitation of his mother.

He bit his tongue but couldn't hide his smile. "Go get dressed, brat."

She made a face at him. "*You're* the brat."

She was so pretty, so much like Gina—or like Gina might've been if her childhood had been different. If she'd known at least one of her parents.

He realized too late that she'd been studying his expression. She played the moment for all its worth. "Can I have a raise in my allowance?"

DINNER THAT NIGHT was served in the dining room, one of Coalgood's great halls, with mullioned and transomed stone windows and crown moldings and rich cherry furniture. Cullen sat between Gabriela and Scout, who was trying to interest him in some Playmobil bandits under the table. While his niece whispered, "Uncle Cullen! Bang bang!" he tried to figure out how to break the news about Gina. Maybe at the door, right before he and Gabriela left?

"Scout." Zeya, one year older than Cullen, frowned at her daughter. "Please put away the cowboys."

"If Uncle Cullen promises to play Playmobil with me after dinner."

"Yes."

Tom Tormey, Zeya's black-haired, blue-eyed husband, winced at the promptness of Cullen's answer. "We're trying not to make a tyrant of our daughter."

Cullen winked at Scout. "Am I the one who opened the biggest toy store in the Appalachians and bought every Playmobil set imaginable?" He and Scout shook their heads at each other, and her black corkscrew curls bobbed. "No, I'm not."

"No, you're not, Uncle Cullen. My parents have the biggest toy store in the whole world."

As Zeya held out a hand for the bandits, her mother said, "Zeya, please don't reach across the table. It sets a bad example. Scout, honey, don't you want some lamb chops?"

That's the problem, Cullen wanted to tell Zeya, *with living at home. Mother wants to raise your daughter.* It was a bigger problem because Zeya, Tom and Scout were all vegetarians, an anomaly at Coalgood and in Guyandotte.

His family lined both sides of the table, Mother at one end and Daddy at the other. Matthew's wife, Shelby, sat on the judge's right beside Scout. Her husband sat across from her, next to Zeya. Matthew was Cullen's half brother, the son of the judge's first marriage. He'd been fourteen when Cullen was born. When Cullen was three, Matthew had transported him halfway to the second floor of Coalgood in the dumbwaiter and left him there. On another occasion, he'd held him by his heels from an attic window.

It was family tradition to fly in Matthew's plane to each newly completed building that he'd designed. Though Matthew was touted as the South's most brilliant architect, Cullen never entered one of his buildings without noticing that a child could be launched down the grand staircase in a red wagon, without seeing all toilets as objects to climb on when trapped in a bathroom with a six-foot black snake.

Scout, deprived of her toys, pulled on one of Shelby's dark red curls, corkscrews like her own. "Shelby, can I go to your office tomorrow?"

Shelby turned serious eyes and gold-rimmed glasses on her niece. "Sweetie, I have to go to court to defend a really creepy guy."

"Oh, Shelby!" Scout frowned. "I bet you'd rather be with me."

The judge muttered, "Shelby likes the low-life sons of bitches, and she doesn't believe in the death penalty, either."

Shelby patted her father-in-law's hand. "But you and I can still eat dinner together, even live in the same house."

"Your husband's a sponge."

Matthew's dense eyebrows lifted. "Her husband, your son, pays most of the upkeep on this turn-of-the-century monstrosity."

The judge's next utterance was profane.

"Daddy!" exclaimed his wife. "There are children present."

Tom scooped up some millet pilaf from his plate. "That's all right, Mitzi. Teaches 'em how to talk. Scout, Gabby, you catch all that?"

Every summer, while Gabriela was at dance camp, Cullen and Tom completed thirty-mile-a-day treks on the country's longest trails. The Appalachian Trail, the John Muir Trail... They grew beards, ceased all bathing and brushed their teeth but not their hair. They yipped with coyotes, cawed at black-winged scavengers and devised elaborate schemes for outwitting fat marmots and bears. They maintained silence in the presence of eagles and hawks. Cullen usually enjoyed his brother-in-law's wit. Tonight, it grated.

Restless, Cullen retrieved his camera and began photographing family members in black and white. Shelby talking earnestly to Scout. Zeya's family eating different food from everyone else at the table. His parents' servant, Lily, bringing the coffeepot. Gabriela scowling at the camera. Daddy blowing out the candles—on Mother's cake.

"It's time for presents," announced Zeya, jumping to her feet. "Mother, this one's from Daddy."

The judge started. "It most certainly is not."

Cullen put his head in his hands and silenced his suddenly giggling daughter with a glance, which she aped to Matthew a second later and her uncle aped right back.

"I forgot her birthday," the judge said. "Like always." He winked down the table at his wife.

Everyone laughed then, at the joke, which was a sign of the judge's sharpness, a sign the disease was moving slowly.

During the opening of the gifts, Gabriela caught Cullen's eye. With an agonized look, she mouthed, "Can I go to Noel's?"

"After the presents."

It would give him a chance to talk to his family

without Gabriela's seeing their reactions. What she'd said earlier still bugged him. She didn't miss much.

The minute Mother had opened her last gift—a framed photo of Cullen and Gabriela—Gabriela said, "May I be excused?"

"Of course, darling."

Her grandmother lifted her face, welcoming a kiss, and Gabriela obliged. "I love you, Grandma."

The judge said, "Thanks for the presents, everyone."

As Gabriela hugged him, too, then left, Matthew opened the sideboard. "Drinks anyone? Chablis, Mitzi?"

His stepmother responded with a dazzling smile that suggested the ritual was annual rather than nightly. "Why thank you, Matthew."

"Health fanatics, I recommend the Merlot. I'm told it's loaded with antioxidants."

"Too yin," Zeya said.

Shelby smiled at her husband. "Nothing for me, Matthew."

Cullen heard the front door close behind Gabriela. "Gina's coming back."

Glass hit glass. Matthew getting clumsy with the wine.

Daddy snapped his head up. "Who?"

"Gina?" exclaimed Mitzi and Zeya.

Tom said, "Your *wife?*"

"She goes by Ivy now. Ivy Walcott." His throat was full, confessing this, that she had changed her name. Especially her last name.

From the sideboard, Matthew coughed. "Guess we all need some excitement, Cully. I'm glad you brought it up tonight at this family gathering."

Out of compassion for Shelby, Cullen let it pass. *Surely* you're *not excited, Matthew?*

"But your wife's dead!" Scout blurted. "People don't come back from the dead."

"She was never dead. But she can't remember her life with me. She has a head injury. Permanent brain damage."

"Oh, God, how awful." Zeya shuddered.

"Oh, Cullen." His mother shook her head. "Surely *you're* not going to take care of her? What about Tracy?"

"An interesting question." Matthew spilled Mother's Chablis in her lap. "Oh, jeez. I'm sorry, Mitzi."

"What's the matter, Joe? Got butterfingers?" Daddy said in that slow voice that wasn't really his anymore.

Joe was Daddy's brother. Joe had died in Korea before Cullen was born.

Lily peered in from the kitchen and hurried for a damp towel to mop at Mother's dress. "It's just the white, Mrs. Till. It'll come right out."

Returning to the sideboard, Matthew collected his own glass of Merlot. "Where's she staying?"

Cullen met his eyes. "With her husband."

Shelby stood up from the table too fast, and he wanted to shoot himself. "Hey, Scout," she said. "Did you mention a Playmobil party?"

THE NEXT DAY, Ivy wondered if West Virginia was a place of gray skies. She hadn't seen blue since she'd crossed the state line, though she'd seen plenty of snow since reaching Guyandotte. And this hollow...

Missing Girl Hollow. Cullen had said "holler" the way people in Tennessee had. She'd grown up here.

There was the oak with three trunks that Cullen had described to her. The road looked rutted, the passage between the trees narrow, but the Saab would make it easily.

Branches wound together above the car, creating a long corridor of tree limbs. They were gray and brown now, streaked white with the snow collecting on them. But in summer, this would be a forest of green.

As her windshield wipers stroked back and forth, she took a sip from her travel mug of nettle tea. She carried tea balls and herbs with her, and she'd made tea with gas-station hot water all across the country. It was almost two days since she'd slept.

That's the cabin. Light-headed, she parked beside a black vintage Camaro with pinstripes and an intake scoop.

The cabin door opened, and through her snow-flecked windows, she saw the tall figure behind the screen. Then the screen pushed out. His hair was light brown, overlong and wavy. His wool shirt hung on broad shoulders, his faded jeans on narrow hips and long, muscular legs.

What am I going to say to this man? What will he expect?

Closing her eyes, she held on to one thought. She'd contacted the midwifery association in West Virginia and been assured that a midwife in the Guyandotte area could provide much-needed services. There wouldn't be much money in it. *You'll be eating rice and beans, but the women in those hollers really need help.*

Naturally, she wouldn't start a local practice until she knew she'd be staying. But Cullen had already said he hoped she'd stay. And her heart and soul pointed in that direction, too—toward honoring their commitment, toward joining Cullen in raising Gabriela.

Any comfort, any sense of continuity, came from one source. She was a midwife. Her key ring, an oversize diaper pin bearing the logo of Mountain Midwifery and holding a cluster of functional diaper pins, reminded her of this and her connection to Tara and Francesca. The same was true of the birthing-woman pendants Francesca had bought for them all at the midwifery conference in Tennessee. And the friendship bracelets Tara had made with kids at the birth clinic in Texas. Ivy was a midwife, the daughter of Francesca Walcott, the sister of Tara Marcus.

And the wife of Cullen Till.

He had left the porch, and when she opened her door, he stood six feet away, beneath the naked trees. His green eyes were the missing leaves, the missing shoots of spring. Ivy's chest tightened oddly, her pulse racing, her stomach hot. Heat ran down her legs, and she couldn't move.

His smile cut grooves on each side of his mouth. Beautiful teeth and a yin-yang post in his left ear.

Precipice, Colorado, was a town of celebrity second homes, a land of handsome adventure-seekers, rugged mountaineers and suntanned skiers. But this was the finest-looking man she'd ever seen, and she'd bet he could climb mountains or hike for miles without rest.

Her lips parted. *Husband.*

He'd come closer, close enough that she noticed a button in the middle of his shirt was white, while the others were black.

Like the hair on his chest.

And his eyelashes and eyebrows.

Cullen searched her eyes, hunting signs of recognition. No, he could tell she didn't recognize him, though he knew her. He knew her smooth golden skin, her fine nose. Her wide mouth. *It's you.*

But it wasn't.

Ivy Walcott wore a cream-colored turtleneck, a sheepskin coat and jeans that made her legs a mile long. Cowboy boots, too. She was ski-resort Western chic, like an ad for Aspen.

Or Precipice.

Gone was Gina in her gingham and secondhand clothes. Gone were Gina's eyes that always looked sideways when she spoke to you.

Ivy Walcott looked right at him, her mouth soft and vulnerable.

He wasn't sorry he'd asked her back.

She held out her hand.

Ignoring it, he stepped close and put his arms around her.

Cullen's body trembled at the contact. *Gina.* He meant the hug to be simple, a welcome.

It was intense and complicated, with her head making one nervous turn against his chest, with her arms reaching to hold him in a way that reminded him that, for her, this was a first meeting. His jaw rested on her hair, and he shut his eyes. Different shampoo.

There was nothing to say, nothing to make it sane.

When he released her, slowly, she said, "That was nice."

Nice was inadequate. Nothing could express what he felt.

He didn't respond.

The black Saab was filled with boxes and a couple of suitcases. There was a loaded luggage rack on the roof, and cross-country and alpine skis strapped to the back. Through the rear window, Cullen saw ice skates and snowshoes, too.

"I didn't know how much snow you have."

"Quite a bit, here. There's actually a ski area a half hour away." He laughed. "Not that I'm sure *you'd* call it a ski area."

Ivy looked toward the cabin. "Where's Gabriela?"

"School. You can come with me to pick her up."

Her watch read two o'clock. Which meant an hour or so alone with Cullen in this deserted place.

But she liked the cabin. It was log and stone, rustic in a way the log houses of Precipice would never be. The roof peaked steeply into the trees above tall windows and a circular stained-glass panel showing a falcon and a red wolf. The upper story looked new, while Ivy could easily believe that the central cabin was a hundred years old. Neatly stacked firewood filled half the porch.

"See anything familiar?"

Was he hoping? She searched his eyes, trembling inside just from the visual contact. "Nothing. I knew I wouldn't. My memory won't ever return. The loss is permanent."

He didn't look away. "Then we have some catching up to do. But I have to tell you, I'm not as sure as you are that your past is all gone."

Oh, Cullen, don't. Don't believe that. Don't hope for it.

"See…" His voice sounded uneven. "Your grandmother was a midwife. And so was your mother. And so were you."

Midwives… She'd been a midwife when she was Gina Till? Was that why catching babies, identifying the sagittal suture, assessing a baby's lie, had always felt so natural to her, like something she'd done before?

I was a midwife, and…

And she didn't remember, nor had she ever seen this man, the husband who'd made love to her, who'd made a child with her. Her mouth filled with saliva, and she felt dizzy, her legs unsteady.

Her head swam, and his face became too vivid, the edges too sharp, and then everything went away.

ON THE COUCH, horizontal, she came around.

Kneeling beside her, Cullen watched her eyelashes flutter, watched the shades of violet appear. Panic when she saw him. She closed her eyes, then reopened them, calmer. "I'm sorry. Did I faint?"

"You fainted. Any idea why?"

She held her hand against her eyes, half-shielding her face. "I, uh, haven't slept real well the last two nights."

Neither had he. "Did you stop last night? On the road?"

"No." It was embarrassing. "I was wide-awake."

"Could you sleep now?"

Ivy tried to sit up, and he let her, slowly.

Sleep… Could she sleep now? No, Ivy decided. Not a chance. Not until she met Gabriela. She shook her head. "I'll be fine till tonight." She put her feet on the floor. The cabin was hot. Roasting in her coat, she pulled it off, and Cullen took it from her to hang up.

When he returned, he moved a pillow on the couch to sit next to her.

As she blinked, catching the details of the room, he said, "I apologize for shocking you. Do you remember what I said?"

"Yes. I'm afraid it's just a coincidence. Please don't—don't hope that my memory will return. It categorically, absolutely, will not. Neurologist certified, short of an act of God. And I'm not talking about one doctor. I've seen a dozen, psychiatrists and brain doctors."

Cullen believed her. "It's okay. Let's talk about something else." If she hadn't slept for two days, she was more nervous than she let on. At the moment, he didn't trust her judgment. "I'll give you a tour in a minute. Gabriela's room is in there." He nodded toward the door. "There's a loft upstairs with a turn-of-the-century tester bed. Narrow. And there's a day-bed up there, too. Also, there's this couch. So…there are options."

Ivy met his eyes. She knew things about him already. That he was a gentle man. That his house was clean and that there was a pair of toe shoes, for ballet, at the end of the couch and a copy of *Seventeen* on the coffee table. That he took his commitment to her seriously. At least, seriously enough to ask her to "come home."

"Ivy, I need to be straight with you. I don't expect a commitment tonight or this week even. But I've never brought lovers to this house. I didn't want to do that to Gabriela. She doesn't need a walk-on in her life."

Ivy had pondered this question ever since he'd asked her back. What would be best for Gabriela? What was reasonable to expect of Cullen and herself?

Now she was here, and she found him attractive and kind.

"I should warn you. Gabriela had a mixed reaction to the news that you were coming back. She's twelve. You know?"

Ivy understood.

"I told her I hoped you'd stay. That's still how I

feel. I know things are different, but I see your face, and you're still my wife.''

The same urges that had prompted her to return to a situation she couldn't foresee urged her answer now. "I will stay."

"You shouldn't make that decision yet."

"It's obvious to me. And better for Gabriela if we decide immediately."

Cullen tried trusting her and could not and knew he should not. He and Gabriela would be at her mercy, at the mercy of a stranger.

As she was at theirs.

"Then—" his mouth was dry "—I think you should sleep upstairs. In the daybed, if you like. You can trust me to leave you alone."

His teasing smile was gentle and friendly, not threatening.

"For a while anyway."

Ivy's heart gave several hard thuds. What would it be like when he *didn't* leave her alone? *I need to say something. To warn him.* Tara and Francesca and ten years of unavoidable awkwardness had taught her that honesty was the best policy. "I haven't had a lover."

Every time she met his eyes and spoke, she ceased to be Gina for him.

Cullen deliberately closed his mouth. No lovers.

He considered the implications. *Think about her.* "Do you remember what sex is like? Do you imagine it?"

Her pelvic floor tingled with increased blood flow. He'd asked like a man who had the right to know.

The space behind her eyes was hot. *He loves me. Or he loved me once.*

As far as she knew, no other man ever had.

Eyes on his lips, she made the words come out. "I…imagine it. I might remember the sensation. I'm not sure. It's probably like being pregnant or having a baby. I *think* I know what it feels like. But I've completely forgotten the experience itself."

Cullen took a long breath. *There's a lot you've forgotten. More than you'll ever guess.*

Her cheeks were bright beneath her tan, and she tensed initially as he relaxed against the back of the couch. A sadness nudged him, and Cullen shoved it away just as something familiar hit him. Her scent. He knew that scent. *You smell the same.*

Did she know his scent? Could she remember that much?

He focused on what she'd said. About sex. It should have been a dream come true—the chance to be Gina's first. But she wasn't Gina. "How do you feel about the prospect of making love with me? It must seem like an arranged marriage."

"No." She drew her lower lip between her teeth, a nervous gesture of Gina's and one that had never failed to excite him. Even now. "It feels safe. I must have liked you."

He had no answer for that. Except to continue putting the pieces on the table. "So. I slept with Gabriela's ballet teacher a couple of times. I've been seeing her…for about a year." He found her steady, clear-eyed gaze. "I thought you were dead. I'm not promiscuous."

"That's an attractive quality."

He laughed. The dark sadness, the highs and lows of familiarity tugged at him again.

"Does she know?" asked Ivy. "The ballet teacher? That I—"

"I told her."

"And?"

"She's a nice person."

Ivy wasn't surprised. "Are you in love with her?"

"No." He'd thought he might be, until he knew it was over. Time to get off this couch, carry in Ivy's things. "Let me bring your stuff from the car, and I'll show you around. A lot of the things in this house were your family's. Your grandmother, your mother, you and Gabby were all born here, in this cabin."

Quilts. It was then that she noticed the quilt on the couch, another quilted piece on the wall. *I know how to quilt.* Gently she touched the soft fabric. There was a beauty and timelessness to this heritage.

He was giving it back to her, and she wanted to embrace him again, to thank him. Before he went out, she said, "Cullen? What about my father?"

"Died in the mines when you were a baby. There are photos of both your parents—and your grandparents on your mom's side—at my studio. They're yours, of course. I'll take you down there before we pick up Gabriela."

"Please." *You have my past. You are giving me my past.*

Had he told her the whole truth about the ballet teacher? Had he made love only twice with a woman he'd dated for a year? And what did he mean by making love?

A new distance had sprung up between them at the mention of his lover. A year was a long time to be involved with someone. Did that explain his sudden quiet, the way he went outside without looking at her again?

Turning to peer out the window, she watched his athletic strides over the snow, watched him stop and put his hand to his face. His shoulders trembled slightly.

I wish I could see your face.

His body told her enough.

Something hurt. And until she knew for certain what it was, she'd sleep in that daybed.

DON'T THINK ABOUT IT. Don't think about it.

Cullen had stifled the thoughts as long as he could. Outside, under the trees, they descended on him like mosquitoes in July.

Memories of a woman with Ivy's looks, an Appalachian lilt in her voice, a down-to-earth practicality and weaknesses he'd loved and loathed. He'd wanted to *talk* to her. All morning, he'd imagined hugging her, talking to her, watching her tomboy ways, watching her assess the change between the two-year-old she'd left and the twelve-year-old she'd come home to, then sit down for a heart-to-heart with Gabriela and turn a mouthy adolescent into an angel.

She'd been at her best as a mom.

But she was gone, and tears came against his will. Postponed grief. Gina was as dead as if her body had died, too.

He was married to a woman he didn't know but whose scent was like Gina's. Who looked like Gina. Who had felt like Gina when he embraced her.

A woman he couldn't help wanting.

A woman he did not love.

CHAPTER THREE

HER CONVERSATION with Francesca was brief—but long enough for her mother to ask, "Ivy, is that wise? Staying there? With him?"

Cullen had put on his coat and was gathering film canisters and manila envelopes—undoubtedly containing photographs or proofs, things for work.

Regretting what she'd told Francesca, Ivy said simply, "I hope so. In any case, it's what I'm going to do."

Francesca's sigh traveled across miles. "I wish I could come out there, at least meet this man."

If only Cullen wasn't listening. "It's not about him." She didn't want to see his face, his reaction to that. "We have a child."

This time, the other woman's long breath contained all the emotion of what motherhood meant. "Yes," she murmured. "I see. And you feel you're safe?"

"Very."

"Well… Then please give your family a hug from me and Tara. I think I can get away after Lori Sheffield's birth, in December."

"I'll love seeing you, Mom."

She couldn't help noticing that Cullen watched her quizzically. When she'd given Francesca Cullen's address and phone number and hung up, she said, "So you're wondering why I suddenly have a mother."

She liked his smile.

"Sure."

"I'll tell you in the car."

THEY TOOK THE SAAB, and she let him drive. On the way downtown to his studio, she told him how Francesca and Tara had befriended her and informally adopted her as an adult. "Charlie, that's Tara's dad, wanted in on it, too, but he and Francesca have been divorced twenty years, and she said one mutual child is enough. Still, I call him Dad. But he lives in Alaska. I've only met him about five times."

What was Cullen thinking? It wasn't till they reached a traffic light, at the turnoff from the highway and onto Main Street, that he met her eyes. "I'm glad someone took care of you. I'll be happy to meet them."

She didn't know how much of what he said was simply good manners, but she trusted it was sincere.

And in her weariness, her sense of unreality in an unfamiliar world, she trusted *him*. Although she wasn't sure she could tell Francesca why.

CULLEN LEFT IVY ALONE with the photos while he went to develop the roll he'd shot at Coalgood the other night. Rather than opening the albums he'd brought out for her, Ivy rose and walked through the studio. The walls were a gallery of photos. Not portraits—more like photojournalism, in black and white

and in color. Appalachian places and faces worthy of
the best magazines. Cave interiors, hill-country farms.
And when she opened one of the books on the
counter, she discovered he had sold to magazines. All
his magazine work was in plastic sleeves in the album.

You're good, Cullen.

Choosing a dark blue overstuffed chair, she finally
settled down with a brown album of faded photographs. *My grandparents.* Each line on their faces
spoke to something inside her. Through these portraits
and snapshots she could know the family, the places,
that would otherwise be completely lost to her.

Mountain faces. Her father's skin blackened with
grime from the mines. In other shots, the grime never
seemed completely gone. Her mother and grandmother, carrying midwifery bags. Her mother was
blond, too, dressed simply in sixties style—so similar
to the clothing worn by her grandmother in the earlier
photographs. It was as though time had stopped in
these mountains.

This is my place. This is my country.

She knew she would never return to Colorado to
live.

She had truly come home.

The second album opened another world, captured
through Cullen's lens.

She'd nursed Gabriela. A newborn. Ivy had seen
the tester bed that day. She'd seen the quilts, on the
tester bed, on Gabriela's iron bed downstairs, on the

daybed in the loft where she would sleep that night, a dozen feet from him.

Gabriela was born at home. But who had been there? Cullen had said Gina's mother died when she was just five, that her grandmother died when Gina was eighteen, two years before Gabriela was born.

She would have to ask Cullen. She turned pages and finally found a single picture of him holding the newborn Gabriela. With a shock of memory, she recalled a detail of her stay in the Boulder hospital. It was something she'd tried to put out of her mind for the last decade—with limited success. The baby photos brought it back. She must tell Cullen, but she couldn't tell him suddenly. He'd be upset.

"Hi."

He'd emerged from the darkroom.

She gestured to the photos on the studio walls. "You're wonderful."

"Thanks."

She turned another leaf in the album. "We look so young."

He peered at the album, at upside-down photos. "We *were* young. Twenty. Our wedding photos are at home. I think they're in Gabriela's room."

"Who attended her birth?"

"Me. You told me what to do."

And these were the memories lost to her? The birth of her child? Nursing her infant daughter?

"What happened? What was the birth like?"

"I was taking photos for the paper. I came home, and you said you were in labor, and suddenly your water broke—all over my shoes.'' He grinned, then averted his eyes.

She understood. Grief. That was why he'd been upset outside the cabin. She whispered the why. "I'm not her."

Cullen crouched beside her to look over her shoulder at the photos. As if she hadn't spoken, he said, "You'd always planned to do your own birth, so you'd lined me up with midwifery books to read. *Spiritual Midwifery* was one of them. We cuddled a lot during your labor. Touched. When she crowned, you talked me through it, checking for the cord and everything. I caught her and put her on your stomach."

Numb, she listened to the rest of the details. Delivering the placenta, cutting the cord, nursing Gabriela.

"You nursed her for almost two years. She'd barely stopped when you...disappeared."

She met his eyes, getting used to his features and the three o'clock shadow on his jaw. Getting used to the idea of telling him what she must. "What did you think had happened?"

"I didn't know. Your wallet was gone, but I had the car. You never hitched rides. Gabby was with me, at the studio." He paused. "You don't have any idea what happened?"

"Not really."

"Tell me about your head injury."

"It's focal retrograde amnesia, basically. I never forgot how to *do* things—which probably explained my becoming a midwife again. But there was a hell of a lot of stuff I didn't know. Presidents, current events. I took some history classes and pop culture, just so I didn't embarrass myself."

He sat back on his heels. "What caused it?"

"A blow to the head. I could have fallen. I could have been hit. It could have been an accident. No one knows. And probably no one ever will." She gathered herself. "I was—I was bleeding from a recent miscarriage." Her breath hurt. "Or a failed abortion."

He was white, his jaw hard.

Cullen wondered how much to say. Now was the time to tell her. He didn't want to. Somehow it was between him and Gina. *But it's her body. Same woman, Cullen. Your wife.*

And now, he'd just learned, she had carried his child.

HARRY S. TRUMAN JUNIOR High School sat on a hillside overlooking Guyandotte. The redbrick walls showed above the trees before her Saab began climbing the hill with Cullen silent at the wheel. It gave Ivy extra minutes in which to be more nervous than she'd ever been.

As they reached the school, following other parents and two school buses, Cullen asked, "Are you all right?"

At last. He speaks. He'd returned to the darkroom after her revelation—more to be alone, she suspected, than to work. "I'm just worried she's not going to like me or is going to resent my presence. She doesn't even know me. And you were dating her ballet teacher.''

He pulled into the parking lot and took a spot along the curb to wait for Gabriela. ''You know, she was really a mess when you disappeared. Now she's resisting the idea of you, and it's probably for reasons she doesn't even understand. But I think she needs you.''

No one had ever needed her that she could recall, except women in labor, and there'd never been a situation in which someone else couldn't have attended a birth. ''Thank you. For saying that.''

''I mean it.'' Should he say more? Why not? Part of his rationale in asking her to come home had been the sense that *she* needed *him*. ''Ivy, after the sheriff came last week, I just sat there for ten minutes thinking about Tracy—the ballet teacher—and about you. Sure, a stepmother was beginning to look like a good second option for Gabriela. But you?'' He met her eyes. ''I think you have the magic with her.''

''I lost my personality.''

''I believe love is stronger than that.''

Ivy heard. He wasn't just talking about her and Gabriela.

He was talking about the two of them, husband and wife.

Her answer came from her heart, not from her mind. ''So do I.''

He broke the eye contact, looking past her shoulder. ''Here's Gabby. I'd better get out. She won't know this car.''

Ivy saw the blond girl applying lip gloss as she walked, a boy on each side of her. As Cullen opened his door, she couldn't stop herself.

She opened hers, too.

OH, GOD. THAT'S HER.

Blinking, Gabriela stopped on the sidewalk. "I'll see you guys later. There are..." They would think she was totally weird if she suddenly said "my parents." She'd been going to school with Roger and Jeremy since kindergarten, and everyone knew damn well she had no mother. "There's my dad."

And the most beautiful woman Gabriela had ever seen, drop-dead gorgeous like her photos.

No wonder he wanted her back.

Gabriela swallowed. For a second, for her dad's sake, she wanted this Ivy woman to love him, too. But how could she when they'd been apart so long and she supposedly couldn't remember his face?

Oh, come on. She's not blind.

Gabriela hoped she wasn't stuck up, either.

Her dad had come around to the passenger side of the black car and was waiting for her. As she came near, he put his arm around her. He cast a glance at people nearby and spoke softly. "Gabriela, this is Ivy. Ivy, Gabriela."

Ivy tried to read her daughter's expression. It wasn't hard. *She's terrified. I'm scared, too, Gabriela.*

Once she'd asked Tara, "Aren't you ever afraid to meet people?" Her sister seemed to greet everyone she knew or met with a hug and a grin. Tara had said,

"Of course I am. Why do you think I act this way? It makes me brave."

Ivy had never been able to greet a new acquaintance with an embrace until today.

And only because Cullen had taught her how.

She stepped forward and hugged her daughter. Slender bones. A child turning into a woman. "I'm so glad to see you. I drove across the country most of all to meet you." She tightened the awkward hug for a moment, then released her daughter, who was already as tall as Ivy. "You're beautiful." *Gorgeous.*

"Thanks." Gabriela's voice was low, flat. "So are you."

Her dad had his arm around her again, which made Gabriela feel better. He tugged on her ponytail. "Let's go home, Gabby."

THE PHONE WAS RINGING when they opened the car doors outside the cabin. Cullen sprinted to get it.

Tom said, "Your mom just called us at the store. The judge is missing."

Gabriela and Ivy trailed into the cabin. His daughter wore the face of a death-row inmate.

Ordinarily, he would have left in a second to track down his father. Not today. "Where's Matthew?"

"Atlanta. I'm about to go look, and Shelby said she'd go, too, but he's got the Lincoln. It could take a few of us."

Hanging up the phone, Cullen found Gabriela and Ivy sitting at opposite ends of the couch. "Grandpa's missing." He turned to Ivy. "My father has Alzheimer's."

Her eyes plunged into his, doing something to him. "I'm sorry."

"He was a district judge."

Wincing, she shook her head.

Ivy noticed Gabriela gazing at her as though she were a creature from another realm. When Ivy caught her eye, the twelve-year-old said, "He really has to explain *everything* to you? I thought you grew up in Guyandotte."

"My earliest memories begin ten years ago."

"So, does that make you like a ten-year-old?"

"Gabby." Cullen's voice was stern.

"Sorry." Her apology carried no remorse.

Ivy took the question as asked. "The answer is no. I still have emotional memory and what's called procedural memory. I remembered how to drive, how to tie my shoes and, to some degree, how to attend births. I'm a midwife," she added, in case Cullen hadn't told her.

"You used to be a midwife, too. That's totally weird."

Her honesty made Ivy smile. "Cullen, do you need to look for your dad? If you'd like help, we could take separate cars."

He considered. "All right. He's driving a navy Lincoln Continental with the license plate SALTILL. Samuel Abraham Lincoln Till. Gabby, you go with her. Grandpa knows you, and you can suggest places for Ivy to look. Try the country club. If he's not there, wait for me, and I'll meet you.''

GABRIELA CHECKED OUT the interior of the Saab. It was the kind of car she'd always wanted. It really annoyed her that her father still drove the muscle car he'd had in high school, even though all the guys at Truman and at the pool in summer acted like it was a Ferrari or something.

She watched Ivy start the car and thought how beautiful her hands were. *This is so weird. She's my mother, but she's not.*

"Okay, you'll have to direct me."

"Sure." Gabriela couldn't stop herself. "Can you remember how you got here?"

The blond woman turned her head and met Gabriela's eyes. "No problems with recent memory."

Her eyes are like mine.

Also, something about the way this stranger looked at her said she wasn't amused by the question. So much for that conversation.

She drove as if she was used to snow, and Gabriela said, "You live in Colorado?"

"I have been living in Colorado."

Gabriela did not like the sound of that. As they headed out of the hollow, she said, "So, how long are you staying?"

The Saab drew to a halt, although the stop sign was still yards away. Ivy faced her. "How long do you want me to stay?"

Her eyes were too direct, like she was already in

charge. Not in a mean way. She seemed like a person used to finding out what people really wanted. Gabriela watched her key ring swing from the ignition. It was a cluster of diaper pins on a larger pin with a blue wildflower on it and the words "Mountain Midwifery."

How was she supposed to answer a question like that?

"I guess it wasn't a fair question," Ivy said.

No kidding, Gabriela thought rebelliously.

"I'd hoped your dad would be the one to tell you this, but he and I had a chance to talk before we picked you up at school. I'm married to your dad. I'm your mother. And I'm going to stay here and live in the house where my grandmother was born, where my mother was born, where I was born and you were born."

"Don't you have a job somewhere else?"

"People in West Virginia don't have babies?"

"Not with midwives. We're not hillbillies."

"Mmm." Ivy put the car in gear and drove down to the stop sign. "Okay, which way? There's a tape case behind your seat if you want to hear some music."

A MARY CHAPIN CARPENTER album was playing in the country club, where a man in a well-cut suit sat laughing with the barmaid.

"Uncle Matthew!" Gabriela crossed the bar as if she owned the place. "Are you looking for Grandpa, too?"

"Is Grandpa missing?" Shifting on the bar stool, he faced Gabriela, then caught sight of Ivy still in the doorway. His hair was the same shade as Cullen's but more coarse and wiry. When he stood, it was to a good four inches taller than Cullen's six feet. "Well. Well, well, well." He paused long enough to make a statement with his distant inspection, then, confident and deliberate, strode toward Ivy and stopped before her. "I recognize this lady."

Feeling like he was hungry and she was what he wanted to eat, Ivy resisted taking a step back. "Then you have the advantage."

Not to be left behind, Gabriela joined him and Ivy. "She doesn't recognize *anyone,* even my dad."

"How interesting for both of you." Matthew sounded as though he wished he was part of the situation.

Why is this man coming on to me? Obviously, he was some kind of relative. Trying to forget Gabriela's coolness on the way to the country club, Ivy gazed at her until Gabriela waved absently at the man.

"Oh, this is Uncle Matthew."

Matthew was more precise. "Matthew Till."

"My husband's brother?"

A smile played on his lips as he gave a faint nod. His head tilted toward the bar. "Will you join me in a drink?"

They had promised Cullen they'd meet him in this place. Clearly his father wasn't here; there was no navy Lincoln in the parking lot. The last thing Ivy wanted was to sit down to a drink with a man sending out these kinds of signals. Particularly if he wasn't Cullen. *I'm too tired to deal with this.*

Had she imagined it all?

His expression left no hope. Matthew Till was a wolf in wolf's clothing.

She gathered her strength.

"We should hang out," said Gabriela. "We're supposed to meet Dad here anyway."

Matthew's smile showed only delight. "By all means, then. Gabby, what can I get my favorite niece? And nothing alcoholic, please, or I believe Corky *will* kick you out. Otherwise, I think she'll be indulgent." He threw the barmaid an affectionate wink.

The woman's expression was less forgiving. "For you, Matthew, anything."

"Do you have Perrier?" Gabriela asked.

"Absolutely." Corky eyed Ivy coldly. "Gina?"

Ivy stepped up to the bar. "Actually, my name's Ivy now. And you'll have to forgive me—"

"She has brain damage," Gabriela interjected. "She can't remember anything or anyone from when she lived here before."

It sounded like an effort to embarrass masked as an effort to be helpful. Ivy glanced at Gabriela. "Thank you for explaining, Gabriela."

"Anytime." She gave her uncle a saucy smile.

Brat. Ivy looked at the barmaid. "And you are?"

"Corky Stone. We went to school together." Her expression had softened some. She was blond and tiny, with a little scar on her upper lip and a blue-and-white crop top stretching over her full breasts.

"I'm so sorry. Everyone wondered what had happened to you."

"If anyone finds out, I hope they'll tell me. I've been living in Colorado for the past ten or so years. I'm a certified nurse-midwife."

"Good for you. I just can't believe you're back! And you've seen Cully and everything?"

Those eyes and ears were avidly gathering news—like hands snatching up twenty-dollar bills dropped in the street. Did this have to do with the ballet teacher? Ivy took a breath. "Yes."

"So—he's happy?"

A silence. What should she say?

"He's *way* happy." Gabriela's voice drew a line on the spotless bar. "My mother's home. He's happy. And I'm happy."

So that's part of who you are, Ivy mused.

She was defending her father.

No.

Her family.

I like you, Gabriela.

"Your mother's return is something to be happy about." Matthew's large hands settled on Ivy's shoulders. "What can I have Corky pour you?"

Her movement was instinctive. His hands were gone, he was busy regaining his balance, and she had put four feet between them. "Matthew, please don't startle me that way. There was a possibility I lost my memory because of an attacker, and you can imagine how I wouldn't want that to happen again. So I tend to react very quickly to someone touching me without my permission. Please don't do it again.''

Behind the counter, Corky danced to ''I Take My Chances.'' ''What can I get you…Ivy, was it?''

''I'll have what Gabriela's having, please.''

Gabriela had gone motionless. Her eyes started to Ivy's. Slowly, she smiled. A real smile, from her eyes. ''I'll get us a table.''

''Thank you.''

''Tell me,'' Matthew murmured when Gabriela was out of earshot, ''does Cullen find you even more intriguing than before?''

Ivy was thankful for ten years of observing relationships between men and women, often at intimate range. Husbands and wives at the birth of a child. Tara's relationship with her ex-husband. Francesca's with hers, which was something different altogether. And dating had given her practice in discouraging unwanted advances.

Easy to tell Matthew, ''You'll have to ask him that. Is Cullen a member here, Corky?''

''Sure. Want me to run a tab?''

''Thanks. I know he'll pick this up.'' Ivy left the bar to join Gabriela at the table she'd chosen. There was no way of knowing why Matthew had behaved as he had, with such confidence, toward his brother's wife.

But it was possible to guess.

And Ivy didn't like her guess at all.

A HALF INCH OF SNOW had covered the Lincoln. The surrounding landscape was all white, even the woods.

On the judge's cell phone, which he'd stopped at Coalgood to pick up, Cullen dialed his brother-in-law's mobile number.

Tom said, "Yeah?"

"I found him."

"Where are you?"

"State park." His father had taken him hiking here, camping in summer, caving. "To be specific, I found the car and his tracks. I'm going after him now." His father's request—to die—hung in the air.

"The store's closed. Shall I pick up Zeya and bring her to drive the Lincoln back?"

"Thanks." Besides, Daddy might give him an argument about coming home. The judge outweighed him by thirty pounds, and Cullen didn't want to risk hurting him. "Will you please call my mother, too?"

"Of course."

Cullen hung up and opened the door of the Camaro.

He slogged through the snow-covered mud, past the Lincoln frosted with white. The footprints led toward the trail to Soldiers Cave.

How strange to have these thoughts. That he was glad for the chance to be here with the judge one more time.

The judge was only twenty feet up the trail, stopped. Maybe he'd forgotten where he was going. He squinted at Cullen as his younger son climbed to where he was standing.

"Cully." Sam Till felt his own lucidity. *That's my son, Cullen. Where am I? What are we doing here?*

He remembered then. Illness. Old age.

Alzheimer's.

He looked around. *What was this place? Oh, yes, Guyandotte State Park. Why did I come?* "They sent you after me, didn't they?" The snow fell softly, drifting down through the trees.

"Want to come back to the car? I'll drive you home. Tom and Zeya are coming to get the Lincoln."

The world was a blank, a place of mystery, where even the simplest things were withheld from him. Cully talked slower than other people, but it didn't help now. And there was something…something…he wanted Cully to do. Oh, yes.

"I'll drive you to Coalgood," his son offered.

Sam wasn't ready. He wanted to decline, which he could do with a single word that he could not remember.

His eyes leaked tears.

Cullen jammed his hands in the pockets of his red-and-blue alpine shell. His ears hurt from the cold. He pulled the hood over his head, half-waiting for a repeat of the request his father had made just the previous night.

Help me die.

It never came. Maybe the judge was past asking.

And maybe past moving on his own initiative. "Come on. Let's go home. To Coalgood."

The judge didn't move.

"Daddy, I need to get back to my family. Gina has

come home. She goes by Ivy now, but she's come home to live with me and Gabby. I need to go. Will you please come with me?''

Sam heard. *Gina*. Gina. Cullen had a future ahead of him. Still sowing his oats, hiking all over the world, caving, still wandering the hills like some hill-billy, but at least he'd sold some photos. He'd been at the right place at the right time more than once.

But *Gina? Cully, did you have to knock up that girl and marry her?* And then…

Time jumped, forward, then back. "You should think hard if you really want to marry that…" What were they, that class of humans? Zeya and Mitzi, his wife. He saw them in droves and tried to think of the word for them. *Woman.* That was it, he thought with a moment's satisfaction. *Woman. Woman.*

The cold seeped into Sam's bones. He saw his own shoes in the snow. Why had he worn these shoes hik-ing?

Cullen had his arm, was helping him down the trail.
I'm old and sick, and my kids are taking care of me.

Another thought followed. Then evaporated. It was important. What was it?

"You know, Your Honor, you're my favorite judge."

"Smart-ass kid."

"I love you."

Sam's tears froze on his cheeks. "I hope you find another wife, Cully. You deserve a woman who loves you."

Cullen steered his father around a snow-covered walk. How was he supposed to answer that one?

Another wife.

A woman to love him.

Well, Daddy, I have the first of those, anyway. "Let's go home to Coalgood. And the woman who loves *you.*"

CHAPTER FOUR

HE STOOD IN THE DOORWAY in his parka, which was purplish blue with bright red lining and trim—good outdoor gear. When she first glimpsed him there, so tall and strong, Ivy felt a trill along her pulse. For ten years, she had tried to feel something for other men and had felt so little that she wondered if her head injury had damaged her emotions, even her attraction to the opposite sex.

Each time she saw Cullen dispelled those doubts. She was attracted to this man. Powerfully.

His eyes barely flickered over her or Gabriela but settled on Matthew, their expression unblinking and cold.

"You must come to Atlanta to see the museum when it's done," Matthew was saying to Ivy, referring to the new Museum of the Confederacy, which he'd designed. "I'll fly you there. In my plane."

"Excuse me." Rising, Ivy caught Cullen's eye. She had to step around Gabriela's chair to go to him.

His slightly parted lips, his hands catching her arms through the wool of her ribbed turtleneck, could have meant anything.

She asked, "Did you find your father?"

"Yes. He's back at Coalgood. I'd gotten him home

before I remembered you haven't slept. How are you holding up?''

''Getting sleepy.''

''We'll leave the Camaro here, and I'll drive you home.''

''Find Daddy?''

Matthew's proximity heated her back. He'd stopped short of touching her, but only just. Ivy's instinct was to slam her elbow into his solar plexus. Instead, she took one long step forward, turning to stand beside Cullen. ''Corky ran a tab for the drinks, Cullen. I hope that's all right.''

''I offered to get them, but your lady was very insistent.''

Cullen ignored the remark. ''I did find Daddy. I thought you were in Atlanta until I saw your car outside.''

''I only just returned and had the privilege of seeing my favorite niece and this beautiful creature.''

Ivy studied their faces, assessed the energy between them. *This isn't about me at all.* ''I'm going to sit down with Gabriela.''

''Sure.''

Cullen watched her legs, her body, her confident walk. She'd always been a good athlete; she probably still was. Maybe this summer he'd take her somewhere instead of going with Tom. For her, he'd shave with ice water.

''She is absolutely the most irresistible woman I have seen in some time.''

Cullen glanced at Matthew. As a teenager, he'd

stopped fighting Matthew. But Matthew had a way of pulling on your shirt, punching and beating on you until you hit back.

Cullen had developed a system for dealing with his brother. Strength through resistance to anger. It worked until human frailty snapped, as it had at Coalgood the other night, when he'd been unable to keep from saying, "With her husband." But Ivy's behavior had met with his complete satisfaction. "She's beautiful," he agreed. "Join us, or are you going home, Matthew?"

"Oh, I'll run along and let you enjoy your wife and Gabriela."

Another subtle dig. One with more dangerous implications—what Matthew knew about Gabriela. Ivy seemed able to take care of herself. Gabriela was a child.

The best protection for her was to pretend indifference to Matthew's insinuations. "Okay. Drive safely. The roads are slick."

"Not as slick as Gina's crotch, I'll bet."

With a sudden intake of breath, Cullen walked away.

At the table, he squeezed Gabriela's shoulders and grabbed a chair beside Ivy. "Does my family want to go home or eat here?"

"Ivy is a black belt in aikido and in tae kwon do. She almost made Uncle Matthew fall down."

"Did she?" He grinned at Ivy, swallowing other feelings. Knowledge. "I'll have to be careful."

"No." Her face was solemn. Honest. "I'd defend you with my life."

He believed her. "It's important to me that you never do that. Defend me in any physical way." Especially from Matthew.

Their eyes held long.

"Do you understand?"

"Not why." A second passed. "But if that's what you want, I won't."

"Thanks."

Gabriela sat up in her chair and all but snapped her fingers for a menu. "Let's eat here."

IT'S HAPPENING, Gabriela thought later that night.

Her dad was totally caught up in Ivy. But the weird thing was, they were both paying a lot of attention to *her,* too.

Like Ivy standing in her room now, checking out her posters. "Okay, tell me who these people are."

"All right, that's Peter Martins. That's—"

"Wait! I know!"

Gabriela couldn't help laughing.

"Baryshnikov." Ivy grinned at her. "Right?"

"That earns you one point out of a hundred as a ballet lover."

Ivy pointed at another poster. "The Alvin Ailey Company?"

"The words kind of give it away, don't you think?"

Ivy laughed, then examined the other posters. "I'm stumped. Educate me."

Jumping off her bed, Gabriela plucked two books from the maple bookcase her dad had made. "Educate yourself."

Ivy read the first title. *Writing Dancing in the Age of Postmodernism.* "Have you read this?"

"Some of it. Tracy—my ballet teacher suggested it. I'm going to be a prima ballerina and then a choreographer. I've got great videos, too. That's what you really need to do. Watch videos." She looked over her shelves again.

"Wait, wait. I want to watch them with you."

"Tonight?"

It was almost ten. "How about tomorrow?"

"Thanksgiving. We'll have to go to Coalgood. That's my grandparents' house. But we could take some videos, and Noel can come over. She's my best friend. I want her to meet you."

Ivy felt her eyes watering. *She likes me.*

"Are you all right?"

"I'm just happy. To be here with you." And Cullen.

Gabriela's whole body seemed to grow light. This was her mother, and it felt good. It felt like it was meant to be. She didn't know what to say, so she said nothing at all.

IVY WAS PRACTICING tae kwon do patterns in Gabriela's dance room when Cullen came in. He sat on a mat by the mirror to do his nightly sit-ups and push-ups. He'd run in the snow that morning, a lifetime ago.

She seemed not to notice him. He watched a few kicks reaching high over her head and decided she was lethal. And she'd dealt with Matthew, though she hadn't managed to discourage him.

He counted sit-ups, keeping his mind empty.

Then push-ups.

When he stopped, she was stretching, and he moved closer. She'd put on some loose black pants and a white long-sleeved T-shirt. He wore sweatpants and a T-shirt.

"Cullen," she said, "I'd like to start a midwifery practice here."

"Sure. You just worked out of the house before. Is that all right?"

"I think so. I'd like to find a backup physician. Anyone you'd recommend?"

"My sister and my sister-in-law like Mata Iyer."

"Is she an OB/GYN?"

"As far as I know. I'm more inclined to notice that she's gorgeous. I think she's Indian."

"Great. I can't wait to meet her." On her back, Ivy stretched a leg over her head. *Matthew. Should she bring it up?* Yes. "Your brother came on to me pretty strong."

Cullen relaxed forward, over his legs, stretching. How direct she was. Not like Gina. Not that Gina would have betrayed him. She just...

He couldn't put it into words.

He'd never wanted to.

"I know." What else could he say? Did one fair turn deserve another?

He got up, checked that Gabriela's door was shut, then shut the door of the dance room. He sat beside Ivy, facing her. "Gabriela is his natural daughter."

The single beat of her heart slammed Ivy's chest.

"You worked part-time in the courthouse. I think he met you there, when he was stopping by to see my dad. You fell in love with him. He was married, you got pregnant."

"Slow down. Please." It obviously wasn't his favorite story to tell, but she needed to know everything. "Was I married to you?"

"No. We were friends from school. I'd…liked you for a long time. You kept guys at a distance, so it seemed easiest to be friends."

"You married me because I was pregnant."

"Wrong. I married you because I was in love with you."

"And I loved your brother."

"Not after the mess he got you into."

Ivy had her doubts. "Gabriela doesn't know?"

"No one knows except Matthew. And it's possible he's told Shelby—his wife—somewhere along the line."

Ivy had noticed Matthew's wedding ring over drinks.

She'd slept with a married man. Borne his child. Married his brother.

Not me. Gina.

How convenient. A blow to the head had changed her into someone who didn't do such things.

No. Francesca and Tara had. Midwifery had. Martial arts had. Most of the ways she'd developed, she'd collected on her own, through the use of her mind, her will, the skills she'd learned.

But she hated this. Hated that Gabriela was Matthew's child instead of Cullen's. Obviously, Cullen was Gabriela's dad in every other way. But...

Could she live with that kind of lie?

It seemed wrong. Maybe Gina would have accepted it from start to finish, to cover her own crimes. But it didn't sit well with Ivy Walcott.

"Cullen, I want her to know. I think it's important."

"Then we disagree."

"But what if your brother tells her?"

Cullen sighed. Matthew was capable of telling her. He hadn't in twelve years, but... "Let's take this up again when you're not tired." He changed the subject. "Think you can sleep now?"

Her limbs were heavy as bags of sand. "I think."

"Why don't you turn in? I'll be up in an hour or two. I have some slides to put in the mail."

Ivy hesitated. "You don't have to. Stay up late, I mean."

She was getting used to his smile lines. "I think we'll both sleep better if I do. Go on up."

LEAVING OFF the overhead light in the loft, Ivy changed into flannel pajamas and left her clothes on the floor beside the dresser. Downstairs, Cullen had put Jackson Browne on the stereo, low.

The tester bed seemed bigger in the dark, the canopy like protection. Gabriela's bed was cast iron; Cullen said it was the bed Ivy had slept in growing up. Both of the beds had been in her family since her grandmother was a child.

This is really my home.

. He was her home.

She had put the box in her top drawer. It was just a small white gift box in which she kept all her earrings and a couple of bracelets and necklaces, most of them gifts from Tara and Francesca.

Her rings were there, too. A gold band and another ring, a circle of lapis lazuli stones set in gold.

She'd been wearing the rings when she was brought to the hospital in Boulder. For days, she'd twisted them on her finger, rubbed them like talismans. One nurse after another had said, "What beautiful rings."

Ivy had loved them, too. And wondered who had given them to her.

While she slipped them on her left hand, Jackson Browne sang "Tender is the Night."

The clean flannel sheets on the daybed smelled faintly of pine. The mattress was firm, and to her left the windows reached to the ceiling. Shadows from the moon, far beyond the trees, cast black shapes on the warm wooden walls, just as the moonlight illuminated the trees through all the windows, including those behind the tester bed.

What had he said today? That she could trust him to leave her alone...for a while?

Was Cullen waiting out of kindness? Or to give his

grief over the loss of Gina a chance to heal? Or was it because of Tracy, the ballet teacher?

Who was Gina? Cullen had promised to tell her things—and he was, gradually—but so far she just couldn't picture the person she'd been at twenty, when she'd married him, or at twenty-two, when she'd disappeared.

Today, she'd instantly pegged Matthew Till as a seducer, a womanizer. She'd seen them in all forms in Precipice, and she'd seen them more skillful than Matthew. How old had he been then? He had to be at least forty now. But maybe not.

I slept with him.

It disgusted her. She really couldn't stand the idea of sex with a man who couldn't control his sensuality, a man who saw women as conquests.

But Gabriela... *I love her.*

What if Gabriela was to find out the truth? Would she hate her mother? Would she hate Cullen for lying to her?

The point of change needed to come immediately. Only now would Ivy have the right to explain, to say, *I'm not the same woman I used to be.* But if she conspired with Cullen and Matthew to keep the secret, how was she different?

Suddenly, a fourth party entered the picture.

Matthew's wife. Shelby.

Cullen had said he suspected Shelby knew the truth. But did she? And if she didn't...

Ivy hugged the sheets around her in the dark. As she'd driven across the country, she'd tried to foresee all the possibilities of what she'd find in West Virginia. A husband she didn't like. A daughter with whom she felt no connection. People with different interests. A place where she'd never feel at home.

Instead, she'd discovered a gentle man who seemed to respect her—a man *she* could respect. Her daughter liked her, and Ivy liked and loved Gabriela without trying. The hill country was beautiful, the cabin a place where she could live and die in happiness.

Her imagination had fallen short in assessing the possible problems.

She'd never suspected that the woman she'd been would have left the kind of unfinished business that Gina had.

And I should have guessed. To arrive at a hospital a thousand miles from home, broken and bleeding. Why? What had happened?

Who were you, Gina? Tell me.

Who was I?

SHE SLEPT IN blue flannel pajamas with pictures of appliances on them. Cullen had seen them earlier when she was unpacking, putting her clothes in the dresser he'd cleaned out. She said she'd brought everything she owned but furniture. She didn't have much—of anything.

In the moonlight, he stripped off his T-shirt. Her blond hair sprayed over the pillow, over her pajamas. She'd already kicked off half the covers. The heat from the stove downstairs collected in this loft all day.

Cullen carefully gathered her grandmother's log cabin quilt and folded it over the back of the rocking chair.

When she sighed in her sleep, he started slightly. She rolled to her side, and the top of her pajamas hung loose, showing the curve of her breasts. There must be some of Gina left in her, something to make her trust him so completely. Or else it was simply that she'd lost years of her life and it had made her naive.

She hadn't seemed naive at the country club.

Before he could turn away, to get in the canopy bed they'd once shared, he saw her hand resting on the sheets, on the bed where Gabriela had slept as a three- and four-year-old.

The moonlight was tender.

He opened the drawer where he'd put her photo, found his ring and put it on.

HER EYES OPENED, and the natural light in the room was wonderful despite the gray day. The limbs of the man tugging a T-shirt over his head held the same warmth as the wood. Ivy admired his abs and pecs and the muscles of his arms. What would his chest hair feel like if she touched him? As the white cotton fell down around his body, he saw her eyes and paused beside the tester bed, his head higher than the canopy. "Good morning."

"Good morning." *We spent the night in this room together.* She'd never heard him come in.

His jaw was shadowed, unshaven. "Gabriela and I have a Thanksgiving tradition that she claims to hate.

We snowshoe to Ganfrey's Pond, about a mile away, and go ice-skating. Then, regrettably, there's a command performance at Coalgood. The family home.''

"That sounds really nice, the skating. So I should dress warmly?''

"When you feel like it. The other part of the tradition is a leisurely, healthful breakfast—as Gabriela says, to make up for what Lily will do to us later. Lily's my parents' housekeeper,'' he added quickly. "And a wonderful cook.''

Before Ivy could bring up the issue of telling Gabriela about her natural father, there came a bump on the floor.

Cullen called, "Hold your horses. I'm coming down.''

Gabriela yelled, "I want to get this miserable day on the road!''

"A lover of the holiday, you can see.'' With a wink at Ivy, Cullen headed for the ladder.

"Cullen.'' He looked back, and Ivy put thoughts of Matthew and Gabriela aside. "Thank you.''

"For what?''

"For welcoming me back.''

"Wait to say that until you pass the ultimate ordeal.''

"What's that? I can cook,'' she offered.

He laughed. "So can I. That's not what I meant.''

His eyes turned momentarily mischievous. "I meant,'' he stage-whispered, "Pass the ultimate ordeal. *Coalgood.*''

CHAPTER FIVE

THROUGH THE CASEMENT windows of the living room and beneath the snowy limbs of the climbing oak, Zeya watched Cullen and Ivy overturn the toboggan in a snowbank. Legs tangled in the snow, they laughed, and Cullen caught her in a one-armed hug before they got to their feet. "I haven't seen Cully that happy in years."

Her elder brother peered over her shoulder for a view. "Gabriela doesn't seem so happy."

"Matthew," his wife called from the couch, "come look at these photos Cullen brought over. He actually got something flattering of me. It's a miracle."

Shelby, Zeya wanted to say, *you're a saint.*

Matthew edged over to the coffee table where his stepmother and Shelby were passing photos back and forth, Mitzi sharing each one with the judge. Scrutinizing the photo of Shelby and Scout, Matthew finally bent over and kissed his wife. "You are a beautiful subject." He tugged absently on a red curl, then returned to the window. "Well, I think I'll go join the lovebirds and my nieces and Tom."

Matthew was not usually a sledder, and Zeya exclaimed, "Good grief, Matthew, why don't you give him some peace to be with his family?"

"Why, Zeya, are you suggesting that I would choose this joyful moment in my brother's life to torment him?"

"Matthew," the judge barked abruptly, "leave your brother alone. Let him play in peace."

As Matthew gritted his teeth, the three women smiled at the judge's twenty-five-year time leap.

Matthew finally smiled. "He's not playing, Daddy. He's outside with Gina."

Rising from the couch, Shelby stretched languorously. "Feeling like going upstairs for a while, Matthew?"

Definitely a holy woman, thought Zeya. No other being in the universe would have so much patience with Matthew or so much compassion for him.

"Gina?" The judge walked to the window.

His wife followed. "She's different now, Sam. This is Ivy."

"That's not Gina. Why the hell did you say Gina was out there?" Before anyone could answer, the judge exclaimed, "By God, there she is, after Tom now, it looks like. Matthew, tell her to go home."

Zeya, her mother and Matthew saw in astonishment what the judge had noticed. Gabriela and Scout climbing off a sled at the bottom of the hill, where Tom had met them. Gabriela.

No one spoke for seconds.

Then, abruptly, Matthew threw back his head and howled with laughter.

CULLEN DRAGGED Gabriela's sled back toward the top of the long run, alongside the sunken garden behind the house.

"Uncle Cullen, take me. No, Daddy's going down. Daddy, wait!"

As Scout ran to join Tom on a toboggan, Cullen gave Gabriela's shoulders a squeeze. "How are you doing?"

"Fine."

Something was amiss, but Cullen had no idea what until Ivy hauled the other toboggan over the snow toward them. "Gabriela," she asked, "when can we watch those videos?"

"Now, probably. If you want."

"I do."

Like that, the sparkle returned to Gabriela's eyes. Cullen debated if he should volunteer to join them, then decided Gabriela wanted Ivy to herself.

Know just how you feel, Gabs.

"Come on." Gabriela abandoned her sled. "Let's go in the back way. Then we won't get the snow-on-the-floor lecture from Grandma and Lily."

A figure in a fisherman-knit sweater and flannel-lined khaki pants trudged around the corner of the house and up the hill toward them, looking like an advertisement for L.L. Bean.

Catching sight of Matthew, Ivy said, "Great, let's go. I'll race you," and sprinted over the snow to the back patio.

Gabriela passed her and wheeled, throwing up both hands to stop her so that Ivy ran into her, and they both stumbled, laughing. "Slow down," Cullen called out. "The patio's slick."

"Mother and daughter," Matthew remarked softly. "Anywhere on earth, a person could see that Ivy is that child's mother. And that Gabriela is her daughter."

Ignoring him, Cullen chose the fastest sled and continued up the hill that rose alongside the sunken garden.

Helping himself to the toboggan, Matthew followed. "Except, of course, the judge. Our father, get this, mistook Gabriela for Gina. 'By God, there she is, after Tom now, it looks like. Matthew, tell her to go home.'" He shouted a laugh. "Let's go to the top, Cullen. I'll race you. Course, you have the faster sled."

Cullen offered his brother the rope.

"No, thanks. I just wanted to point out that you have the superior equipment so you'll feel a greater sting of humiliation when you lose."

They found the launching point, the highest launching point on the property, too high for Scout—and Gabriela was too aware of her future as a dancer to risk a sledding accident. Cullen settled on the sled, using one foot behind him as a brake. "You say when."

"Now." Matthew caught Cullen's arm and yanked him along.

Cullen had intended to give his brother a solid head start. Now he was ahead, though Matthew's heavier weight evened the contest some.

The snow had crusted to ice in places. Through the clatter of the runners, he heard Matthew's words, the judge's words. *There she is, after Tom now, it looks like.* His thoughts pulsed red. White flew at his eyes.

"Get over!" Cullen yelled.

Matthew nudged the side of the sled with the toboggan.

They were at the right edge of the run. They needed to move left, not right, to avoid the cluster of oaks separating Coalgood from the Nathans' place next door.

Cullen gave the sled a sharp jerk all the way to the right and rolled off it to the left, coming to within a foot of the second oak.

"Yee-haw!" Matthew yelled, lifting a fist as he rode the rest of the way down the run. "You're a chicken, Cullen! You always were."

Cullen dragged the sled to the house, then walked down the hill to meet Matthew.

Getting up from the toboggan, his brother reached out and patted his cheek with a snowy wool glove. "Still Daddy's little puppy, aren't you, Cully?"

"Why would Daddy think Gina was hitting on Tom?"

Matthew's face changed, became overly concerned with the question. "Now, why *would* he think that—when she was always so faithful to you?" He tossed wiry, gray-flecked golden hair back from his eyes. A second later, he grinned and slammed Cullen on the back. "You're so *easy*, Cully. You're easy to bait."

He hugged Cullen and kissed his cheek loudly, then whispered, "He never said it. Ha-ha-ha!"

Staying behind, Cullen watched Matthew drag the toboggan back up to the house.

Tom came up behind him. "I recommend a padded cell for that man."

"Uncle Cullen." Scout tugged on his coat. "Will you take me down the big hill?"

The front door shut behind Matthew. "Sure, Scout. Let's go."

"Can you pull me up on the sled?"

"Dream on."

Tom laughed. "Start walking, kid."

"I'll beat you both!" she yelled and ran.

"I never met Gina, but Ivy seems nice."

"She is."

"Not exactly a dog, either."

"Not exactly." Cullen was glad when Tom continued up the hill after his daughter, leaving him to grab a sled, to be alone.

There she is, after Tom now, it looks like.

The judge's words.

Matthew was mean, but he just wasn't that clever.

"OH, WHAT WOULD YOU GIVE?" Noel exclaimed. "Did you *see* that?"

Gabriela had invited her friend over to watch the ballet videos, and two hours ago Noel had arrived with the news that Zeya and Tom had gone to the toy store to prepare for the start of the Christmas season tomorrow, and Cullen was building "snow creatures" with Scout.

In Coalgood's rec room in the basement, Ivy listened to the two girls' ballet dreams and watched some of the most phenomenal dance she'd ever seen. Postmodern ballet and more.

She wanted to encourage Gabriela's dreams, but she wished they were less tied to the prospect of fame.

"Look at all those flowers," Gabriela said. The ballerina's arms were overflowing.

Ivy asked, "How would it make you feel to get so many flowers?"

"Great!"

Ivy wanted to help her through this adolescence, help her make the transition to womanhood. From needing to be loved, from needing approval, to loving and nurturing.

But for now, her immediate concern was that Gabriela be told Matthew was her natural father—before Matthew decided to tell her. That meant first convincing Cullen, then telling Matthew and Shelby their intention. One meeting with Shelby had made Ivy suspect that Matthew's wife did know the truth. It had also made her admire Shelby, who was an unlikely partner for Matthew Till.

But she really hadn't had a second alone with Cullen since that morning. When she'd come downstairs, she'd found him cooking breakfast while Gabriela photographed him with his camera and begged him to let her go away to New York City to ballet school. Ivy had the feeling that it was the continuation of a long conversation on the subject because they both did a lot of laughing.

And who, Miss Gabriela Till, would steal all the hot water in the morning if you were gone?

Ivy.

And who would talk back to me?

I'll teach Ivy how.

They ended the conversation with a hug and Gabriela saying, *Okay, I'll stay and torment you for one more year.*

He was a good father, and Gabriela was a wonderful girl. *How did I get so lucky?*

"Hello, ballet fans. We've been summoned to dinner."

Noel and Gabriela perked up at Cullen's entrance.

"Dad, can I sleep over at Noel's? Her mom said it's okay."

His hesitation lasted no more than a moment. "Yes."

"Hooray!" The girls sent up a cheer, and Noel jumped to her feet.

"Okay, I'm going home. Come over as soon as you can. We've got a toothbrush and everything, Mr. Till. It's nice meeting you…Mrs. Till."

As Gabriela shut off the VCR, Noel went through the big arched doorway of the rec room. Instead of heading up the stairs, she turned down the hall to the right. Leaving the room with Gabriela and Cullen half a minute later, Ivy peered down the hallway. Noel had disappeared.

"There's a mudroom down there—and stairs up to the sunken garden," Cullen explained.

"The laundry room's in there and the dumb-waiter," Gabriela added. "Once, Uncle Matthew pulled my dad partway to the second floor in the dumbwaiter and just left him for a whole afternoon. Can you believe it?"

Ivy couldn't tell how Gabriela felt about the event. Perhaps she viewed it as an amusing family anecdote. Or maybe she was alarmed on behalf of the boy trapped in the dumbwaiter.

"How old were you?"

"Three." Cullen nodded toward the stairs. "Let's go up. You can see my family in full color now."

"It's always *so weird*," Gabriela confided.

Ivy wondered if that was why Cullen hadn't met her eyes once since he'd come downstairs.

SHE SAT ON the judge's right.

He said, "You aren't a vegetarian, are you?"

"No."

"Good. Glad Cullen's met a nice girl."

Gina wasn't?

Mitzi Till threw Ivy an apologetic look and shook her head, a sign to pay no attention to the things he said.

On Ivy's right, Cullen ate silently, never looking up at her.

What was wrong? She couldn't escape the feeling that something had changed for him since they were last together on the sledding hill.

"Ivy *is* a nice girl," remarked Matthew. "Incorruptible, I'd say."

"You would know," the judge muttered.

"Daddy!" Mitzi Till shook her head. "Please be nice. This is Thanksgiving. Matthew, help him with his turkey."

But Lily had appeared over the judge's shoulder. "Let me help you, Judge Till."

"I can cut my own food!"

Cullen's arm went across Ivy, keeping her back from the brandished steak knife. "Easy, Daddy."

Ivy trembled, and Cullen rose. "Switch seats with me," he said.

She did, without a word, and found herself next to Scout.

"How gallant of you, Cullen," Matthew murmured.

Scout nudged Ivy's leg. She held up a small plastic figure. "Aunt Ivy, watch out. *An alien!* He wants to steal your heart."

Ivy started to giggle at the idea when Matthew's smooth voice overrode her laughter. "I'm sure he's not the only one."

Courtesy kept Ivy from casting a look at Shelby, on Matthew's left, to see how she was taking this behavior, the incessant digs at his younger brother.

"Zeya, take the toys away from Scout, *please*. Scout, honey, it's not good manners to have toys at the table. Grandma says please put the alien away. Honey, don't you want some turkey? It's so good."

"Did you take my bread?"

Matthew sat back from the judge. "No, Daddy, I most certainly did not take your bread."

"Mitzi." The look the judge threw his wife was suspicious.

"Daddy, you *ate* it." Zeya passed Ivy a bowl. "Ivy, try this rice pilaf."

"I did *not* eat it."

Cullen lifted his chair and set it back on the patterned Karastan, then retrieved his camera. "Daddy, sit next to Matthew. Let's have a photo."

IN THE FRONT SEAT of the Saab, he started the car without a word.

Instinctively, she touched his hand. "Cullen."

His glance was a snake's bite, that quick and sharp. She never flinched. "What is it?"

He switched off the ignition, sat back in his seat and watched snow falling in the headlights. In a row along the curb, the snow bandits and snow Martians he and Scout had built were losing their shape. Should he share what Matthew had told him, what the judge had said? Pride rebelled against letting Ivy know... know what?

It was all guesses. A suspicion Matthew had raised, preying on his own insecurity. An insecurity with powerful reason behind it. The most powerful reason of all. And even if the judge had said it, what did that mean? He could have just confused times. Perhaps he'd seen Matthew with Gina before she was pregnant with Gabriela....

Though he'd never said so.

The judge didn't know about Gabriela.

Cullen finally answered, "Too much Coalgood. Let's go home."

She stopped him before he could start the car again. "Cullen, please don't keep things from me."

"All right. My brother said something that led me to think my wife—that would be you—may have betrayed me with him after our marriage." With a bright, mirthless smile, he started the car.

"I'm sorry. If it's true. I'm not that kind of person now."

"If it's true, your apology is inadequate. Keep it." He drew the Saab away from the curb and into the road, making the first tire tracks on a blanket of white.

Ivy shut her mouth, opened it to argue, then closed it again. Who else, after all, should be expected to suffer for Gina's wrongs?

The Saab made its way around the island, and Cullen glanced toward a house on the left where a light burned. Ivy had learned from Noel and Gabriela that Tracy lived on this street. "Was that Tracy's house?"

"Yes."

Ivy changed the subject. "Have you given any more thought to telling Gabriela the truth about Matthew?"

"About Matthew and you, do you mean?"

There was no point in saying he had no proof. The signs were there. "Yes. About who her natural father is."

"Her natural father." His tone was bitter.

She winced. *Don't do this, Cullen.*

Still, to have taken blame for the unplanned pregnancy, to have married her and then been betrayed...

He was right. Sorry would never be enough.

The wipers crossed back and forth on the windshield in sweeping arcs. Dark miles passed on the highway before he turned up the road that led toward the hollows.

They didn't speak again until the cabin.

Shutting off the engine, Cullen said, "It's better for her not to know. You have to understand this about Matthew. He has limits. He wants to hurt me, not Gabriela."

"I don't think he'd hesitate for a second to hurt me, Cullen. Or any other woman he wanted. Obviously, he doesn't mind hurting his own wife. What makes you think he'd be more sensitive to his niece's feelings, especially since she's your daughter?"

"His daughter, you mean."

"And since you brought it up, what is it with you two?"

Cullen released his seat belt, tried to get comfortable with his back to the door, his knee behind the gearshift. "He's fourteen years older than me. His mom died when he was Gabriela's age."

"Ouch."

"And Daddy remarried pretty fast. Also..."

When he didn't finish, Ivy guessed. "You're Daddy's favorite?"

His silence was no denial.

She made a face. "He'll tell her, Cullen. And I don't want him to be the one to do it."

Cullen shifted in his seat, opened the door. "Let's continue this discussion inside."

EIGHT HOURS EARLIER, if someone had told him Gabriela would be spending the night at a friend's, he would have rejoiced. Now the last thing he wanted was time alone with Ivy.

Gina.

Building the fire in the woodstove, he contemplated nature and nurture. Ivy must still possess Gina's nature. Was it a lack of nurture that had made her unfaithful? He wanted to believe it—and didn't.

"Care if I put on a CD?"

He glanced up. She was picking over his collection of CDs and the few of Gabriela's that were jumbled in with them. "Go ahead."

She chose Neil Young, keeping it low so they could talk.

For a second, in the car, she'd almost convinced him about Gabriela. "Ivy, my name's on her birth certificate."

She digested that. "I can see your point, Cullen. I just—don't feel at ease with it."

Sitting on the rag rug, Cullen felt a little of his rancor fading. How many nights would they sleep in separate beds? He stood and turned up the stereo. Not sure it was what he wanted, sure only that he needed to start somewhere, Cullen beckoned her from the couch.

"What?"

"You'll see."

Slowly, she rose in her socks and jeans and white turtleneck with diamonds on it. When she neared him, he took her left hand in his right and lightly wrapped his free arm around her as Neil Young sang "From Hank to Hendrix."

Cullen sang to her, and she couldn't help smiling.

Their smiles faded simultaneously, changing into something else.

He angled his head down, and she brought hers up.

Their lips touched, trying to answer the questions, trying to figure out if they could travel the long road together as they'd promised thirteen years ago—and the day before.

His lips were warm. Nothing familiar in them, but she liked his scent, liked his taste, liked the gentle pressure on her mouth. But his body was so big, so hard. Her other contact with men had been…different. More like the encounter with Matthew at the country club. Touches she didn't want. Dancing with Cullen, kissing him, was like skiing the backcountry, like snowshoeing in solitude through the forest, like the speed of skates on the ice of Ganfrey's Pond that morning.

"I've never…liked a man before."

He drew back, to study her face. Her eyes.

Slowly he smiled, but not with trust. "Lucky me."

Cullen released her, mostly so he wouldn't tell her his thoughts, which were bitter. *Unfortunately, I loved you. And you broke your vows.*

He told himself again not to leap to conclusions,

but it was too late.

In his heart, he had always known.

THERE WERE NO MORE KISSES that night. He settled down with some slides, she phoned Tara for the least candid conversation she'd ever shared with her sister, and finally, sensing he wanted her to turn in first, like the night before, Ivy did.

This time, sleep came slowly, and she was still awake when Cullen came up. Not wanting to surprise him, she said, "Hi."

He glanced toward the daybed. "Can't sleep?"

"No."

He indicated the canopy bed. "Want to get in here?"

She'd have to sometime, unforgiving husband or not. This wasn't the way she'd imagined it. *It probably isn't the way he wanted it, either.*

"I'd prefer to wait until you want me there."

"Oh." He unbuttoned his flannel shirt and hung it on the rod in the small closet. "Then don't let me disturb your insomnia."

Beside his bed, he stripped off his pants and underwear, and she knew it was his way of saying he was through giving her special treatment.

Starting with his discovery that day. Which had nothing to do with Ivy—and everything to do with Gina.

She closed her eyes, listened to the bed creak as he climbed in.

He sighed, expressing that his was the more comfortable bed. "Good night, Ivy."

"Good night, Cullen."

"Let's see," he muttered. "Gabriela will probably spend the night with Noel again in…May."

She knew what he meant, but…

"Those aren't the magic words."

"If only I knew them. Like—like *Matthew* does."

His bitterness chilled Ivy. Maybe he'd always doubt her, even knowing how much she'd changed with the loss of her former personality.

She was the one who needed magic words, and there were none.

She did the best she could.

Abruptly, she got out of bed, went to the far side of his and lifted the covers, remembering belatedly that he was naked beneath. The sudden realization made her sway on her feet. *What was she doing?*

Too late to back out.

It had been too late yesterday, when he'd met her with an embrace.

It was too late a week ago, when she'd promised to come home.

She got into bed and prepared her apology, while he eyed her as one might an affectionate coyote.

"My unfaithfulness to you was abominable. I'm sorry for hurting you. You can rest assured that the woman in your bed tonight would never do such a thing."

He didn't blink.

"I'm really sorry, Cullen."

"More sorry. Be more sorry."

"How can I be more sorry for something I don't remember doing?"

"So who did it? Where did she go? She looked a lot like you, and she called herself my wife, the way you do." He had sat up.

Cowering against a second pillow that smelled faintly of him, Ivy wondered how he expected either of them to get any sleep in this bed.

"I apologized. What else do you want me to do? Wear sackcloth and ashes for a year?"

"That would be a start. But you know what? You're right. There's nothing you can do. Except wait."

"For what?"

"For me to pay you the compliment of sharing my heart with you again."

"Well, don't expect to share my body in the meantime!"

"Tonight, it would be a chore." He fell back on the bed to stare at the canopy. "Good night."

She started to climb out of bed, but his hand locked on her wrist. "Oh, no, you don't."

"What?"

"I think it's time for you to start sharing your husband's bed—if nothing else."

This is ridiculous. What does he want? Irritated, Ivy eased herself back into the bed, careful not to touch him.

Slowly, he released her wrist. "Sackcloth and ashes for a year, did you say?"

"I want to go to sleep now, if you don't mind."

He ignored her. "A year... And what else did you say earlier tonight? I remember! 'I've never liked a man before.'"

Ivy shut her eyes and put her hands over her ears.

He moved them, pressing them to the pillow on either side of her, and when she opened her eyes, his gazed down at her and just enough of his weight covered her to make her want to feel the rest of him.

"Sleep well, *Gina.*" He didn't kiss her but released her and turned away.

BEFORE AN HOUR HAD PASSED, Cullen realized that her penance was going to be his hell. He wished he'd accepted her apology and left it at that.

The only problem—he didn't forgive her.

He didn't forgive *Gina.*

Ivy had had the last word, then drifted off to the sleep of the innocent. *I'm not Gina.*

In the night, he massaged his forehead. He'd been a jerk, and he was going to suffer unless he took back the things he'd said.

Suffering seemed more appealing.

She shifted in her sleep, her face resting against his upper arm. He didn't want to push her away but didn't want her close. She smelled so good. The scent hurt.

Gina, how could you? With a baby?

She'd had opportunity galore. She and Matthew could have met in this bed while he was at work.

And it explained...things he'd never wanted explained.

His eyes stung.

It was Gina's scent doing this to him, the familiarity.

But Gina had never slept with her head against his arm.

Gently, he moved, turning his back to her.

She slipped toward him, filling in the part of the bed he'd vacated.

Cullen flipped back and lifted her to move her over.

She jerked awake, eyes wide and mouth open in a cry, terrified, and her hands began to react. Not wanting to know what they could do, these hands, he caught her arms gently. "It's just me."

She relaxed.

A woman who had not slept with a man.

When he moved her over in the bed, she allowed it, like a sleepy child. *No one's going to hurt you again.*

The darkness reminded him that whatever wrong she had done him, something much worse might have been done to her.

To both of them.

She'd lost herself—and their child.

It hit him for the first time.

Gina had been pregnant when she was hurt. Pregnant with whose child?

To suspect Gina of sleeping with Matthew was one thing. But the other...

She wouldn't do it. Not that.

If only he knew.

Ivy's eyes, gazing at him, made Cullen realize that

he was propped on his arm, staring. At her. He lay down again.

"What were you thinking?"

"Wishing I could get your memory back for you. Every bit of it."

She didn't ask why. But after a long time, she said, "I don't want it so badly anymore."

CHAPTER SIX

SHE AWOKE SOMETIME in the night with her face on his skin and remembered his anger. Carefully, she shifted away, and he turned in his sleep, his head nearing hers.

Who's he dreaming of? Tracy?

Or Gina.

I don't want Gina to have done what she did.

I don't want to have done it.

Maybe she hadn't. Undoubtedly, that was why Cullen wished her memory would return. So that he could learn the truth.

She'd spent nights yearning to regain her memory the way Cinderella must have yearned to go to the ball. But her memory would never return. If Cullen wanted the truth, he should ask Matthew.

And what kind of answer would Matthew give?

Whatever answers would pain Cullen most.

But there was another solution. *What if I asked?*

"DON'T FEEL TOO SPECIAL. It happens every morning."

Ivy knew she'd been staring. She'd tried not to, but she found him beautiful.

Quelling an inner flush, she averted her eyes as he pulled on his sweatpants.

Cullen remembered, too late, that his was probably the first erection she'd ever seen—that she could recall. Anger over infidelity warred with other things, feelings that had more to do with Ivy than with Gina.

Anger won.

Taking clothes for the day out of his closet, he said, "I'm photographing kids with Santa Claus at Zeya and Tom's store from ten until two. I need to head downtown soon, get ready. Noel's mom said she'd bring Gabriela by the store after lunch. So the day is yours." *Invite Matthew over, if you like.*

"Is there anything I can do to help you?"

"Nothing," he lied.

Then she could run some errands, start advertising her midwifery practice. Only one thing troubled her. She sat up in bed but had to duck down again to see his face, he was so tall. "Cullen, I need to know something. I understand you're angry, but do you still want me to stay?"

His eyebrows lifted. "Thinking of leaving your husband and daughter already? Two days—"

"I'm not thinking of leaving. I'm asking if you wish I would."

"I wish you'd never screwed my brother."

I didn't.

The protest died inside her for the hundredth time. "Me, too. Though I can't regret our beautiful daughter."

He was silent. When he shut the closet door, it was

one degree short of a slam. He went downstairs without another word.

CLOTHES FOR SALE.

The table sat by the edge of the road, behind an old mini pickup with a camper shell, and the woman beside it wore exhaustion in her skin and her bones. It was the exhaustion of poverty, apparent in her gauntness and the slump of her shoulders. Ivy drew the Saab to the side of the road and got out, just as another woman came from the snowy woods, carrying a bag of dried vines. For ornamental wreaths, perhaps?

The woman who had emerged from the woods was pregnant, and Ivy instinctively assessed the size of her abdomen, how she was carrying. Was she getting prenatal care—or would her family do it the old way, at home?

Remembering Gabriela's reaction—"We're not hillbillies"—Ivy bet on a hospital birth.

Trudging through the snow from the car, Ivy called, "Good morning."

"Morning."

Ivy stopped at the table. The clothes on it were faded and tattered, with the exception of a satin affair that looked like a prom gown. But one of the older dresses was quite pretty, a blue calico, and there was a gorgeous quilt, too, a wedding-ring pattern.

"Can I help you?" The heavy mountain twang resonated in the older woman's voice. Her cigarette puffed clouds into the cold as she eyed the Saab distantly. Clearly, Ivy couldn't have appeared more foreign had she arrived on a camel.

"This dress is lovely. And the quilt." Ivy considered. The quilt looked newly made, albeit from well-worn fabric. There were plenty of quilts at the cabin—quilts Cullen said she and her grandmother had made—but the wedding-ring quilt would make the perfect Christmas gift for Francesca.

How much should she offer? She wanted to help, yet the last thing she needed was to appear too different from her client pool. And truthfully, she would earn less money working as a midwife here in Guyandotte.

The midwife in Morgantown to whom she'd spoken on the phone had said, "Get used to the idea of working for barter. A lot of these people won't even take public assistance, so there goes any possibility of medical insurance. More than half the time, you'll be paid in quilts and curtains and jars of Grandma's blackberry preserves. Be sure to find out who the people with money are and socialize some. You'll need at least a few paying clients."

Ivy asked, "Would you take ten for the dress and sixty for the quilt?"

"These quilts sell for two hundred in Morgantown."

It was worth that, at least, but Ivy couldn't pay it, and the woman didn't expect it. "The most I can give you is ninety for the quilt and ten for the dress."

"That'll do."

Ivy fished in her bag for her wallet, glad she had

the cash. The woman had hidden the hunger in her eyes, but...

"By the way, I'm Ivy Walcott." She held out her hand, and the woman could do nothing but take it—warily. In the frigid day, Ivy felt the calluses, the veins and wrinkles, of her hand. "I'm a midwife, and I'm just starting a practice here." She started to address the younger woman and faltered for a moment. *She's just a child...* Fifteen, perhaps, but *still.*

The older woman stared as though Ivy's profession had nothing to do with her.

"I know you've probably established a relationship with a doctor, but I just want to let you know in case you haven't. I grew up around here. My grandmother and mother were midwives, too."

"You don't say. Who was your grandmother?"

"Mrs. Naggy. I was Gina Naggy. I'm married to Cullen Till."

The woman squinted at her oddly. She stuck her cigarette back in her mouth. Ivy's hundred dollars had found their way into the pocket of the woman's quilted coat. "I thought that was you, but I was afraid to hazard a guess. I don't suppose you remember me. Emma Workman."

She thrust out her hand, and Ivy shook it again and hastily explained about her memory loss.

"That explains it. We were never close, but you would have seen me four or five thousand times in your life."

Emma swiftly changed topics. "Actually, Devon's not seeing a doctor. I've had four children and six grandchildren, including Devon. The doctors just want to run all kinds of tests, and we're keeping this baby. Doesn't seem a need for tests.'' She paused. ''How much do you charge?''

''I have a sliding scale. It depends on what you can pay.''

Emma sucked on her cigarette. ''Say we give you back fifty dollars of your money. Would that be enough?''

''Yes.'' Devon was far along. Thirty-two weeks? Thirty-three? *I have to get a backup physician.* But surely that wouldn't be a problem here, where poverty was rampant; any physician with a lick of sense could see that a midwife's services could only help. ''Do you have a phone at your house?''

''No. But we live up Missing Girl Hollow, too. I know your place.''

The girl should be seen without delay, and Ivy told Emma so. ''I need to know what to expect.''

''Our family births easy.''

''Nonetheless. May I visit with Devon for a bit?''

She retrieved her midwifery kit from her car—she always kept it there for emergencies—and took Devon's history on the rear bumper of the pickup, writing with her wool gloves on. Devon was sixteen, and the father was her boyfriend, Rowdy.

Ivy listened patiently, glad that Mrs. Workman stayed at a distance, allowing them to talk privately.

''Are you sure you want to keep this baby, Devon? You're young. A baby changes your whole life.''

''I want her. I think it's a girl. Rowdy and I are

probably going to get married anyway, but if we don't, there's always Gran to help.''

"Do you live with your grandmother?''

"Yeah. My mom has to work up in Morgantown. It's the only place she could get a job.''

"Well, I'll need to do a home visit in the next few days. Do you mind if I feel your abdomen, to see how your baby's lying? That way, I can also start to assess how many weeks pregnant you are.'' Devon didn't know the date of her last menstrual period.

"All right.''

IVY LEFT THE ROADSIDE a half hour later, excited at the prospect of an upcoming birth yet uneasy about Devon's future. Undoubtedly, she would spend the weeks up until the girl's delivery and through the postpartum period dealing with those emotions. She'd never expected that her first client in Guyandotte would be sixteen years old and pay her fifty dollars for all prenatal services and the birth, but at least she *had* a client.

She needed to talk to Cullen about money. In Precipice, she'd been paid two thousand dollars for each birth, including prenatal services, and nearly everyone could pay. Did Cullen mind another mouth to feed?

Judging from the country-club membership and Gabriela's ballet lessons, he was doing well, and it was possible he had family money, too. She wasn't going to worry about it right now.

After parking near Guyandotte Toyland, three spaces from Cullen's Camaro, Ivy consulted her list of errands. "Backup physician" was at the head of the list, followed by a Yellow Pages listing, flyers, finding an answering service. Mata Iyer's office was at the medical clinic on First Street. She was on Main now.

Ivy struck out walking, turning down Cardinal. Yes, there was First Street. It began to snow as she peered down the block at an official-looking building with a wheelchair ramp in front. Clinic or post office? She gambled and hurried toward it.

The medical clinic. Mata Iyer, M.D., was listed with several other doctors.

An Oldsmobile idled at the curb in front of the clinic, and an unshaven man with unkempt gray hair stood before the building, staring vacantly toward the street. His fly was open, and he was masturbating.

Ill.

Wondering if he belonged inside, Ivy started up the stairs to the clinic just as a woman emerged from within. "Sam!" She clutched the man's arm, and as she turned to lead him toward the automobile parked at the curb, Ivy recognized both her and the man. Cullen's parents. "Come get in the car, Sam."

The man seemed to recall himself but couldn't get zipped.

"Just get in the car."

"No!" Querulous, he started back to the clinic. "'Pointment."

"We already went."

The judge opened the glass door, preparing to walk inside.

Ivy hurried over. "Your Honor." She grasped his arm.

His eyes did not recognize her.

"Please get in the car. Your appointment is over. This way." She tried to lead him down the steps. His wife took his other arm.

In increments, he allowed himself to be led. He folded himself into the automobile, sat down, then began playing with himself again.

Mitzi Till shut the door. "Thank you, Ivy." There was no gratitude in the words. "You must excuse me." She hurried around to the driver's side and got into the car.

The Oldsmobile left Ivy in low clouds of steam and exhaust.

Should she walk to the toy store and tell Cullen?

His mother just wasn't big enough to handle the uncooperative judge. She would've gone to Coalgood herself, make sure they were all right, if not for Mitzi's coolness, the message that Ivy should really mind her own business.

In that case, she'd make an appointment with Mata Iyer, then hurry to the toy store. She'd find three family members there. Surely someone could get away.

A BLACK-HAIRED MOPPET planted herself at Ivy's feet before she'd progressed a yard inside Toyland. "Santa Claus is going to bring me a flying saucer with aliens."

It took Ivy a second to realize who was addressing her. "Scout! Hello."

A sea of bodies, parents and children playing with toys, banging shopping bags, separated her from both the dais in the center of the store and the ringing cash register. While a mechanical unicyclist pedalled on a wire overhead, Scout held up the alien of the night before. "This alien wants to steal your heart, Aunt Ivy."

Ivy lifted the five-year-old to hug her. "I think you've stolen it for him." It was a madhouse in here. Would Cullen really want to know about his father right now, in the midst of this chaos?

Yes. She would offer to go over to Coalgood and check on things. With Cullen's blessing, Mitzi might be more receptive.

"Will you take me to the ice-cream store?" Scout asked.

How could Zeya and Tom keep track of her in here? "If your mom and dad say it's okay."

"Hooray!" Scout squirmed out of her arms and zigzagged through the shoppers to the cash register.

A foam football sailed over Ivy's head, almost colliding with a mobile, as she made her way around the Santa Claus line to the place she'd seen Cullen's flash.

When she saw him, she sighed. He'd told her this morning he didn't need help. It would have been true if he were an octopus. Forms and pens and a camera on a tripod. While he worked, a mother leaned toward him and yelled, "Excuse me! Excuse me! Can you tell me how long it's going to be?"

Santa Claus addressed the girl on his lap. "A bunny! Did you see the bunnies over in the corner?"

Ivy found herself standing between Cullen and the mother. "Can I help you?"

"Yes. I want to know how long the line will take."

The girl scooted off Santa Claus's knee.

"Well, it looks like Santa Claus is taking about two minutes with each child. And I see, oh, eight children in line. Fifteen or twenty minutes?"

The mother eyed her watch, which had a watercolor palette on the face. "All right, Amy. Get in line. And thank you."

"You're welcome. I'm Ivy Walcott, by the way." A woman with two toddlers in tow might have more children in the future. "I'm a nurse-midwife, and the photographer is my husband."

"Oh, nice to meet you. Karen Beck." They shook hands. "Well, time to deal with this line."

"I think you need to fill out one of the envelopes on the table."

Shortly after, she had a second to speak to Cullen as he paused to change film. She spoke quietly, under the happy din of the store.

"I just saw your mother and father outside the medical clinic. He was masturbating, and she had trouble getting him in the car. Would you like me to go to Coalgood and make sure they're all right?"

His glance told her nothing. Eyes on his camera again, he said, "Matthew should be there." His gaze shot up. "You'd like that, though."

"I don't deserve that."

He finished loading the camera. "Please tell Zeya or Tom what you just told me and ask one of them to call Coalgood. If my mother needs help, you can go over. Otherwise, you can help me, if you want."

The words—and his tone—said her help was immaterial to him.

Ivy kept calm. "Thank you. I'm happy to help. If you can refrain from insulting me."

"Has anyone made you wear a scarlet *A?*"

Someone played a musical toy so loudly all the parents in the store winced or covered their ears. *That one won't be selling well.*

"Bitterness doesn't become you," she murmured.

"Or infidelity, you."

"You're talking to the wrong person."

He stepped back, looked her up and down, met her eyes. *I am?*

She turned away. "I'll tell Zeya and Tom."

ALL RIGHT, HE WAS BEING a jerk. But how much of the past was changed by the fact that she'd hit her head? She'd been unfaithful, she'd hit her head. Now, she was suddenly both trustworthy and unblemished? He didn't buy it.

Little Penny Jones tugged hard on Santa's beard. Cullen caught it on film.

"Your beard's real, but I don't believe you're Santa Claus at all!"

"Well, Penny, we'll have to see about *that* on Christmas morning, won't we?"

Tom shouldered his way alongside Cullen. "Matthew's at home. An interesting conversation, as always.''

''What did he say?''

''Among other things, to give the puppy a pat on the head and tell him everything's all right.''

Cullen made an indifferent sound. ''Thanks. For checking on them.''

''He also suggested a family forum to convince your mother to hire an attendant.''

''Good luck.''

''Tomorrow night at eight.''

After dinner at least. He could digest his food at home. *An attendant.* This was what his father had dreaded. Just two days ago, he'd been able to talk about his illness and death. Now he was masturbating in public.

It was almost as though some stress had caused the sudden deterioration. *Gina's return?* But his father hadn't recognized Gina. Instead, he'd mistaken Gabriela...

''And by the way, Ivy's taken Scout for ice cream. She said to tell you she'd be back soon. I told her you like mint chip.''

''Thanks,'' Cullen repeated. He took another envelope from a parent, made a notation.

''She's pretty special. I can see why you waited so long.''

Cullen stared at him.

Tom exclaimed, ''Don't look at *me* like that. I was merely celebrating your good fortune. And now I think I'll go celebrate mine.'' He rubbed his hands together, scanned the floor-to-ceiling toys, the store packed with shoppers, and hurried back to the cash register.

THE FOLLOWING MORNING, Saturday, Gabriela had ballet class, and Cullen drove her into town, then went to the studio. He had sittings from ten until two, so Ivy was supposed to pick her up.

Not wanting to think about the inevitable meeting with the ballet teacher, Ivy used her free time to phone Tara in Sagrado, Texas, for a heart-to-heart.

She tracked her down in the communal housing at the clinic and for half an hour did most of the talking.

"Let me get this straight," Tara summarized. "Your former persona was unfaithful—with this brother—and he's treating you like a murderer who's found God on Death Row."

"An exaggeration, but you have the gist of it."

"And you're sleeping in the same bed, where he treats you like a leper."

"That's a bit of a contradiction, but yes. He knows I'm interested in him, and this is some kind of repayment. I don't know how *he's* sleeping, but it's been lousy for me."

"You're in some kind of narrow Victorian bed, and you don't know how he's sleeping?"

"I think he fakes. Sleeping."

"I'll bet he does. You know, I can solve your problem with the unaffectionate spouse."

"I'm not sure I want to hear this."

"Well, listen anyhow. I know you and I don't own

armloads of the stuff, but I've *never* met a man who wasn't fascinated by lingerie.''

In spite of herself, Ivy began laughing. "I needed to talk to you. Just for this laugh."

"Imagine it. You, Ivy Walcott, in a clingy… Okay, Victoria's Secret isn't really you—"

"And I refuse to wear a red teddy with black lace."

"Okay, anyhow, you put on some gorgeous ivory silk number and come downstairs to say good-night. I guarantee his eyes will pop out of his head. You did say, the other night, that he's cute?"

"You asked if he's cute, and I said yes. The truth is, he's the only man I've ever found attractive in my life."

"As Ivy Walcott."

With a sudden vision of Matthew Till, Ivy whispered, "Shit."

"Is the brother cute?"

"If you like the type."

"Which is?"

"Okay, the *Anne of Green Gables* movie. The second one. The captain?"

"Mmm. Interesting. He was an appealing guy."

"A cross between that and, you know, Gregory Peck—but he acts like he's on a soap opera."

Together, they went into peals of giggles.

Ivy sobered first. "It would be funny, except he's married. His wife is a public defender. Nice. With the most beautiful red hair you ever saw."

"Anne of Green Gables?"

"Shelby of Coalgood. She's really lovely. And you

get the idea that she knows he's unfaithful and yet she loves him.''

"I've seen it before. Didn't work for me.''

Ivy flinched. For a moment, she'd forgotten that Tara's husband had left her for her former midwifery partner just two years ago. *That swine.* It didn't help that he and Solange hadn't consummated their relationship until they'd told Tara they were in love.

In some ways, that had probably made it worse.

Ivy hunted for something to fill the silence and found it quickly. "I almost forgot!" She told Tara about Devon. "We have our first prenatal on Monday. I also have an appointment with a woman who I hope is going to be my backup physician.''

"Good luck." Tara's experiences with the medical community had made her pessimistic about dealing with physicians. "But I'm glad you've got a practice going, Ivy. What are you going to call it?''

"I don't know." She squinted, thinking.

"Oh, come on, it's so obvious. And Mom won't mind. She'll love it.''

Suddenly, Ivy laughed. "Okay. Mountain Midwifery it is.''

LINGERIE.

She had an hour before she was supposed to meet Gabriela. Surely that was time enough to find something pretty in Guyandotte. Biting down a grin, Ivy grabbed her coat and purse and headed for the door.

Downtown, she visited Regina's Dress Shop. She was going through the racks in the back when she noticed another woman browsing nearby. She would've recognized those red curls anywhere.

"Shelby. Hi."

Matthew's wife glanced up. "Oh. Ivy. I didn't see you. I was in a pre-court trance."

Had Ivy imagined it, or did her eyes turn wary when she saw the rack Ivy had been studying, full of satin and lace? *If something was going on before, she has to be at least a little worried it'll start up again.*

"Shelby, do you have a minute?"

The wariness became tangible.

"I'm trying to figure out something to interest Cullen, and I need someone whose taste I can trust."

Shelby pushed between two circular racks. "*You* need something to interest Cullen?"

Ivy grimaced. "Believe it or not."

Lifting her eyebrows, Shelby turned her attention to the racks, but Ivy could see her mind wasn't on shopping. Maybe she'd start talking if Ivy waited.

Ivy flipped aimlessly through long gowns. Not what she wanted. "Think…think irresistible. I want something that'll make me irresistible to him."

"Ivy."

Shelby's sober tone drew her attention, but Ivy saw that the other woman was still fingering garments.

"Did you really lose *all* your memory?"

Let's get this on the table. If Shelby didn't know about Gabriela, Ivy didn't want to be the one to tell her. That was Matthew's burden. But she did want to reassure Shelby, make sure she knew the past was done.

"Yes." Ivy found a place close enough to Shelby that no one else in the store could overhear their conversation. "And I've come home to some unpleasant surprises that don't reflect the person I've thought I was for the past ten years."

The lenses of Shelby's glasses winked at her. Behind them, she assessed Ivy with pale eyes, as she might a person she was expected to defend in court. "I'm forgiving," she said at last.

Ivy bet she'd had lots of practice. "And I'm sorry."

Unexpectedly, Shelby took her hand. "Don't be sorry for Gabs. She's a great girl."

She knows. A huge feeling of relief went through Ivy—and wonder at the kind of person she was dealing with. She couldn't stop herself from reaching out and embracing her. The arms that hugged her back were surprisingly strong, firm and sure.

"Changing the subject—" Shelby straightened her glasses "—I wanted to ask if you know any natural fertility treatments. I'm not big on fertility drugs." She was blushing.

"Sure. There's a lot to talk about. Do you want to get together at the cabin some day?"

"Tomorrow works for me."

"Cullen and Gabriela will be around, but we can go up to the loft and talk."

Shelby smiled. "I'd like that. And I'll pay you."

Ivy waved her hand, dismissing it.

"Hey, sister, let me give you a clue about working in Guyandotte County." Shelby lowered her voice conspiratorially. "When someone offers you cold hard cash, *take it*."

A few minutes later, her voice distracted Ivy from two lukewarm lingerie possibilities.

"Hey, Ivy."

She glanced over.

With an elfin grin, Shelby held a scrap of cream-colored stretch cotton lace against her blazer. "Yes?"

"That's not clothing. That's a Kleenex!"

But Regina herself chose that moment to appear, and Shelby pointed from the garment to Ivy as though to say, *What do you think?*

The shop owner looked Ivy up and down. "For you?" In a heartbeat, she pronounced her judgment. *"Perfect."*

CHAPTER SEVEN

MATTHEW WAS LEAVING the dance studio as Ivy arrived. Since she was still two doors down and he was going the other way, he didn't notice her. Her mind leaped through questions. What had he been doing at the studio?

Not talking to Gabriela?

Well, he's going to talk to me now.

"Matthew."

His eyes showed interest if not pleasure. "Why, hello, Ivy."

She reminded herself that he'd lost his mother young, that he behaved as he did because something inside him was broken. "Matthew, I'd like to ask you some questions."

He raised his eyebrows.

They had the cold sidewalk to themselves. She plunged in. "Did you and I have an affair after I married Cullen?"

"You really can't remember?"

He wanted to play with her, she could see.

She didn't play. "True."

He smiled. "Then I suppose that's for me to know."

No, Matthew, this isn't how it's going to be. "Matthew, the sheriff may not feel that way. I suffered an injury. If I suspected you—"

"My dear girl, whatever *your* suspicions, the sheriff would not suspect me. He would suspect Cullen. And surely you don't want him to know about Gabriela?"

Matthew was fishing. He couldn't possibly know whether or not Cullen had told her the truth. "What earthly advantage," she asked, "do you see in not telling me the truth?"

He seemed to consider, then smiled. "I simply like the idea that there's something I have that you want. It promotes a certain intimacy between us."

"On your side, maybe. Not on mine. And there's something else I want to know. I was pregnant around the time I left Guyandotte. Do you know whose child it was?"

He stared unblinking. "In fact, this is news to me, Ivy. You don't say!" He seemed delighted with himself.

Oh, shit.

"Does Cullen know?"

"Of course. We have no secrets."

Matthew smiled. "But I do. I like this. Let's be friends, Ivy." He offered his hand.

She didn't take it. "I'm going to think very hard about speaking to the sheriff, Matthew."

"Suit yourself. I think you'll decide it's not such a good idea after all. What if the truth should get back to Gabriela?"

"That may be for the best." *You are not going to hold one card over me, Matthew Till.*

"Cullen surely doesn't agree with you. This is his virility on the line."

"Somehow I can't help thinking *you're* the one with your virility on the line, Matthew. Why else would you persist in harassing your younger brother?" She'd gone too far and wished she could retract the words.

"It so happens," he answered calmly, "that you're wrong. And now I'll leave you to pick up our daughter." The last word firmly in his favor, he began walking away.

Ivy rubbed her forehead, her face. Matthew had won that round. She'd given him a feeling of power. Still, she didn't regret it. She'd been straight with him, which was the only way to deal with people. Maybe the answer was to see the sheriff. But what crime had been committed?

Did someone hit me on the head?

She tried to imagine Matthew becoming violent with a woman. It wasn't out of the realm of possibility. But he'd been right. If she started raising questions about how her head injury had occurred and in the process revealed the suspected affair, Cullen would become the primary suspect. That was the last thing they needed.

Only when she turned to enter the dance studio did she remember one question she'd neglected to ask Matthew. What had he been doing in there? At the doors, she checked quickly to see if the building contained any other businesses. No. Then why had he come?

Ivy pulled open a glass door and went in, entering a world of sweaty adolescents removing pointe shoes and heading for the lockers. She spotted Noel and Gabriela and waved, and Gabriela beckoned.

There was a sign about shoes at the arch into the dancing room, so Ivy removed her hiking boots and ventured inside in her socks. She saw Tracy Kennedy.

She's beautiful. Her less classic features, like her nose and prominent chin, only made her face more arresting. Ivy swallowed, remembering Cullen glancing at her house the other night.

The dance teacher walked toward her, regal and graceful.

That skin.

The possessiveness and jealousy gripping her stomach surprised Ivy. This woman had made love with Cullen. *I don't like this feeling.*

It gave her more sympathy for Cullen's recent behavior.

"Hello, Gina. I understand you probably won't remember me. I'm Tracy Kennedy."

"It's Ivy." She'd never felt anything like the tightness inside her now. She tried to remember Shelby's graciousness and use it as her model, then told herself there was a big difference between a woman who'd slept with your husband ten years before and one who'd done it a few weeks ago.

No, there's not that much difference. And you bore Matthew's child. Grow up, Ivy. She'd never be as gracious as Shelby, but she could behave like a civilized adult.

"I changed my name," she explained to Tracy, then changed the subject. "Gabriela is very excited about your class."

"She's a good student."

There was a pause; Tracy didn't attempt to fill it. Instead, she took a breath and looked quickly around the emptying studio. "Well, it looks like Gabriela's ready to go."

She's not over him.

Maybe Cullen wasn't over Tracy, either. Was that why he was able to sleep beside Ivy without touching her?

Maybe the lingerie was for nothing.

Her daughter approached them both. "Tracy, this is my mom, Ivy."

"We were just meeting. Gabriela, your pas de bourrées are much better today."

"Thanks to you. Oh, wait. Ivy, Tracy's taking a group of us up to Morgantown to see *Nutcracker* in two weeks. It's at the university. Can I go?"

"Need to ask your dad." Morgantown was a long way. The capital, Charleston, was far closer. But clearly, Gabriela was eager to spend time with her teacher. "Do you have a permission slip?" she asked Tracy.

"Gabriela has one."

The comment seemed to suggest things were taken care of between the two of them, that Ivy was an afterthought. Her own insecurity talking. She told Tracy, "I'll ask Cullen."

"Of course. Bye, Gabriela. Goodbye, Ivy."

Ivy's legs were rubber as she and Gabriela walked to the car. She wished she could say something both sincere and gracious. *Your teacher seems nice.* But the more accurate assessment was, *Your teacher is ladylike.*

Think about her feelings, Ivy. You just met Cullen three days ago. She dated him for a year.

But that was it. It didn't *feel* like days since she'd met Cullen. He seemed familiar already, and she couldn't help believing it was emotional memory kicking in from long ago.

Suddenly remembering, Ivy asked, "Did Uncle Matthew come into the studio to talk to you?"

"No. To Tracy. I don't know what he wanted.

"Hey, Ivy, will you take me shopping in Charleston? I get my clothing allowance today, and I want something cool for *Nutcracker* and the Christmas dance."

A dance? Well, she was in junior high. "You're pretty sure you're going to *Nutcracker.*"

"Oh, Dad'll let me. He trusts Tracy." Her face suddenly froze, and her eyes shot up at Ivy's.

Ivy smiled patiently.

Gabriela said, "You know...?"

"I know."

"Sorry for mentioning it."

She really was a sweet girl. Thinking uneasily of Matthew and wondering if Gabriela would stay sweet, knowing the truth, Ivy said, "Let's walk over to the studio and ask your dad if he minds our going to Charleston."

THE FAMILY GATHERED in the living room of Coalgood that night. Cullen had left Ivy and Gabriela at home, listening to Jewel, making popcorn and getting ready for a movie. Matthew's "family forum" began half an hour late, after Tom and Zeya had struggled to get a wound-up Scout to bed.

Shelby was upstairs with the judge, interesting him in a computer game. The rest of them clustered around on various pieces of spotless furniture.

"No fair bride tonight, Cullen?"

"No, Matthew."

Matthew sat back against the couch, then moved suddenly. Produced a lemon from behind him.

Mother held out her hand for it. Shaking her head, she explained, "The judge hid it there. He thinks I'm stealing his food. Can you imagine? Now, I don't understand the nature of this meeting. Daddy and I do fine together. I want to care for him."

Matthew surrendered the lemon. "That's commendable, Mitzi. But eventually, he'll require lifting. I think it's time to look at a full-time attendant."

"He's nowhere close to needing lifting, and he's certainly not dangerous."

Cullen, half-lost in the quagmire of his father's request to die, waited for someone else to say it. The judge yelled at all of them. He threw things in the kitchen when people didn't understand what he wanted to eat because he couldn't remember the word for bananas or steak. Not to mention that he suspected his wife of stealing his food. "Let's take shifts," Cullen suggested. "The men. Do you mind, Tom?"

"Does it matter if *I* mind?" Matthew asked.

Cullen stared at him.

"This is unnecessary, Cullen. *And* Matthew. Daddy and I get along fine. There is absolutely no reason for my children to act as bodyguards. Or to hire an attendant."

"Not bodyguards," Zeya said, "but, Mother, wouldn't you like help?"

"You children have your lives and your work."

"Cullen has flexible hours." Matthew worked on a glass of Merlot. "He's Daddy's puppy anyhow."

"Matthew, I wish you wouldn't say that. Heaven knows what you mean," exclaimed his stepmother.

"It's affectionate. When he was little, don't you remember Daddy putting out his arms to get Cully to run to his chair?"

The recollection brought sudden tears to Mitzi Till's eyes.

Matthew's look was sardonic.

"Affectionate?" Cullen asked.

Matthew blew him a loud kiss.

"Not now, you two," Zeya snapped.

Mother stood up. "None of you need put yourself out. Cullen's wife will want him at home, and the rest of you are busy. Now, I'm going up to the judge. Shall I have Lily bring coffee?"

The subject was closed.

When she left the room, Tom murmured, "I think we're in denial."

"Speak for yourself," Matthew muttered, as though not understanding the remark. Setting down his wineglass, he rose. "Tell Shelby I've gone for a walk. I'll be a while." He smiled at Cullen in particular. "Doctor's orders."

He left, and Tom and Zeya and Cullen stared at each other glumly.

Zeya shook her head. "This is crazy. He *is* too big for Mother to deal with. What are we going to do?"

Cullen and Tom exchanged looks.

"Okay, I know it's the coveted shift, but I'll volunteer to take the evenings. Zeya and I are really going to be swamped until Christmas and for at least a week afterward. I'll sit with the judge every evening, even Christmas Eve."

"Thanks, Tom." Cullen shook his head. "But Matthew was right. My plan was bad. I need to work. You need to work. He needs to work. And someone has to be with Daddy during the day."

"An attendant," Zeya said. "It has to happen, whether she likes it or not. You know it's not the money that's stopping her. Want me to start asking around on Monday?"

"Okay. Let me know if you want to do it together." He got up. "I think I'll head home."

Zeya's eyes, the same green as his own under hair the same shade as his, sparkled up at him. "Ivy's sweet, Cully. Sweeter than she used to be."

For just a second, Cullen was tempted to ask his

sister if she'd ever noticed anything between Matthew and Gina. But he couldn't expose Ivy that way. And Matthew was the one to ask.

But Cullen wouldn't waste his breath.

HE DROVE SLOWLY around the island, half-dreading his return home. After Gabriela went to bed, there would be an awkward hour, at least, when just he and Ivy were awake. Every attraction he felt toward her would rouse his anger and distrust. If he was cold, she would be calm. If he was rude, she would be fair. Then, finally, she'd retreat to bed, and when he came up, the cycle would begin inside him all over again.

Also, the more time he spent around her, the more he noticed ways she *hadn't* changed. Many of her gestures. The way she brushed her hair. Cooking, dishwashing and laundry rituals.

She was the errant wife who swore she'd reformed.

What if he was wrong? What if she'd never slept with Matthew once she was married? What if his whole reaction had grown out of possessiveness and insecurity?

He couldn't believe it anymore. He knew how little passion there had been between him and Gina.

If Ivy would just keep to her own side of the bed at night!

But it was her habit to lie on her side, facing him, with a bundle of covers tucked under one knee. When he came to bed and moved the covers, she rested her knee on him instead.

There was Tracy's house, her porch light on. Her

door was open, and she was letting a man inside, and the man was Matthew.

Neither of them noticed the car passing.

The front door shut.

Cullen drove thoughtfully to the bridge. Tracy knew Matthew was married. She'd invited him inside in innocence, Cullen was sure, and Matthew wouldn't get far with her.

Did Matthew really think this would hurt him?

Cullen still felt protective of her, but other tender feelings had disintegrated. Now their memory was lukewarm.

Only one woman in his life had ever awakened his deepest feelings, good and bad. He'd given her his heart, promised her his life, raised her child.

Her betrayal had cost her his respect. And Cullen didn't see how she would ever earn it back. The only answer was time.

As GABRIELA SAID good-night and went off to her room, Ivy tried to quiet her nerves. What was the worst that could happen? She'd put on the silly teddy, and he would lift his eyebrows once and proceed to ignore her.

No, I'll put it on and go to bed. He can notice when he gets into bed. She absolutely could not parade in front of him in that thing.

She spent some time stretching in the dance room before she went up to bed. As she was leaving, Cullen came in to do his usual sit-ups and push-ups. ''Good night,'' she told him.

"Good night."

Indifferent. She headed through the living room to the sunroom and the ladder to the loft, her eyes burning. He'd loved her once. She couldn't remember those days, but she'd seen evidence of that old, never really extinguished love when she'd first arrived in Guyandotte. Seen it in a dozen different ways.

But now... This discovery he'd made had killed it. *I killed it.* More than ten years ago.

The worst part was what she felt for Cullen. As Gina, she must have loved him, too, or how could she feel something so strong now, in such a short time?

Why did she do it?

Why did I make love with his brother?

If only she knew at least that much, could somehow understand. Did Cullen have any idea why she'd done it?

In the loft, she undressed and put on the teddy she'd bought that day with Shelby's help. She'd bought it with such hope, and now she couldn't help thinking that hope was doomed to failure.

She glanced in the mirror.

She looked beautiful, long-legged and lithe, the lace creamy against her flushed skin.

But Cullen's rejection wasn't about her looks.

She should tear the thing off and put on her flannel pajamas again.

Oh, come on, Ivy. Think what it might do if the two of you could just touch tenderly. He loved you once.

He'd loved Gina.

No, if she was to be blamed for Gina's crimes, she

would take the good, too. Nursing her child, being loved by Cullen, making quilts with her grandmother.

I should teach Gabriela. I should pass on this tradition.

She climbed into the old bed, comforted by its creaks. This cabin, these mountains, were her home and her birthright. Her thoughts wandered—from planning her rural midwifery practice, to sewing a quilt with Gabriela, the carrying on of tradition. She tried to blot out the simple human want so keen inside her.

To know her husband's love.

CULLEN CAREFULLY drew back the covers. She stirred, and as the covers fell from her, he saw her bare arms. It took a second to register. No flannel pajamas.

Uneasy, he tried to see what she was wearing, and as he did, her moonlit eyes opened and blinked at his.

From where he sat on his side of the bed, naked, he glimpsed lace. A bodysuit or something?

Unable to resist his curiosity, even though her eyes still watched him, he lifted the covers.

Oh.

He let the sheet and blanket fall and got into bed, turning his back to her.

Ivy couldn't bear it. Maybe he really was in love with Tracy Kennedy. If so, what was she going to do? *I can't lie here in this thing while he ignores me.*

He might have loved Gina, but obviously he didn't love Ivy Walcott. Or maybe it was because she'd *been*

Gina. She couldn't sort it out anymore—who she really was, who he was really married to.

But she was through sharing a bed with a man who didn't want her.

She sat up, climbed out of bed and retrieved her pajamas from her drawer. And damned if she was going downstairs to change at this hour.

"What are you doing?"

"Putting on my pajamas. You don't have to watch."

But he had sat up, too, his hair mussed, to squint at her in the dark as she tugged down one strap and began to maneuver her arm out of it.

Tracy had taught him about teddies.

Ivy had never worn one before, or she wouldn't be struggling with shoulder straps. Gina had never worn one, either. Something inside him cracked gently, starting a slow melt that wasn't about sex but about tenderness.

"Stop."

"What?" She glared at him. "I *said* you don't have to watch."

"Was that for me?"

"No. Actually, it's for Gabriela. In fact, maybe I'll give it to her. Just leave me alone. I can't deal with nasty remarks right now. And I'm—"

He was getting out of bed, standing before her, naked and tall.

Male.

His hand gently caught hers, to guide it back through the arm loop. He eased up both straps, then rubbed her shoulders. She shivered, afraid to look at his hands, afraid to look anywhere but at his chest.

He said, "Come back to bed."

She squeezed her eyes shut. "I need to be loved. I deserve to be loved. I'm *good*. I'm not what you think."

Cullen wished he could agree. "Come back to bed."

Ivy opened her eyes. "No." She tugged down the straps again.

"It snaps at the crotch." He remained where he was.

Stanching tears, she undressed, and Cullen watched, aware of a dark force inside the room, inside himself. Failure to forgive. He was hurting their chances now and couldn't stop. He wanted to wound her as she'd wounded him.

He wished he didn't feel like this.

Ivy pulled on her pajamas, aware of the new barrier between them, of the way things had changed.

Cullen said, "Come back to bed."

Maybe, Ivy reasoned, that was as far as he could go.

And she would have to take a small step, too.

She did. Back to the tester bed.

IN BED, CULLEN EMBRACED her, holding her tight. He couldn't speak, but he could do this. Gather her close and closer.

Ivy had never felt anything so wonderful as this man keeping her against his body, surrounding her with his body. And when she looked up, he kissed her, slowly.

Their mouths opened gradually, and she felt his tongue. It was a match to the never-lit tinder inside her. The strongest force she'd ever known urged her closer to him, directed her hands to his bare shoulders, directed her arms to clasp him around the neck.

Cullen kissed her cheek, her jaw, her throat. "I love you."

He spoke so softly she wasn't sure she'd heard him right. She was still wondering when his mouth covered hers, when their tongues touched again, a prelude to greater intimacy, like the erection she felt against her leg, like his hands on her arms. Her body simmered. She writhed as he unbuttoned her pajama top and lowered his mouth to her breast.

This is making love. This is what it's like.

He drew down the bottoms, tossed them out of the bed. His touch was tender, in her wetness.

"Cullen."

He kissed her again as he stroked her, teased her. He'd never seen Gina like this, and he knew what he was seeing in Ivy.

Innocence.

Gina had somehow never been innocent, not even in high school, before she'd met Matthew.

"Open your eyes."

She did, and could hardly meet his. He kissed her more and embraced her, feeling her hair against his cheek. She was tremulous heat, and his hands memorized her. *Lover.*

Tracy had never been...

He cleared his mind, but it was too late. His penis grew limp.

He kissed Ivy and remembered Gina and Matthew. *This woman is different. This woman is mine.*

His body would not obey him.

What in hell? He needed, wanted, to make love to Ivy. *Now.*

Cullen drew back the covers to see her body, and she trembled, opening herself to him slightly, obviously wanting to give. He turned her, to put his mouth to her. His erection was back. She moaned, and he gently stroked her legs. She invited him to deepen the intimate kiss, and he did and had to hold her still.

"Cullen." She dragged his head up.

Kisses, her body beneath his. "I'll be right back," he promised, and left the bed to find condoms. He saw her teddy.

Tracy's had been purple and black, another turquoise and black. *Don't think about her.*

By the time he returned to bed, he'd lost his erection.

Ivy knew. His kisses were the same as before, but—

"Are you in love with Tracy?"

Was she psychic, to know he'd been thinking of Tracy? "I am not in love with Tracy," he said quietly. It was the truth.

Then is it because of my head injury? Am I not human enough?

His lips lowered to hers again, and she kissed him

back, trying to infuse him with the passion they'd shared moments earlier. But there was no awakening in him, no change at all.

Cullen could imagine fifty bad scenarios that would be better than this. Even Matthew telling Gabriela he was her father...

Was it discovering he'd been made a cuckold that had done this to him? Was it something about her, or about the two of them?

Forcing himself to relax, Cullen rolled onto his back and drew her against his chest. She settled with her head on his shoulder, her hand in the hair on his chest. Her hand reached down.

This should do it. Cullen felt her tentativeness, her nervousness. It coaxed desire from him.

He was unprepared for her mouth.

He hardened immediately. "Ivy."

Her hands were healing hands, honest hands. She was giving herself to him, and he gave himself back.

"WELL, DID THE TEDDY WORK?" Shelby asked that afternoon, when she and Ivy had gone up to the loft to talk fertility. "You look sort of...pink and glowing—if you'll pardon the cliché."

She'd felt flushed all day, and happy. She and Cullen had made love again this morning, and this time he'd had no trouble keeping an erection. "Yes, it worked. Thank you for your help yesterday. Now tell me how I can help you." She sat on the edge of the tester bed, and Shelby took the rocking chair.

"I want a baby. We've been trying for maybe... two years?"

"Have you had any tests at a fertility clinic?"

"Yes. Everything indicates we should be able to get pregnant. And we've been given the whole scoop about what position is best, things like that. What I want to know is, are there any herbs that could help?"

"Sure. I can set you up that way. In fact, I have some on hand." She made another mental note; in the spring she should begin gathering herbs. She could take Gabriela with her and teach her.

But Gabriela didn't care about herbs or midwifery. She wanted to be a dancer.

"Also, I've got a book to lend you." She handed Shelby *Conscious Conception.* "It's...different, but it can be fun to read about different perspectives on fertility."

"I'll enjoy that. Thanks."

"Now, let's talk herbs and diet."

For half an hour, they visited together, discussing fertility-promoting foods and herbs. As they finished, Shelby fingered one of the quilts folded at the foot of the tester bed. "This is beautiful. I've always wanted to know how to do it. It seems like such a West Virginia thing. I don't know if I can get my New York fingers around a needle."

"Sure you can. I want to start one with Gabriela. Want to join us?"

"Oh, it would be an intrusion. It's a mother-daughter thing."

"The more hands the better. Let's go ask her."

They went downstairs and found Gabriela practicing dance.

Ivy wasn't one to foresee disasters around every corner, but it still troubled her some to see Gabriela focusing all her hopes and dreams on what seemed like a fickle profession. And the idea of fame. Those dreams should be part of childhood, but Gabriela was on the cusp of womanhood.

I want her to know other things, to understand how to nurture.

The onset of menstruation was a special time. Perhaps some special initiation into womanhood was in order, to help Gabriela celebrate becoming a woman.

She asked Gabriela if she was interested in starting a quilt with her and Shelby.

Gabriela paused in a movement. "Oh, sure. I guess. You mean, like, now?"

"As soon as you finish practicing."

"Okay. I'm almost done."

Cullen was out of the house photographing a wedding, but Ivy knew there was a cedar chest full of fabric scraps in the day room, enough to start with. When she'd first seen them, she'd known they must have been hers or maybe her grandmother's. "I've seen a book around here, Shelby. I'll let you and Gabriela choose the pattern." Ivy searched the living-room bookcase and plucked out the book of patterns, then collected fabric scraps from the cedar chest. A decent pair of scissors was harder to come by, but she found a ruler, pencil and paper for drawing patterns.

"Mom—Ivy." From the door of the dance room, Gabriela blushed.

Ivy hurried to her side and put an arm around her. Low, she said, "You can call me Mom. I'd love that."

Gabriela's eyes watered, and she suddenly hugged Ivy.

Hugging back, Ivy blotted the specter of Matthew from her mind. *Don't let anyone destroy this happiness.*

"What I wanted to say—" Gabriela wiped her eyes "—is that I know where your sewing box is. Dad sort of said I can have it."

"Then it's yours. But go get it, okay? Because we'll need it."

Gabriela and Shelby sat on the couch to look through quilt patterns and finally decided on the Variable Star.

"Good choice. Okay, let's get started."

It was five before Shelby left, with a bagful of scraps to work on at home. As she drove away and Ivy went to the kitchen to begin making dinner, Gabriela said, "You know, I think we should let Shelby keep the quilt. What do you think?"

Ivy smiled, terribly proud of her. "I think that's a great idea." She gave Gabriela another hug. She'd never imagined such a wonderful relationship with her daughter.

But an aura of darkness hovered around them. The secret Gabriela did not know.

CHAPTER EIGHT

THE BLACK CURLS THAT FELL past Mata Iyer's shoulders sprang slightly as she moved. "Ivy, I'm so glad you came in. I'd be happy to provide physician backup for you. This community desperately needs a way to reach out to low-income women, and I've often thought that a certified nurse-midwife might be the answer, might help reduce poor outcomes. I see so many fifteen-year-olds coming into the ER with no prenatal care behind them. These teenagers really have a difficult time, both before and after the births."

It was the perfect opportunity to bring up Devon—and the family's concern about finances.

"You know, Ivy, we're always willing to work with low-income families, but people are just afraid. They really don't know the situation. Anyhow, I'm happy to see Devon. Check with the receptionist on the way out for an appointment."

Before Ivy left, Mata shook her hand warmly. "I'm so glad you're here. If you don't mind, I'll start spreading the word about your services."

"I feel blessed," Ivy answered sincerely. "Thank you so much for your help."

THAT AFTERNOON was Ivy's first prenatal with Devon Workman. Ivy put her midwifery kit in her mountaineering pack and hiked down the hollow to the Workmans' trailer. Gabriela had ballet class, and Ivy had asked Cullen to pick her up. The thought of his seeing Tracy troubled her—but that was why she'd wanted him to get Gabriela. *We have to walk through these things.*

The Workmans' was the place closest to the main road, a single-wide trailer that had been patched and added to with a hodgepodge of building materials. Seeing homemade curtains in the windows, a collection of antique bottles along one sill, Ivy felt a renewal of pride in her heritage, pride in people who kept things clean and well repaired even in the face of poverty. Remembering the quilt she and Gabriela and Shelby had started, she thought again of planning an initiation ceremony for Gabriela.

But how could she honestly participate in that if Gabriela didn't know the name of her natural father? *She needs to be told.*

Ivy could imagine nothing worse than Matthew insensitively telling her. She probably wouldn't even believe him.

That thought made it easier to accept the lie.

And more difficult to accept herself.

THE TRAILER WAS CLEAN inside, and Emma Workman gave her a tour through the rooms, hers and Devon's. "There's space for the baby in Devon's room."

"Devon, are you still in school?"

She shook her head. "Not just now. But I'm going back after the baby comes."

Ivy hoped so. She wanted to mother this girl and wished for Devon that her mother was there. "Will your mom be able to come down for the birth?"

She shrugged.

Emma looked faintly disapproving.

So Mom's not involved with her daughter's life anymore.

Devon had said she'd needed to go to Morgantown to work. What kind of world made such a thing necessary?

"Where's your father?"

"Oh, he lives in South Carolina with his girlfriend."

Emma refrained from sighing, from uttering a disapproving word. But Ivy could see her eyes over Devon's shoulder and guessed her feelings. She made a wordless promise to Emma Workman. She, as midwife, would be present for this girl, too, would help her on the rocky road ahead. She made a mental note to stop by two or three times a week until the birth and more often afterward.

"Okay, why don't we go sit down in your bedroom, Devon, and we can talk about the kind of birth experience you'd like to have."

THE LAST PERSON CULLEN wanted to see was Tracy Kennedy. He resented her intrusion into his thoughts when he was making love with Ivy. He keenly regretted ever having asked her out.

And when he entered her studio that afternoon, he immediately saw his brother. Tracy lounged in the arched doorway between the foyer and the dance room, smiling up at Matthew, while he stood with one hand braced against the arch over her head. On the make.

Cullen considered walking outside and waiting there for Gabriela, but Tracy spotted him.

What are you doing with Matthew, Tracy?

Could she switch that easily from him to his brother? Did she *want* to?

Matthew turned his head and caught sight of Cullen. "Well, look who's here. How's my baby brother?" He hooked his arm around Cullen's neck, tight, and rubbed his knuckles against his scalp. Hard.

Cullen escaped the headlock. "Hello, Matthew. Nice to see you."

"Dad, can I go to Morgantown with everyone to see *Nutcracker?* Tracy's driving."

"Yes, Gabs."

"Morgantown," remarked Matthew. He gave Tracy a quizzing glance.

"Field trip." Her smile tilted wryly at Matthew.

She does like him. How can she like him? Cullen experienced a pang on Shelby's behalf. Matthew was an idiot.

"Ready to go, Gabriela?"

"Yes. Where's Ivy?"

"She has a prenatal appointment."

"Pregnant?" Matthew asked. "Already? After only a dozen years of marriage?"

"She's taking care of a midwifery client," Cullen clarified, hyperaware of the unspoken—that he and Ivy had never conceived a child together. Unless... "Bye, folks."

"CULLEN?" IT WAS the second night they'd gone up to the loft at the same time.

He slid between the sheets. "Mmm?"

"I have a strong need to tell Gabriela the truth. I think it's wrong not to."

"As I said before, we disagree. It might be easiest for you to tell her—to get it off your chest—but the greatest gift you can give her at this point is to maintain the lie. She believes I'm her father. Do you think this secret has been easy for me?"

Ivy didn't answer right away. "I guess not."

"It's truly for her, Ivy. She has a strong identity, and part of it is that she's your child and mine."

"It's a lie."

"I don't believe all lies are bad. This one is best for her."

"What if Matthew tells her?"

"We deal with it then and explain why we kept the truth from her."

"That frightens me. Can you imagine what it would do to her to learn it from him?"

Cullen echoed her own thought of earlier that day. "Frankly, I doubt she'd even believe him."

"Would we then tell her more lies?"

"Maybe. It's protecting her, Ivy. I don't fear Gabriela's anger. Revealing the truth would be a load

off for you and for me, but I can see no way it would
benefit her. She's not going to get a father-daughter
relationship out of Matthew."

"Maybe that's what *he* needs."

Dead silence.

"What?" she asked.

"Why are you concerning yourself with what Matthew needs?"

She'd better get out of this conversation fast. "Because I like his wife." She changed the subject. "Cullen, at the country club, you asked me never to defend
you physically. Why is that?"

"If Gabriela hadn't been there, I would have been
more specific. Sure, if someone threatened this family, I would welcome your help in a fight. Matthew
was on my mind. I decided long ago not to rise to
the bait, not to fight him. And I'd hate it if you did
my fighting for me."

Ivy remembered her conversation with Matthew
outside the dance studio. "Is he violent?"

"He can be."

Did she dare bring it up? She must. "Cullen, do
you think there's any chance he hurt me?"

He was quiet so long, she said, "It just occurred
to me for the first time the other day."

"I don't think he'd hurt you. I can't picture it. Me,
yes. But a woman? I don't think so."

"Why won't you fight with him? Even to defend
yourself?"

Cullen hesitated. Describing the things Matthew
had done would make him sound like a psychopath,

a maniac. Cullen couldn't say why, but he loved his brother and felt a need to protect him. There were things about Matthew that people outside the family would never understand. He wasn't sure he could make Ivy see them, either.

"Because I did once."

"Fight with him?"

"Yes."

"Did you lose?"

"No. I won."

Ivy rolled over to face him. "What would you do if he seduced me now? Some things are worth fighting for."

"Seduced *you*? What makes you think you were so innocent? What makes you think you didn't play a role?"

Chagrined, Ivy fell quiet.

"Yes, some things are worth fighting for," he said quietly. "But have you ever noticed that as a culture we almost never consider *not fighting*? Being able to kill makes people feel powerful."

Ivy swallowed. Being able to kill did make her feel powerful. It was a need for that power that had led her, in part, to tae kwon do. She thought he could teach her something, yet it was just out of her reach, unspeakable and unexplainable. "Didn't defeating Matthew give you a sense of personal…strength?"

"Truthfully, when it was all over, I felt slightly foolish. It was only fighting. It didn't make me stronger or better." He kissed her, drawing her close. His hands cupped her bottom, and his penis stirred, but he was distracted. She thought Matthew might have hurt her. Cullen was sure he hadn't.

But *had* someone hurt her?

ON HIS WAY HOME FROM WORK the following day, Cullen stopped at Coalgood. Zeya's search for an attendant had so far yielded nothing they liked, and the judge's unruliness made Cullen uneasy. When he entered the kitchen that afternoon, his father had just knocked a bowl of macaroni and cheese to the floor. Lily was cleaning it up while his mother tried to find something to placate him.

"White!" he yelled at Mitzi. "White."

Cullen's mother showed him a box of spaghetti from the cupboard. Lily took out the Swiss cheese. Milk. Cottage cheese. Yogurt.

The judge yelled again and swept everything that was on the table—salt and pepper shakers, butter plate, coffee cup—to the floor.

Cullen helped pick things up. "Where's Matthew?"

"Atlanta, working."

And Tom was at the store.

Standing suddenly, the judge knocked over his chair.

"Daddy." Cullen touched his arm, and his father slammed into his face with the back of his arm. Blood spurted over the table.

"Oh, Cully. Daddy. Sam, sit down."

His father seemed surprised by the blood.

Cullen grabbed a dish towel and held it to his face. "Sorry, Lily."

"It's all right, honey. You just don't touch him when he's like that, you hear?"

Cullen heard. And saw. These two women were alone with a big man who could turn violent over being offered the wrong food.

"White!" yelled the judge.

Opening the refrigerator, Cullen searched the shelves, the drawers, the door, for anything white. Still holding the towel to his bloody nose, he held up an egg.

His father grunted.

Cullen set a couple of eggs on the counter and pulled a skillet from under the sink. His father liked them scrambled.

"I'll do that. You just sit down." Lily took over.

Mother tried tucking a napkin under his father's neck, and the judge pulled it out.

Bad. Daddy didn't know his own strength, and he was querulous, his faculties impaired.

Cullen stayed while his father ate, then helped him upstairs. His mother got out the judge's medications, and her husband took them with a glass of water while Cullen examined the bottles.

He's just getting sicker and sicker.

The judge hadn't wanted this to happen. He'd asked his son to keep it from happening. Cullen pictured it for a moment, losing his father somewhere dangerous, letting him die in the cold and the snow.

He could sit with him and let him die of exposure, for instance.

And bear the weight of the secret.

I should do it. It's what he wanted. It can be my last gift to him.

"When's Matthew going to be back?"

"Dinnertime."

"I'll stay till he comes home."

The judge spoke up. "They're all ungrateful, Mitzi. Where are they? Our children don't give a shit. Spending our money and never coming around." He seemed to see Cullen. "Except you. You get everything, Cullen, when I die."

"That is not true!" his wife exclaimed. "I don't know where he gets these ideas. Cully, will you sit with him a minute? I just have to call Joanne." Her sister. "She called last night, and I haven't had a chance to phone her back."

"Sure."

"You get everything, Cully. Everything I've done, I've done for you."

Cullen entertained a notion of the judge taking up this train of thought at dinner. It was fleeting. "Daddy, you still want me to help you die?"

"What?"

His mother returned to the room, and Cullen decided not to repeat the question. She put one of her sweaters in a drawer.

"You get everything. Your brother's worthless. He screwed your wife. You know that? Walked in on 'em."

Mitzi had straightened up. She stared at the judge. "Is that true?" she demanded, turning to her son.

Cullen shook his head. "Of course not." The judge had walked in on Gina and Matthew? Where? When? It must have happened at Coalgood. It explained his father's comment about Gina being after Tom.

His mother slanted a look at him but didn't challenge his answer, and Cullen was glad when she left the room.

He was alone with the judge. And the truth.

It was no longer a suspicion. It was a fact.

His wife had committed adultery.

WHEN HE GOT HOME, Ivy had cooked dinner. He ate it in silence while Gabriela talked about ballet and Ivy cast questioning glances toward him. They were just finishing when the phone rang.

Ivy picked it up. "Hello?"

"Hello, is Gabriela there?"

A boy. A boy with a deep voice. Ivy said, "Who's calling?"

"Brad. Sorry."

Ivy bit her bottom lip and at last said, "One moment. Gabriela, it's Brad."

She leaped up, wiping her mouth. "Oh, thanks. I'll take it on the cordless." It took her three seconds to locate the phone, carry it to her room and shut the door.

Ivy shook her head and checked Cullen's reaction. Something in his expression went beyond Gabriela and Brad. It had to do with her. *Is he angry?* If so, he could tell her later. "How old is that guy?"

"Ninth grade."

"Have you met him?"

"Only on the phone."

"And you didn't say, 'Excuse me, my daughter will call you back in a few years?'"

"No, I didn't. She's not dating him. She swears they're just friends."

"That was not the reaction of one friend to another."

"She does the same thing when Noel calls."

"Oh, come on, Cullen. You were fourteen once."

He didn't answer except to say, "Let's go for a walk."

And leave her alone with that guy?

Relenting, Ivy helped him clear the dishes from the table, then put on her boots and her coat and stocking cap.

They went out into the snow, and she let him choose the path, back through the woods behind the cabin.

"You screwed my brother."

"What?" Not this again.

"My father confirmed it. He walked in on you two, apparently."

Oh. So the imagined was now reality.

She felt the ridges of a scar inside her, the scar of who she'd been, the sins she must carry. The cold numbed her face, made her slur her words. "Cullen, do you have any idea what might have made me behave like that?''

"It's behavior I don't understand at all, Gina. Ivy," he corrected.

"Truly?"

Cullen obviously didn't have the patience to psychoanalyze an unfaithful wife. "Lack of character?''

"No father in the house?''

"It's no excuse." Abruptly, he grabbed her, and she found herself pinned against a tree. "I want to kill that bastard!'' It was a guttural confession, hissing and lethal. His breath warmed her face. His hands on her arms hurt.

"Take your hands off me *now*.''

"No." He grabbed the waistband of her jeans.

"Don't do this,'' she warned.

"You know how to stop me.''

She didn't stop him, and he thrust inside her there against the tree. It felt good, and she clung to him, her arms around his neck, wanting an orgasm he didn't allow. Only his.

Warmth dripped on her legs. She drew up her pants as he closed his fly.

"What was that about?'' she asked. "It wasn't love.''

"You have to ask what that was about?''

No. She didn't. It had been a primal assertion, a statement of possession, of maleness. Proof of the power men had over women—and women had over men.

She wanted to touch him, to soften edges that had grown hard.

She chose not to.

He led the way onward in the snowy woods, away from the cabin, into cold and darkness. She followed, like Enid following Gereint in the old story from *Mabinogion*.

Except Enid had been innocent.

So am I.

No, she wasn't.

She grew cold. She tripped over a root.

He continued walking, never slowing his pace until he stopped suddenly, eased her against another tree, more gently this time. Unzipping her jeans, tugging them down. The bark was cold behind her. Snow dripped on her legs.

He filled her, and she squeezed back.

"Come," he said. He kissed her, stroked her tongue with his, whispered words. "You're going to come on me, and I'm going to come inside you again. And again tonight. And maybe again."

She shuddered over him and was limp.

WHEN THEY GOT HOME, Gabriela was off the phone. "Brad asked me to the Christmas dance." She beamed.

Ivy gave Cullen a look of superior knowledge.

He said, "Good for Brad. I'm sure he won't mind if your mother and I accompany you."

"Dad!" Gabriela moaned. "No way. I mean, you can drive us, but I think his brother's going to."

"Oh, no, he's not."

"Why not?"

"You're twelve years old. That's why not."

"Oh, please. I'll be thirteen in May."

"Talk to me about that in May. If you're going to the Christmas dance with Brad, the two of you ride in the Saab with us."

She shut her eyes and reopened them. "That's *mortifying*. I'm not a child."

"Could Brad's father drive them?" Ivy suggested.

"He doesn't have a father," Gabriela answered.

Cullen didn't like that at all. He felt for Brad, but Brad's older brother would not be the one driving them to this dance. "You tell Brad that I'm going to drive."

"It's too embarrassing. Everyone'll laugh if we drive up to the dance with my parents."

"Brad won't. I guarantee he'll understand perfectly."

"How do you know?"

"Because I'm a man. Tell him I look forward to meeting him."

"I won't go." It sounded like a threat.

"Have you already accepted?" Ivy asked.

"Yes."

"Then you're going."

"Oh, you'll *make* me go to the Christmas dance?"

"We'll make you keep your promise, yes."

"I'll get the flu."

Ivy had been wondering when she'd see this side of Gabriela. "You will not get the flu."

"Stop me."

Cullen had been hanging up his coat and Ivy's. "Apologize."

"For what?"

"For being rude to your mother."

"I'm being *honest*."

His eyes nailed her. She stared defiantly back. He said, "I'm waiting."

"Oh, I'm really scared."

Ivy knew she should say something. But what? What would make an impact on this child? Then, she knew. "No *Nutcracker*."

Gabriela stared as though Ivy had betrayed her. "Since when are you making the rules?" she exclaimed.

"I'm sure your father agrees with me."

Gabriela shook her head. "Uh-uh. He totally supports me about ballet."

"Gabriela."

She looked at him.

"I agree with her. Get used to the idea that when it comes to you, sooner or later we agree about *everything*."

Gabriela addressed Ivy. "Why don't you go back to Colorado?"

Cullen gritted his teeth.

Ivy seemed unfazed. "Because this is my home. I love your father, and I love you, and I'm here to stay."

Something changed in Gabriela's eyes. They no longer met those of her parents. Abruptly, she turned on her heel and walked to her room. The door shut behind her with a firm, calm click.

WHEN SHELBY CAME BY the following weekend to work on the quilt, Gabriela claimed to have too much homework to join them. Ivy and Cullen were both getting the silent treatment. Gabriela remained cold and unfriendly when her mother picked her up from ballet or school. At home, she practiced ballet and spent the remainder of her time in her room with the door shut.

Ivy could see that Cullen was hurt by it, but he didn't suggest relenting about the trip to Morgantown. When Ivy mentioned it, he'd said, "I'm not really crazy about Tracy as a role model at the moment."

Probably he was talking about the time Ivy had met him for lunch downtown, and the two of them had seen Matthew drive past with Tracy in his car.

Now Ivy found it hard to be with Shelby and not mention what was going on. *If Cullen was driving around town with another woman, would I want to know?* The answer was a definite yes. Did that make it right to tell Shelby?

"Let's go up in the loft and work," she suggested.

Ivy sat on the daybed, leaving the rocker for Shelby, and they took out their needlework. Ivy admired the two squares Shelby had stitched at Coalgood. "They're beautiful."

They set to work in silence.

Ivy said, "I think Matthew's seeing Gabriela's ballet teacher."

Shelby slowly laid down the piece she was sewing. Her lips were tight. She met Ivy's eyes. Finally, she said, "No one's told me about that one yet."

Why do you let him get away with it?

And Tracy... Ivy gritted her teeth. She knew better than to let jealousy color her impression of someone. But... She closed her eyes. "I really want to trash that woman just now, and I know it's partly because of Cullen. However, I think it's more than that. As a culture, we need to criticize that kind of behavior in order to protect the social order. I mean, if it's okay for one woman to sleep with someone else's husband, that seems to make it okay for the rest of us—even though we know it's not."

Shelby resumed stitching, then laid down her work again.

Ivy wished she'd kept her mouth shut.

"It'll burn out," Shelby said. "And in this case, I'm sure it's not about Tracy. It's about Cullen."

Parts of Ivy's body hurt, as though they'd been stretched too hard. "As it must have been with me."

"Yes." Shelby was so calm. She must be enraged beneath the surface.

"Do you ever confront him?"

"Sure. It's always nasty."

"Do you ever confront the woman?"

"And say what? 'My husband can't keep his pants zipped. I'd appreciate if you could help him with his problem by not sleeping with him.'"

"Well, it's a start. It might make you feel better to take a part in stopping it."

"Nothing's going to make me feel better at this point but a child. *That* would make me feel better. And fortunately, Matthew's with me, as far as it goes."

Ivy thought of Cullen. He obviously wanted a child, and she wanted to have one with him. After their walk through the woods a week ago, he'd ceremoniously dropped the condoms in the trash without asking her opinion. They were of one mind. She wanted to carry his child as badly as he seemed to want it.

He made love to her at least twice a day, once in the morning and once at night.

But Matthew was the subject here. "You've never considered divorcing him?"

Shelby smiled ruefully. "A very long time ago. But you know the sad part?"

She was crying, and Ivy set down her own work to go to her and embrace her. She knew what Shelby was going to say.

"I love the jerk. I understand why he does the things he does, and I just want to keep him."

GABRIELA WAS PISSED OFF. The *Nutcracker* field trip was next weekend, and she wanted to go. Good grief, she hadn't been *that* rude to her mother. Did they want her just to sit there and do nothing when they made up some totally stupid rule? Her father absolutely had to back down about driving her to the dance. She was afraid to mention it to Brad; he might not want to go with her anymore.

How am I going to make them listen?

The dilemma sucked all her concentration from ballet practice, and she finally quit her workout in frustration and stood in front of the mirror, checking out her body, looking for cellulite. She had pretty good muscles, and Tracy said thin wasn't necessarily in; healthy bodies were. *Well, I look healthy.*

In fact, when she looked in the mirror, she liked what she saw. And Brad Petersen had asked *her* to the Christmas dance.

Brad was not going to ride to the dance with her parents, Gabriela just knew it. She fought for other solutions. Maybe if Noel had a date and went with them?

No. They wouldn't go for that, either.

Ivy sure had a nerve. If she hadn't started butting in, her dad would've let her go with Brad and his brother. Gabriela was sure she could have talked him into it, but now there was no way.

Whatever I do, I don't want to grow up to be like her.

A midwife. It sounded so gross. Every time Gabriela saw something being born on the Discovery Channel, she changed the station.

Also, the quilt... Part of her thought it was neat, but another part thought it was embarrassing that her mother was so into these hillbilly things. Midwifery, quilting. Bad enough they lived up in this hollow. She'd much rather live over by Noel, even at Coalgood.

A horrible thought came to her. If Brad's brother

drove, they'd have to come to the house to pick her up!

Oh, well, I'll show them this room. They might even think the cabin was kind of cool when she told them it was a hundred years old.

Except *they* wouldn't be coming up here.

Frustrated, she tapped her foot in rhythm with Michael Torke's music, a CD Tracy had suggested. There had to be some solution.

But she couldn't find one.

She could feign illness the night of the dance.

Or she could tell Brad.

She had a feeling her parents wouldn't let her be sick. In fact, at this point, even if she had pneumonia, they'd probably make her go.

She shut her eyes. Well, Ivy wasn't coming. If her dad had to drive, so be it, but for her mom to be there would be the ultimate in gross.

I'll tell Brad tomorrow.

It was going to be the worst day of her life.

SHELBY TILL RARELY TOOK walks at night, but no one had blinked when she'd said she was going out. Matthew had said, "Want company?" And she'd considered it.

Maybe the best thing was to be close to him, to show her love for him. But in the end, she'd said, "No, thanks. I won't be long."

And now she stood on the snowy sidewalk outside Tracy Kennedy's house. The porch light was on. *Expecting company, Tracy?*

Damn Ivy anyhow. But once Ivy had put the idea of confronting Tracy in her head, Shelby began to derive some satisfaction from the prospect of telling this woman to keep her hands off Matthew.

And after she told Tracy, she'd go home and tell Matthew.

She hesitated.

He'd be sardonic. She'd be a bitch.

So be it.

She walked up the flagstone steps to the front door and pressed the bell.

"STILL NOT TALKING TO US."

"She's strong-willed." Ivy studied the underside of the bed's canopy. It could stand a new cover. That would be fun to sew. "I think that's good."

Cullen sighed. "I'd practically forgotten who I was living with before you came back. Meet Gabriela."

"I think it's normal." Ivy thought of Devon. Did Emma quell her rebellions?

"She hasn't told Brad yet. I know she hasn't. He's called twice. She would've said something if she'd told him."

"The only person whose opinion matters to her is Brad, and I think you were right. I think he probably expects it."

"Maybe. You never can tell. I'm just glad I'm going to have the chance to meet him."

"Were you serious about chaperoning the dance?"

"Why not? It beats bringing cupcakes to class parties."

He had done all that, she realized. Reaching for him, wanting to love him for all his gifts of love, she thought of something else. "Is she menstruating yet?"

"For a year and a half now."

"How did you handle that?"

"Carefully. Actually, I asked Shelby to talk to her before it happened."

"Why Shelby? Why not your sister or your mother?"

He considered. "I don't really know. There's something real about Shelby."

"I like her." Ivy liked her enough not to talk about her tears over Matthew. Instead, she shut her eyes and envisioned Shelby wonderfully pregnant—and Matthew miraculously reformed.

But Cullen's hands found her, and thoughts of conception came closer to home.

TRACY'S SMILE DIED when she saw who was at the door.

A rude comment sprang to mind, but Shelby didn't utter it. She felt too sorry for the other woman. *He doesn't love you. He'll never leave me and marry you.*

Maybe the favor she should do Tracy was to tell her so. "May I come in?"

Tracy drew back to allow her inside, then shut the door.

Shelby checked out her surroundings. She hated the decor too much to say anything complimentary. It tried for the elegance of Coalgood and failed, and

Shelby would have preferred a tattered sofa and worn rug. *Matthew must hate it, too.*

She wandered into the living room and sat on the mauve velveteen couch.

Tracy asked, "Can I get you something to drink?"

"No, thanks."

Tracy did not sit but stood poised beside a wing chair as though waiting for Shelby to explain her presence.

Shelby decided to keep it as short—and dignified—as possible. "You may find this hard to believe, but my husband loves me deeply."

Tracy's jaw was tight.

"I'm the big love in his life." Shelby got up and managed to smile at Tracy. "I just thought you'd like to know." She showed herself to the door.

Tracy stayed silent. But just as Shelby reached for the door handle, she said, "I apologize. Obviously, you're staking your territory, and I can respect that."

If you respected my territory, you would have told my husband to kiss off the first time he approached you. "Actually, that's not it at all."

No smiles from the other quarter. Just cold eyes.

"I'm trying to keep you from getting hurt."

"I don't believe that for a minute."

Shelby shrugged. "What can I say? Good night." She grasped the door handle.

"I don't care about Matthew."

Oh, she cared about someone else. Shelby could hardly blame Tracy for being embittered about Cullen. He'd seemed free when he and Tracy had dated. *But he's sure not now.*

Shelby wished she hadn't come over. Tracy made her sad. Here was a beautiful woman, teaching kids, and... *What made her like this?* Shelby said, "I hope you meet the right man soon."

Tracy's eyes were cool, and she didn't answer.

Feeling like a jerk, Shelby left. She'd never been anyplace so sad.

CHAPTER NINE

BRAD HAD STARTED ASKING her to eat lunch with Tyler and Jim and Ellen Watts. Gabriela was going to have to catch him alone in the hall to give him the grim news. She usually saw him as she was leaving math, and sure enough, he was at his locker, alone.

When he saw her, he smiled. "Hi!"

"Hi." She moved closer to the lockers. If anyone overheard this, she would die. "I have to talk to you about the dance, and, I'm warning you, it's bleak news."

"What?" He wasn't smiling anymore.

"My dad has insisted on driving us."

Brad made a face. "No way."

"It's true. I'm sorry. You don't have to go with me if you don't want. I guess these are the perils of seventh grade."

She felt him glancing at her, considering.

"I thought Ben could drive us."

"I told him that. But I'm his little girl." She batted her eyelashes to make clear to Brad that she was *not* a little girl. Then something occurred to her. This guy really didn't want to go to the dance with her because her father would be driving them? Her father wasn't some nerd. Impatient, she said, "So, make up your mind. If you don't want to go with me, I want to find another date."

Brad tossed back his dark bangs. His lips were full and expressive, and he had some hair on his upper lip, which Gabriela found interesting. "No, I want to go with you." He made a face. "It would've been cool to go with Ben, but oh, well."

"Oh, well," Gabriela agreed.

Surely her dad had been kidding about actually coming to the dance.

THE QUILT WAS GROWING. Gabriela joined in again and actually sewed some squares with Ivy in front of the television, usually watching ballet videos. Ivy was impressed with Gabriela's discipline in ballet, how she chose to dance every day on her own initiative. And she was beautiful when she danced.

Tracy Kennedy deserved some credit, and when Ivy picked Gabriela up from her last class before winter vacation, she decided to tell her. Shelby had told her about going to Tracy's house, and Ivy somewhat regretted butting in—except that apparently Matthew's affair with Tracy had ended.

While Gabriela gathered her belongings after class, Ivy watched Tracy smile at parents and encourage students. But whenever she turned away, her features were etched with exhaustion, her eyes lifeless.

Ivy took off her boots and wandered out onto the floor.

Tracy looked surprised.

"I just wanted to tell you how much pleasure it

gives me to see Gabriela dancing. You must be a very good teacher to inspire the habits she has."

"She loves ballet." Tracy seemed to hesitate, then plunged in. "I know this is hard for parents to hear, but you and Cullen might want to think about letting her go away to a performing arts school. I enjoy teaching her, but she really has something, and she could use more than I can give her in a two-hour class a few times a week."

Go away to school? The suggestion tore at her. But if Gabriela loved dance so much... "Tracy, will it hurt her chances in the future if she continues as she has been, taking classes from you?"

Tracy didn't answer at once. Slowly, she said, "To do what she wants to do, yes. She's more committed to excellence than..." She left the sentence unfinished.

There had to be another solution. *I just found my daughter. I don't want to lose her again.*

"Would private lessons help? And would you consider doing that?"

"I'd do it. It would help, but frankly, I'm not that good—as a dancer or a teacher. I wouldn't be saying this if she wasn't so serious about dance."

"Saying what?" Gabriela had suddenly appeared, standing at her shoulder.

Ivy needed to talk to Cullen, but she saw no point in keeping this conversation from Gabriela. "Tracy just suggested that you go away to a performing arts school. How do you feel about that?"

Gabriela's eyes shone. "Yes."

"Yes, you want to?"

"Yes."

Ivy chewed her bottom lip. *I can't stand this. What's the right thing to do?* She turned to Tracy. "Thank you for mentioning this, and thanks, also, for all you do for Gabriela."

"It's my job." The smile in Tracy's eyes was bittersweet. "And she's a wonderful girl."

You wanted to be her stepmother.

The thought was useless. Understanding Tracy could not change what was.

"No," CULLEN SAID.

"Just like that?"

Gabriela was in bed, and her parents were using the dance room, both stretching after their workouts.

"Just like that."

"Why not?"

"Being part of a family is more important than ballet."

"Tell that to Baryshnikov."

"A perfect illustration of my point."

Ivy understood, but he needed to see the other side. "Cullen, the world needs great artists, and Gabriela wants to be one. It's not just wanting fame. At first, I thought it was. But she cares about dance. She loves it. I think this might be a time to give her what she wants."

Cullen quit stretching. "I can't believe I'm hearing this. From you, who visits the sixteen-year-old down the road practically every day."

The phone rang, and he got up to answer it. Ivy heard him speaking but couldn't tell who it was. Finally, he came to get her. "Your mom."

Ivy raised her eyebrows. Though she spoke with both Francesca and Tara once a week, until tonight neither of them had even heard Cullen's voice. After she finished talking to Francesca, she would ask Cullen what had been said.

Francesca said, "Hi, Ivy. I just finished a birth, and I'm exhilarated, but it made me miss you so much."

"I miss you, too. Hey, I think I might have another client on the way. Emma Workman, the grandmother of the girl I told you about, said her sister's daughter is pregnant. She was going to give her my name. Emma was nearly certain she'd be interested."

"Wonderful!" Francesca sighed. "You know, Ivy, however much I miss you, you have to know that my heart just feels *full* that you've found your family and your roots and that you're practicing midwifery where your mother and grandmother did. Sometimes I cry about it," she admitted.

"Me, too."

A slight pause. "Cullen seems very nice."

"He's a wonderful man. Good inside."

"I'm eager to meet him in person. In fact, that's part of why I'm calling. How would you feel about a couple of visitors for a few days at Christmas? We don't want to intrude—we'd stay at a hotel—"

"Just a minute." Ivy put down the phone and hurried back to the dance room.

Cullen was doing extra push-ups. He stopped in the middle of one, then quit to give her his attention.

"Do you mind if Francesca and Tara come for Christmas?"

"I'd like it."

"She plans to stay in a hotel—"

He shook his head. "If they really want to. But they're welcome here. We can put mattresses in the sunroom—or in here. Or someone can sleep on the couch."

Ivy walked over to him and kissed him on the mouth. He responded so earnestly that she had to pry herself away to return to the phone.

Cullen watched her leave, listened to the tones of her voice and used his T-shirt to wipe the sweat from his body. He wandered out to the living room just as she was hanging up.

Ivy said, "So you talked with her. What did the two of you say?"

"She said she was eager to meet me and Gabriela, and I said likewise. She asked about the weather, and I told her."

Gabriela. Ivy remembered what they'd been discussing before the phone rang.

"Want a shower?" Cullen asked.

They wouldn't get any talking done in there.

"I'd like to go upstairs for a bit. And finish our conversation."

"It is finished."

"Cullen, that's not fair."

He gestured elaborately for her to precede him into the sunroom and up to the loft.

She sat in the rocking chair.

Cullen imagined her rocking their child there, and he remembered her rocking Gabriela—and remembered that during the same period she'd been sleeping with his brother. He sat on the edge of the tester bed closest to her. "Do I need to explain myself further?"

"Yes."

"I hope the world always has great artists. I hope, if Gabriela wants to become one, she will. But it's also important to me that she become a great adult."

"There's probably a performing arts school in Charleston. It's not that far. We could see her frequently."

"Tracy and I have discussed this before. I understand from her that Gabriela should go to New York."

New York?

"But I want to see her every morning and every night," Cullen added. "Right now, she's the sun and all the rest of us are planets spinning around her, and she never notices unless we displease her. She needs us more than she needs to attend a ballet academy."

"Even so, I can't help thinking that we may be standing in the way of her dreams."

Cullen touched his chest. "Great is inside."

Ivy got up from the rocker and went to embrace him. "And you're pretty great, Cullen."

"DAD, CAN I ASK A FAVOR?"

Saturday morning. The dance was that night. Ivy

had gone down the hill to see Devon. Cullen scraped an omelette onto Gabriela's plate. "You can ask."

Gabriela's expression reminded him of Ivy with a dilemma or with bad news. "Can you drive us to the dance by yourself?"

He turned off the stove and took his own plate to the table. He knew his answer, but he wanted to hear her reasons. "Why?"

"It just seems more dignified than having both my parents in the car."

He cut into his omelette. "Eat," he suggested.

She sat down across from him and didn't touch her silverware. "Please?"

"Can't do it."

"Why?"

"Because your mom is my date, and it would be rude."

"Your date?"

"Chaperons for the dance."

Her eyes went wide. "No. No. Please, no. I really couldn't handle it. It's more than I can bear."

"We won't look at you. In fact, once we get inside, we'll pretend to be someone else's parents if you like. We'll even take assumed names."

She didn't laugh. "I will never forgive you if you do this to me."

"Never's a long time."

Desolately, she regarded her meal. "I can't eat."

He swallowed another bite. "What's bugging you? We clean up good."

Her eyes slanted away from him. "You wouldn't understand."

"Try me."

"I'm going to this dance with a *ninth grader,* and you're treating me like I'm in grade school."

"Actually, I'm treating you like you're extraordinary and special, which you are. The chances that your future is with Brad Petersen are slim, and you're twelve years old—"

"Stop saying that!"

"You are not yet thirteen."

She glared at him. "I want to go away to school."

"I know."

She softened. "Did Mom tell you what Tracy said?"

"Your mother and I don't agree with Tracy. But..."

She hung on his every word.

"We reached a compromise. Tracy has said she'll work with you privately, in addition to your regular class. And we think you can go away for the whole summer next year, instead of just three weeks."

Her eyes glowed, and she leaped up from the table and hugged him around the neck.

"Thank your mom. She talked me into it."

"I will, I will." She turned a pirouette there on the floor, and she shone.

His heart twisted. He never wanted anything to go wrong for her.

He resumed eating his omelette, and she sat down and began eating hers. After a moment, she stopped.

"You know, Brad's going to hate me for you guys being chaperons, but I guess I don't care. I have cool parents. It's not like you're nerds."

Cullen quirked his eyebrows. "Thanks."

"But I have final approval on your clothes."

He could live with that and imagined Ivy could, too. "Deal."

GABRIELA WAS SO GLAD her mother had taken her shopping. She never would have found this dress otherwise.

It was ivory and long and totally elegant, and Ivy had suggested these incredible long gloves, too, and helped pin her hair up. She felt like Audrey Hepburn in *My Fair Lady*.

"Okay," she told the mirror, "it's time to check *them* out."

They were sitting on the couch together, going through their wedding pictures. They looked kind of cute, except for... "Dad. The tie." When he glanced up, Gabriela made a slicing motion across her throat. "No patterns. Wear your red tie." She contemplated her mother. "Stand up."

The two of them exchanged a look that meant they were *letting* her boss them around. So what? The most important thing was that they not embarrass her tonight.

Her mother's dress was retro, a flapper look in purplish blue, and it looked suspiciously like she'd bought it at a used clothing store. Well, retro was cool. And Gabriela supposed she could live with the ballet-slipper shoes. Her hair should be up, but then it would all seem too planned.

"Just a minute." Gabriela sped into her room. Her dad had come downstairs with a better tie, the narrow red cotton one. She flashed him the okay sign and told her mother, "Turn around."

Ivy obeyed, and Gabriela moved her hair and fastened something around her neck. Ivy reached up to touch it.

"It's my locket, and it has Dad's picture inside, so everyone should be happy. Don't lose it."

"I'll certainly try not to. Thank you for lending it."

"Okay, get your coats."

"Can you get mine?" Ivy asked. "It's in our closet upstairs."

"Not the sheepskin." Gabriela seemed alarmed.

"No."

"Vintage?"

"Yes."

With a satisfied nod, Gabriela headed for her own room to get her wrap.

"WANT TO GO UP in the bleachers?"

Yes. Oh, yes. She wanted to go up in the bleachers with Brad, but where were her parents?

"They just went out to the front area." Brad must have read her mind.

"What lousy chaperons." Gabriela laughed. "Sure. Let's go."

She kept one eye on the doors as they reached the

bleacher level and climbed up into the darkness. Then she had to concentrate on keeping her dress out of the garbage scattered everywhere.

She remembered reading in one of her dance books that one thing you didn't want to do in a dancing career was kiss strangers on the mouth. You would catch their colds and their cold sores.

Brad wasn't a stranger.

"They can't see us up here," he said, holding her hand as she sat down. He put his arm around her and kissed her, like that.

Oh, wow. Kissed by Brad Petersen. Then she felt his tongue and just about gagged. French kissing was supposed to be cool, but why had no one ever said it was gross? She pulled away.

He looked irritated.

Okay, she'd try again. Nervously, she scanned the area below one more time for her parents. Oh, shit, they were back.

And they were staring right up at her and Brad.

"They're looking at us," she said. "I'm going to the girls' room. Meet me by the pop stand."

She would absolutely die if her mother followed her into the rest room.

AS SOON AS BRAD SAW Gabriela's dad appear by the bleachers, he knew he was going to have to go through some real bullshit. This girl was turning out to be too much trouble. *Friends. We'll be friends.* He'd find someone else to ask out.

He started to get up, but Gabriela's dad sat down beside him.

If he starts lecturing, I'll just leave. I don't need some father breathing down my neck.

"You like to take photographs?"

What was this? Brad smelled a big-brother act coming on, and that was worse than the cop routine. He wasn't going to put up with it. "Look. I just kissed her. Okay? No hard feelings. I'm not trying to lay your daughter. Frankly, she's not my type."

The man beside him didn't say a word, just looked at him.

"And I'm not going to be your little photographer's apprentice. I don't want your help or your guidance or your mentoring. I don't *need* it. My brother and I take care of my mom, and you probably don't understand it because you grew up in your big house with your big happy family. Well, I don't need your shit." Brad wanted to punch him.

"Okay." He stood. "What you need is to come down from the bleachers."

Brad watched him spot another couple several sections down. They were already leaving in a hurry. Stupid rule.

"I can make a camera from an oatmeal box," Gabriela's father said.

That was a load of shit.

"I can even make a camera from a bus."

"You're multitalented. What can I say?"

"Would *you* like to make a camera from an oatmeal box?"

"Kindergarten." But Brad had a flash, a great flash that would prove once and for all that this guy was full of shit. "Your car. I want to make a camera out of your car."

SHELBY CAME OVER THE DAY after the dance to work on the quilt. "I'm pregnant."

"Shelby!" Ivy hugged her.

Gabriela blinked back and forth between the two of them. What was the big deal? She never wanted children. They were so *loud*. Whenever she was around them in restaurants, she wanted to leave.

She stood up and went to the loft window to look out. Ben was supposed to drop Brad off so he and her dad could make a camera out of the Camaro, which was about the stupidest thing she'd ever heard in her life. She really wanted to kiss him again.

"Do you know your due date?"

Gabriela tuned them out and went back to sewing. As soon as she heard them coming up the road, she was going to put on her workout clothes and start practice. She would totally ignore Brad.

Restless, she returned to her seat on the bed, relieved her mother wasn't the kind of person who would follow her into the rest room at a dance.

"OKAY," CULLEN EXPLAINED to Brad. "I've got this worked out *perfectly*. The thing we want to avoid is dumping chemicals in the car, so we've got to be careful of the tubs."

Brad really couldn't believe it. They were going to

make a camera from a Camaro? "I guess the photos won't be that great."

"Oh, yes, they will. Provided the people do well."

Brad looked from the Camaro to the bins and rolls of paper and tape, to the red light and timer and a five-gallon container of water, all amassed in the passenger seat of the car. "What do we do first?"

"Black out every inch of light inside the car."

GABRIELA FINISHED her workout. Brad had barely said hi, the jerk. *He was friendlier when we were just friends.*

She heard the screen door. "Gabriela! Ivy! Shelby! We need bodies."

She rushed out of the dance room to see her father in the doorway. "You did it?" She knew he'd made a camera from a school bus once. There were huge photos at his studio of miners at MinCo.

Her father nodded. "Put on something warm. You'll be standing out there a while. The exposures are long."

IVY, SHELBY AND GABRIELA stood against a tree, each with her back to it, Gabriela in the center. Cullen moved Shelby over some, closer to Gabriela, then did the same with Ivy.

Ivy whispered, "I love you."

He kissed her. "Okay. Ten minutes. If you decide to move, be sure to hold each pose for a *long* time. No more than, say, three poses."

"It's cold out here!" Gabriela said. "Hurry."
He jogged back to the car.

EVERYTHING THEY NEEDED barely fitted inside the car, with the thin black hose for water reaching in through careful taping. Cullen made a quick check for light, double-checking the rusty section on the floor, making sure no chemicals were slopping onto the back seat, where they'd set up a developing station.

He said, "Ready?"

Brad held the electrical tape on the window, prepared to remove it from the windshield.

Cullen set the timer. "Go for it."

Brad peeled off the tape, and light came through the windshield onto the photographic paper. *It's going to work,* he thought. The test strips had blown him away. Cullen had explained how it all happened, but he hadn't really gotten it. Well, they had to do something for the next ten minutes. "Okay, tell me again how all this works."

"Wow!" IVY AND SHELBY shouted in unison.

Gabriela's mouth hung open. "You took that with the *car?*"

The three women looked both ancient and lovely. *Women.* Cullen realized he'd thought of Gabriela that way, too. Young woman.

Brad shook his head. "That's incredible." He shot a glance at Cullen. "Can we do it again?"

"Oh, yeah. We can do it till it gets dark. Let's not waste this light. Okay, what are we doing this time?"

Ivy, Shelby and Gabriela were still checking out

the photo, and Brad edged away from the group. Sensing he wanted to say something, Cullen followed.

"Tell me if this is too much of a favor. But would you mind if I asked my mom and brother to come over so we could take a picture of them? I'd pay you for the paper."

"You don't have to do that. Sure, go call them." Cullen smiled and whispered loudly, "This group is going to start whining about the cold in a minute."

IVY ROLLED OVER SLEEPILY to hug Cullen. Brad had gone home with pictures of himself and his family, and him and Gabriela. About five pictures in all. "You're great, Cullen."

"No. I'm just lucky." But he thought of his father and of Matthew. Zeya had finally found an attendant, a black man named George, and he would be at Coalgood every day except Christmas Eve and Christmas Day. Cullen had liked him but was glad to avoid the family during their period of adjustment to the change.

"I'm so happy Shelby's pregnant. I'm really hopeful this will change Matthew."

"Don't hold your breath."

"Shelby says he wants a baby."

Cullen changed the subject. "When are Tara and Francesca arriving?"

"Wednesday. That's the twenty-third. They're leaving on the twenty-sixth."

"You know, if I borrow one of my parents' cars we can all go to the airport."

"The Saab would get kind of crowded. Let's do that. Thank you!" In the dark, she worried her bottom lip. "But you know, Cullen, I'm a little concerned about the possibility of Devon going into labor. I'm not sure I want to be that far from town." She'd hired an answering service and now wore her pager everywhere.

"I thought she wasn't due for weeks. January tenth? And you've got a backup physician."

"That's less than a month away."

"And you're particularly attached to this client."

"I care about *every* client."

"How about if just Gabby and I go to the airport?"

"Would you mind?"

"If you don't think they would."

"You don't know these women."

He had the feeling he was going to be descended on by witches. "Tell me."

"Well, Tara will give you this big hug, and I'm warning you, she's—"

"What?"

"Exciting."

"Oh." He made a sound through his teeth. "Maybe you *should* come to the airport."

"Oh, no. She's very loyal. I trust her completely. Anyhow, Mom—she'll smile and shake your hand and be kind of reserved, and on the way home she'll ask you ladylike questions about your work, and after a while you'll realize you've told her your most interesting secrets."

Witches. Just like he'd thought. Well, he'd meet

them at the airport with Gabriela, and she could absorb some of the conversation. He reached for Ivy. "Guess who else wants a baby."

She shaped her body against him. "Me."

CHAPTER TEN

ON MONDAY, IVY GATHERED her midwifery kit to take out to the Saab. She would stop briefly at Devon's before heading up to Thousandsnakes Hollow to see Emma's niece, who was expecting her third.

Gabriela, who had been drooping a little since the day Brad came over, asked, "Can I come with you?"

"Sure. Get your coat."

Surprised by the quick decision, Gabriela hurried to get her coat. *I can't believe she's letting me do this.* It had just been a whim, asking to come along, but she did have some curiosity about what her mom did for these pregnant women. And she knew she'd been born at home, with just her mom and dad there.

Climbing into the Saab and shutting the door, she said, "I just don't want to see anything born. It grosses me out on TV."

Ivy contemplated that. It was the third time Gabriela had mentioned being disgusted by birth. It almost seemed as though she wanted someone to convince her that birth *wasn't* gross. Ivy didn't argue with her. She started the car. "Okay, I'm taking you with me because you're my daughter, and my grandmother took me with her when I was your age. But there are some rules, and if you're going to have trouble with any of them, you need to stay home.''

That sounded both interesting and serious. What rules could be so important?

''First, we care for the pregnant woman and her family. That's why we're there. Second, if you want to tell your friends at school that you went to work with your mom or that you helped a pregnant lady, that's fine. But gossip has no place in this profession. We're there to support and nurture each pregnant woman, to celebrate her strength. You're no better or worse than she is, and she's no better or worse than you.''

Gabriela waited. ''That's it?''

Ivy smiled. ''That's enough for now.''

''Okay. I agree.''

Her mother's smile came from her eyes now, a smile that said she, Gabriela, was special and wonderful.

They pulled up in front of the Workmans' trailer, and Gabriela couldn't help staring. *We're going in here?* These people were poor, really poor, and pretty tacky.

Well, I'm not here to be friends.

But what had her mom said? ''You're no better or worse than she is…''

Do I really believe that? Gabriela wondered.

Her mother was opening the driver's door, and Gabriela opened hers to get out.

''GABRIELA, I'M MEASURING the fundal height. This tells how much the baby has grown since the last time we measured. It also helps tell us how many weeks pregnant Devon is.''

Gabriela found the place on the chart for fundal height. So far, she'd written down a lot. The results of the glucose test, Devon's and the baby's heart rates, blood pressure... Her mother told her what she was doing in each case, and Gabriela's head was spinning. At first, she'd sort of tuned out the explanations. But it was actually pretty interesting.

''Thirty-seven centimeters.''

Gabriela wrote it down.

''Now, let's see what baby's up to.'' Ivy smiled at Devon. She'd accepted Gabriela's presence when Ivy had said, ''This is my daughter, Gabriela. She's going to help me today.'' Now Devon was relaxed, smiling a little. Good. Ivy knew what the baby was doing. The baby was breech, but the presenting part wasn't engaged. With Devon relaxed, she should be able to turn her. Where was that heartbeat? She found it, measured. One hundred and thirty beats per minute. *Okay, kiddo, let's see if you want to turn around.*

Gabriela watched her mother's hands. What would it be like to be able to feel someone's stomach and know which way the baby was lying inside her, know what was the head or a foot or anything? It seemed almost magical.

Her mom was listening to the heart again. ''Oh, baby, you're doing so well.''

When her mother smiled at Devon, Devon's whole face brightened. *She's excited about having a baby.*

Only a real loser would get— Gabriela heard her mother's voice, telling her she was no better or worse than anyone else. *Okay, she's not a loser. She did something dumb, but she's not worse than me.*

Support and nurture? How was she supposed to do that?

Forget this stuff, Gabs. You're just an observer.

IVY SHUT THE CAR DOOR and resisted asking Gabriela how she'd enjoyed the experience. In her heart, she longed for Gabriela to become a midwife. But Gabriela's passion was dance, and she absolutely must follow her own heart, no one else's.

Her daughter was silent as Ivy started the Saab. But when they reached the stop sign at the foot of the road, Gabriela asked, "Where are we going now?"

"Thousandsnakes Hollow. I have directions, but maybe you can help. Do you know where it is?"

Gabriela shook her head.

Ivy handed her the map Emma had drawn for her. "This lady is Emma's niece, and she already has two toddlers. It would probably be helpful if you played with them and kept them out of our hair while Rhonda and I visit. This is a first visit, so we won't be doing much more than talking, getting to know each other."

"Okay." Gabriela sounded grim, but she said nothing else.

"CULLEN, THEIR *HOUSE*. I've never seen anything like it. It was hardly more than a tar-paper shack, and her boyfriend was drinking from a bottle, and the kids, neither of whom are his, were dirty, and one of them was still in diapers, and…it was despair. They have no car, no phone, no utilities. Their water isn't potable, and they're boiling it to drink.''

"How did Gabriela take it?"

Ivy stared. "That's all you can say?" They were talking in the dance room again.

Cullen kept his head down. "I guess I'm not shocked by it anymore."

"Have you ever been in one of those places deep up in the hollows? Ours is practically a neighborhood in comparison."

"No. I haven't." *It's not that I don't feel, Ivy.* It was just that he didn't *know* any of these people. And people were touchy about charity around here. He thought a minute. "What were they doing for heat?"

"A homemade stove that didn't look safe."

"What are they burning?"

"Coal."

"I take it you'd like to change this situation."

"I can't in good conscience *not* change it. Or try to."

"How are you going to get them to let you do that?"

"What do you mean?"

"You don't know the people here, Ivy. They're proud."

"She's not of that generation."

He cocked an eyebrow.

"So you're saying I should do nothing?"

"No." He rubbed a hand through his hair, getting

sweaty bangs off his forehead. "Okay, so this is what we need to do. We go up there, and you say, 'You know, I'm really concerned about how you're going to get along after the baby's born, Rhonda. As your midwife, I really need to make some provisions for you and the baby, so I brought my husband along to see if he can look at your stove and check out your water.' Then I go to work and use whatever I can find on their property to fix things."

"But the water—"

"I'll take care of it if I can. Is her boyfriend violent or just drunk?"

Ivy drew in a breath. "He seemed like a hell-raiser to me, so the answer is...possibly violent."

"I'm coming with you on these visits. All of them."

She didn't object.

He repeated his first question. "How did Gabriela take it?"

"Total shock. You saw her tonight."

"Probably didn't hurt her a bit." Cullen smiled at Ivy and touched her arm. "Ready for bed?"

TWO DAYS LATER, he and Gabriela drove to the airport in Charleston to pick up Tara and Francesca. They planned to spend some time Christmas shopping before the plane arrived. He and Ivy had already planned Gabriela's big gift, and they both had a few smaller things for her. And Cullen had one gift for Ivy—a photo of the three of them that Brad had taken with the Camaro. Ivy had seen it, but he'd framed it for her. Still, the incident of the lingerie continued to bother him. He'd like to buy her a pretty nightgown, and Gabriela could help with that.

It was a two-hour drive, and after half an hour of silence, Cullen said, "You sure haven't had much to say the past couple of days."

More silence.

"Are you upset about going with your mom on Monday? She said the place was pretty bad."

"I don't want to talk about it."

He had to accept that. The experience was changing her, and he had to let that take its own course.

"Mom is like…like Mother Teresa or something. It makes me feel guilty."

"What do you have to feel guilty for?"

"Caring about clothes and ballet. I feel like I should be doing what *she's* doing."

"You're twelve years old, and she would not want you to feel that way. Guilt is totally useless. It doesn't make anyone a good person. Whenever you start to feel it, stop thinking until the feeling goes away. Because when you stop thinking about what you should do, you do the right thing."

"I don't believe you."

"Try it. Anyhow, Ivy told me you did a great job looking after the kids while she talked with their mom. You really helped."

Gabriela began to cry.

He saw a gas station with a convenience store up ahead and prepared to pull in.

"I'm fine." She dug a tissue out of her backpack,

which she'd brought with her. "You don't have to stop."

"Yes, I do. We need gas." He turned into the lot and pulled up to the pumps. But before he got out, he asked, "Can I do anything?"

"No."

He smiled at her. "Don't think."

Through her tears, she giggled.

"DAD, WHAT ABOUT THIS ONE? I know it's flannel, but she's kind of old-fashioned."

The nightgown was blue with white flowers and white ruffled trim and flower-shaped buttons. He pictured Ivy in it. "I like it. Let's get it. It'll be from both of us."

Gabriela frowned. "What can I get her? She doesn't seem to want anything. When we went shopping for my dress for the dance, she just didn't look twice at the stuff in the stores."

Cullen took a moment to consider. "I think she liked wearing your locket to the dance."

"But *you* should give her that."

"Why not put your picture in it, Gabriela? She'd probably treasure that the most."

Gabriela stared up at him for only a moment, then exclaimed, "Okay. Let's find a really cool one." A second later, she thought, *My dad's the best.*

THIS WAS SO WEIRD, standing in the airport waiting for total strangers. Her mom called them her mother and her sister, but they weren't related to her by blood or… It made Gabriela's head spin, and she felt totally conspicuous carrying a sign that read, "HI, TARA" followed by a big exclamation point with a heart at the bottom. And her dad had one just like it for Francesca.

The passengers were coming out of the gate. Ivy had told them what to look for. Tara was tall and beautiful with long, dark hair, and Francesca had longish, curly, dark auburn hair. Tara would be bursting with energy, and Francesca would seem aloof.

They were midwives. Gabriela sort of hoped they'd talk about it on the way home in the car. But it probably wouldn't be like that.

"Ah! There they are."

The voice came from a tall woman with long, walnut-colored hair and a huge grin. You almost couldn't notice anyone else around her because she was so…dynamic?

"Let's see—Gabriela, right?" Her brown eyes were bright, and she really had the friendliest smile Gabriela had ever seen.

Gabriela said, "Tara, right?"

Tara laughed, drew the sign toward her to examine it, then set it down beside her and gave Gabriela a hug. A second later, she drew back. "You probably get sick to death of hearing this, but you look just like your mom."

"I have my dad's chin."

"Let's see." Tara compared the two of them.

The other woman who'd been speaking to her dad now turned to her. "Hello, Gabriela. I'm Francesca."

While she shook hands with Francesca, Tara grabbed her dad in a huge hug. He smiled, returned the embrace and took a step back from her.

No kidding, Gabriela thought.

He asked them, "The baggage claim?"

"Nope," Tara said. "We've got everything with us." She wore a backpack, and Francesca had a big garment bag. "We're yours."

GABRIELA HAD ANSWERED all the questions about school and ballet, and Tara was busy exclaiming over things outside the window. Everything out there seemed to excite her. "No way! Look at those trees!" Gabriela actually thought they were both nice, although Francesca didn't say very much.

How could she get them to talk about midwifery?

"I went with my mom to see a pregnant girl the other day."

Both midwives immediately looked at her.

"So..." Tara's grin was coming back up. "Tell us about it."

"Actually, there were two." What should she say? She wasn't supposed to gossip. Gabriela searched her mind. "She turned this baby who was...upside-down?"

"Breech," they both said at once.

"She didn't even say she was doing it. She told us all about it after it was done, and then she had Devon go for a little walk, told her to stand up for a while so the head would stay down."

"Become engaged," Tara said. "It means the wid-

est part of the baby's head, or its butt if it's breech—
the presenting part—has passed through the mom's
pelvic inlet. It's exciting for the mom because it
means the big day is getting pretty close. So, anything
else?''

Gabriela thought. ''I wrote down stuff for her.
That's about it.''

''And then you saw another lady?'' Tara was asking the questions, but Francesca was still turned
around from the front seat. These two acted like people having babies was the most exciting thing on
earth.

Another lady. ''Yes. She had two little kids, and I
took care of them.''

''That must have been a big help to your mother!''
Francesca said. ''If you want to come to Colorado, I
have a job for you.''

Gabriela admitted, ''It's not my favorite thing.''

The women laughed.

''Gabby.'' It was her dad. She could see his eyes
in the rearview mirror, and they were smiling.
''You're a million-dollar girl.''

Her mom had told him how hard things were for
that lady, Rhonda. *He's glad I didn't gossip.* Warmth
spread inside her.

Tara said, ''Okay, now. Tell me every little detail
about your dancing. I don't know squat about ballet,
except that it's really, really hard.''

This was going to be fun, having her mom's…well,
family visit.

IVY HUGGED TARA, then Francesca. "It's so great to have you here, to see your faces."

"And yours!"

"Look at this incredible place," said Tara.

"I grew up here, when there was only this cabin. Or so Cullen tells me. Let me give you the tour."

While Cullen carried in their bags, Ivy and Gabriela showed them around the house. Ivy was surprised how much Gabriela knew of the history of things in the cabin. Cullen must have told her all he knew.

"We thought you'd like to sleep in the sunroom. It stays surprisingly warm in here at night, and we've got these foam futons."

"It's lovely, Ivy." Francesca embraced her again. "And your family's so nice. Gabriela said she went with you to see two clients."

Ivy met her daughter's eyes. "She really helped out."

The look on Gabriela's face was full of feeling, recollection of their visit to Rhonda's house and perhaps other things. Ivy would try to talk with her alone before she went to bed.

She caught up on all the latest with Francesca and Tara as they were preparing dinner together, the way they'd done so many times in Precipice. Tara was planning to leave Maternity House soon. "I'd like to hook up with IHS or else go back to Chile or Mexico."

Francesca sliced a carrot. "I wish you'd stay in the United States where it's safe."

"You don't want me to come to Precipice and work with you."

"You're not legal in Colorado."

"So what?" Tara grinned. "I'm good."

"Your total disregard for the law floors me."

"I don't disregard the law. I hate it. I fight it. And I am *not* caving in."

Ivy had heard this conversation, in different versions, a hundred times. Francesca felt Tara should go to school to become a certified nurse-midwife. Tara said she already had tremendous experience and would learn very little in school that she didn't already know; becoming certified would be no more than caving in to the medical establishment. Ivy tended to agree with her. Tara's decision was born out of integrity, out of her objection to the profession of midwifery being regulated by physicians instead of midwives.

Francesca tensed. "Alex is moving to Hawaii, Ivy. He's selling his house and the Victorian."

The place she rented in Precipice. Either a family might buy it to live in, or a new landlord might raise the rent. In either case, Francesca would be looking for a new home in a town where rents were already high. It was entirely possible she'd have to move her practice somewhere else.

"Any offers yet?" Ivy asked.

"A lot of people looking. It's out of my control."

"Which you can't stand," Tara tossed over her shoulder. "In general."

"Of course I can stand it. Birth is never within my control."

"Which is why you'll do anything for the physicians—so you don't lose hospital privileges."

"Let's drop this, Tara."

Ivy caught the look on her mother's face. "Is something happening?"

"Dr. Henry is retiring," Tara answered. "And guess who wants to do physician backup for home births."

"No one?"

"Bingo."

"What are you going to do, Mom?"

"I haven't decided."

Ivy hugged her. To try to put her mother in a better frame of mind, she told them both about Mata Iyer. Ivy's good fortune seemed to encourage Francesca, but Ivy knew that her mother was going to have to make some choices she herself wouldn't want to make.

"You should have *me* come to Precipice," Tara volunteered. "You can do the hospital thing. I'll do the home births and take the fall if we need to bring someone to the hospital. In fact, I might come up there anyway."

Francesca tensed but fell silent, and Ivy said, "Okay, let's get this dinner on. Tara, how's the rice coming?"

WHEN GABRIELA WENT to her room to turn in, Ivy went with her. She shut the door and came over to sit on the bed, which had become an evening ritual. "How's everything?"

Gabriela shrugged.

Ivy waited to see if she'd speak.

"I'm just confused. I want to be a ballet dancer, but I liked helping you."

"Can you do both?"

"Well..." Her shoulders slumped. "What you do is so important. I wouldn't want to make any mistakes."

Ivy smiled gently, trying to reassure her. "What kind of mistakes?"

"Well, say if you let me hand you things, and I gave you the wrong thing."

What's behind this? Obviously, Gabriela wanted to explore midwifery, but she seemed almost afraid to. "Gabriela, are you afraid that if you help me, I'll think you want to become a midwife?"

"Kind of."

Yes. "I know where your heart is, Gabriela. I would only be disappointed if you ever gave up your dreams, whatever they are. Those are for you to choose. And I'll always be happy to have you help me and to let you learn, if you want. If you think midwifery is interesting, you can learn about it as much or as little as you like. And continue reaching for your dreams."

Gabriela searched her face. "Are you sure?"

"Of course I'm sure. And I had another idea. You're really at the age where you're beginning to turn from a girl to a woman. I think it would be fun if you and I did something special to celebrate your becoming a woman.''

"Like what?"

"Perhaps go on a camping trip where you'd spend part of the time alone, thinking about what it means to you to be a woman, the kinds of qualities you want to develop."

Gabriela squinted. "That sounds cool. After, maybe I could help you more. Learn to feel where the baby is, which direction it's turned."

"That's called the lie. The lie of the baby." Ivy smiled. "Let's take one day at a time. It's cold out. Wouldn't you like to wait till it warms up?"

"My dad—Dad's taken me snow camping before. We could go during vacation. We could just go out here somewhere, on the property."

"Let me think about it. We can decide after Christmas. For now, we have guests, and tomorrow we're all going to Coalgood for dinner." She hugged Gabriela. "Good night."

"Good night, Mom."

"I love you."

"Love you, too."

Happy in this experience that she'd never known— to remember—before returning to West Virginia, Ivy stood to leave. *If only Matthew never tells her the truth.*

It didn't seem like a secret Cullen's brother would trouble to carry to his grave. It seemed like a secret he'd use whenever and wherever it would hurt Cullen the most.

"ARE SHELBY AND MATTHEW here?" Cullen had just made introductions, and Francesca and Tara had met everyone but Shelby, Matthew and the judge.

"It's George's day off," Zeya reminded him. The attendant. "Shelby and Matthew are upstairs with Daddy."

Cullen nodded and made no move to go find them. Neither did Ivy, although the whole group, assembled in the main hall at the center of the house, peered up the long grand staircase to the balcony overlooking the hall.

As if on cue, Matthew appeared at the top of the stairs and started down. Seeing the group gathered, he lifted his eyebrows but seemed preoccupied.

The judge and Shelby walked slowly behind him. Mitzi Till said to Tara and Francesca, "Why don't you all come into the living room? We'll have some Christmas cheer, and I know everyone will join us."

The two midwives took the initiative and followed her lead, with Zeya, Tom and Scout in tow, Scout chattering eagerly to Tara.

Ivy lingered to speak with Shelby, and Cullen and Gabriela started haltingly for the living room.

"Here, Your Honor, take my arm." Shelby offered it to him.

They were on the third or fourth step from the top, and the judge hesitated.

"Come on, Daddy," Matthew coaxed wearily from the foot of the stairs.

Shelby caught his arm gently, and the judge jerked

away. She began walking down the stairs alone. Suddenly, the judge pushed her hard from behind.

She fell, in slow motion.

Ivy reached up and stepped forward as though to catch her. But Shelby tumbled down, and her head struck a stair, and she lay still.

"Shelby!" Matthew's hoarse cry echoed through the hall. He ran, taking the stairs three at a time and gathered his wife in his arms. "Shelby. Oh, God, Shelby."

Ivy and Cullen both charged up the stairs, and Cullen said, "Gabby, call 911."

"Matthew, don't move her. She might have a spinal cord injury."

Shelby's eyelids fluttered, and she gave a slight moan.

"Shelby, try not to move," Ivy said calmly. "We're right here with you. You fell down the stairs."

"The baby." Her eyes reached into Ivy's, begging reassurance.

"We'll just have to see."

Matthew said, "Please don't move, Shelby. I picked you up, and I shouldn't have. Now we need to wait for the paramedics."

Cullen had stood, and he climbed slowly toward the top of the stairs.

Behind him, Ivy said, "Shelby, I'm going to hold your head to help keep you from moving it."

"Shelby! Oh, Shelby," cried Mitzi.

Cullen glanced back at the others and continued up

the steps. His father stood near the top, confused. When he recognized Cullen, his eyes cleared some. "Cully. Cully, she was no good." His mouth was open and words deserted him.

Cully, she was no good.

His first instinct was that Gabriela must not hear any of what his father was saying. Only as he guided the judge back up the stairs did the past suggest itself to him.

Patient. If he wasn't patient, he'd never learn the truth.

He might not anyhow.

As they entered the bedroom, he asked, "Did Gina fall on the stairs, Daddy?" *Did you push her?*

In his new, slow, slurring voice, the judge said, "Forget her, Cully. Whore."

"Did you push her down the stairs?"

The judge blinked, suddenly lost.

Cullen nearly grabbed him, shook him. He wanted to break his hand, choke him until he got the truth. He stood in front of his father. "My wife, Gina. Where is she?"

The judge's look had turned vacant.

"Did you take her to Colorado?"

No answer.

"My wife. Did you push her down the stairs?"

"A…" His voice trailed away.

"Daddy, please answer." Cullen spoke more slowly. "Did Gina fall down the stairs?"

His father shoved him.

He should be in a nursing home. He can't be trusted not to hurt Mother.

Some people kept their parents with Alzheimer's at home for years. But the judge was big and violent. The doctor had said to do whatever was necessary to keep him calm. But he'd just pushed Shelby down the staircase.

Cullen picked up the judge's stuffed tiger from the bed and handed it to him.

I have to know.

He tried a new tactic. "I'm angry you pushed Gina down the stairs."

"She fell."

Cullen's chest twisted tight. Now he was losing the power of speech. "You shouldn't have grabbed her that way."

"No one hurts Cully. Cully gets everything."

Cullen sat, trapped in the room with his father. He'd discovered a man in his family who could hurt a woman.

He'd discovered who had hurt his wife, accidentally or on purpose. The judge had concealed the truth, and he must have taken her somewhere and left her. Maybe all the way to the Rockies.

The minutes dragged by. The judge held his tiger. "Checkers."

I am not going to play checkers with you. "No."

No one hurts Cully. What about Matthew? Ivy in lingerie; no wonder he hadn't been able to keep an erection. His brother and his father had stolen from him.

*You hurt my wife and lied to me. You lied to me.
You lied to me about my wife, Gabriela's mother. I
hate you. I'll never forgive you.*

He could not utter the words. He never would. It
wasn't in him to strike back at a sick old man.

And Mother had never known, or she wouldn't
have been so shocked when the judge said what he
had about Matthew and Gina.

Gina.

That he loved Ivy more and was loved more in
return did not subdue his anger.

"Ivy went with Matthew to the hospital. She
wanted to be there for Shelby in case she has a miscarriage."

It was Tom.

Ivy with Matthew? Were they alone? His trust
trembled.

"Where's Gabriela?"

"Downstairs with Tara and Francesca. That's why
I came to relieve you. She's pretty shaken up and
worried. She wanted to go to the hospital."

"Thanks, Tom." He started to leave the room. "He
wants to play checkers."

MATTHEW DROVE SILENTLY, occasionally wiping his
eyes. Ivy had offered to drive, but he had taken the
wheel.

Within a block of the hospital, he said brokenly,
"She wants that baby."

Ivy didn't answer. She could have told him to show

Shelby lots of love, but there was no need.

Matthew was in love with his wife.

"HOW COULD GRANDPA *do* that?"

Tara and Francesca had suggested they go back to the cabin, and Cullen and Gabriela had just dropped them off there.

"He's sick. His brain is sick." The effort to speak was Herculean. Why had Ivy gone with Matthew?

He pictured her comforting him in one of Matthew's genuine moments, which were intense when they came. *Where is my wife?*

"Is Shelby going to lose the baby?"

"I don't know." His father's face and body, his confusion, flashed through Cullen's mind. His decision was immediate and final. It wasn't revenge or fury. It was prevention. The judge was serving no one anymore. He was hurting people instead.

I'm going to help him die.

The only question was how.

He parked the Saab near Matthew's XKE. *Did you like the car, Ivy?* Where was she? He unfastened his seat belt.

"There's Uncle Matthew."

Matthew was standing in the snow among trees strung with lights in front of the door. He had seen the Saab, and he strode toward it. His eyes were wild as he flung open the driver's door and grabbed Cullen by his parka, yanking him from his seat. "You little piss."

Cullen stood, and his brother slammed a fist in his face.

"Daddy!" Gabriela opened her door and ran around the car. Her uncle hit her father again. "Stop it, Uncle Matthew! Stop it!"

"Hit back! Hit me, Cully. You can do it."

Cullen drew up his throbbing head and met his brother's eyes. "No."

Matthew smashed his groin.

"Daddy!"

His face. Everything was red.

Gabriela ran for the hospital doors. Her mother was coming out. "Mom! Uncle Matthew's hurting Dad!"

Cullen had walked away from his brother, moving amongst the trees, dripping blood on the snow. Matthew stalked him, and Ivy and Gabriela hurried after them.

"Stop him! Stop him!" Gabriela cried.

"I can't."

Gabriela stared at her mother. "Help him!"

"Yes, help him, Gina. He needs help. Don't you, Cully? You better hit back, or your wife is going to do it for you."

"No, she won't."

Matthew punched him again.

Gabriela ran toward her uncle and punched him ineffectually.

"Now your daughter's defending you." Matthew pushed Gabriela out of the way with little force.

Your daughter. Ivy heard the words with a strange disbelief. Even at this moment, when Matthew plainly wanted to hurt Cullen, he'd chosen not to reveal the truth to Gabriela. And he must know the truth was his most potent weapon.

"Stop hitting him!" Gabriela screamed. "Are you crazy? He's your brother."

"Defended by your little girl, Cully?"

Your little girl.

"Daddy, hit him back!"

"Yes, hit me back, Cullen, or you'll lose face in front of your family."

Your family.

Ivy had moved closer. *I can't do anything. How can I let Matthew do this to him in front of Gabriela? How can Cullen let it happen?*

She knew then. This was the competition. Not to lose control. To win over Matthew again by never hitting back.

Cullen, don't do this to us.

"You're Daddy's little piece of shit, you know that?" His brother shoved him to the ground and kicked his ribs.

Cullen wondered if Matthew would actually kill him. *I can't die. Gabby would never get over it.* He lay on his back in the snow, seeing the trees overhead, his face sticky and cold. He saw his own stupidity in red. He was no better than Matthew. "You win, Matthew. If you come down here where I can reach, I'll hit you back."

"Get up and fight like a man, Cully."

"Daddy." His daughter was crying.

"I'm okay, Gabby." He sat up, battered, and gathered handfuls of snow to wash his face.

Ivy could not bring herself to move, to help.

As Cullen got to his feet, Matthew came over and put his arm around his brother. "I'll help you inside, puppy."

Cullen lightly punched him in the stomach and leaned on his brother.

Ivy and Gabriela slowly followed them to the hospital doors. While Cullen and Matthew went into the men's room, Ivy and Gabriela sat on a bench outside.

Gabriela asked, "What if he kills him in there?"

"I don't think he will. I think they're done."

"Uncle Matthew's insane."

A nurse stopped in the hall and saw the trail of blood into the bathroom.

"It's all right," Ivy said.

"What happened?"

"Christmas tension."

How can you make me part of this, Cullen? She was torn between the need to wait outside the door and the desire to return to Shelby. Shelby, grieving.

Ivy hugged Gabriela. "I love you, Gabriela."

"Why didn't you stop Uncle Matthew?"

"Your dad asked me not to, and I said I wouldn't."

"He could have killed him. Would you have let him kill him?"

"No." *But I basically did. Matthew could have killed him.*

"Why didn't he hit him back? He didn't even try."

"You'll have to ask him."

CULLEN'S HEAD WAS over the sink. Again and again, he pressed water to his face. Matthew stood beside him, and Cullen didn't ask about Shelby's condition because he knew why Matthew must have attacked him.

He dried his face, then turned and hugged his brother, hugged him around his arms, stretching because Matthew was bigger, and Matthew cried. "She wanted the baby."

THEY LEFT MATTHEW at Shelby's bedside and started home. Ivy drove, and neither she nor Gabriela spoke. Cullen's face was cut, his jaw and eye swollen, but nothing broken. She would make a poultice for him when they got home. But what was she going to say to Tara and Francesca?

When they parked in front of the cabin, Ivy said, "Gabriela, will you please go on in? We'll be there soon. You don't have to tell them anything. I'll take care of it."

The door closed behind Gabriela.

Cullen said, "I'm sorry."

Ivy hardly knew what to say. That he should have defended himself against Matthew? Then two people would have been hurt instead of one. *Tough.* "I will defend you next time. I am not going to stand there and watch anyone do that to you. What are you going to say to Gabriela?"

"That I didn't want to fight my brother."

"You were fighting him by not fighting him. You wanted to win, and the price you asked us to pay was too high."

"I recall telling him he won."

"Nobody won. You two better sort out your differences or this will continue until one of you dies, and then the other one will be left with things he wished he'd said or done."

Until one of you dies...

Cullen remembered. The judge. The stairs. *Tell her. You can't keep this from her.*

But if the judge died, would it matter anymore?

Protecting your father who hurt your wife?

His head spun. He knew right, saw it before him.

"You fell down the stairs." He repeated every uncertain word of his conversation with the judge.

Ivy saw Shelby falling.

Cullen played the rest through his mind. Helping the judge wander off. *Whatever happens, I mustn't go to jail for this.* He needed to know the law. In this case, he didn't care about the spirit of the law. Only the question would he or would he not go to jail?

But the life insurance...

His mind cleared slowly. A nursing home. The judge had to go to a nursing home. He tried to avoid the thought that it would be the perfect punishment. *I don't want to punish him. I love him.*

But he might have hurt Ivy—Gina. And he'd concealed her fall down the stairs. What had he done with her once she fell?

The same questions raced through Ivy's mind. Had she fallen? Or had the judge pushed her? In any case, why hadn't he helped her, called 911? If he'd done that, she would have been with her husband and child all this time.

And might never have known Tara and Francesca.

She'd read somewhere that trying to change the future was like trying to handle a master carpenter's tools; she would cut herself.

The judge had chosen her future.

And now he was losing his mind, his memory.

She didn't believe one had caused the other. Still, it was ironic. But the greatest irony was that the justice offered by the law would be useless now. The man was dying; his existence was sad.

He's my father-in-law. I don't remember what he was like when he was well. But he's Cullen's father. Without him, there would have been no Cullen.

Cullen said, "Ready to go in?"

SHE MADE A POULTICE for his face, explaining to Tara and Francesca, "Matthew has some unresolved rage."

Neither of them commented. Cullen suggested, "Why don't you let Gabriela and me make dinner? You three could take a walk or go out on snowshoes."

Ivy accepted the suggestion.

She and Tara and Francesca wrapped up in coats and hats and mittens and went out to the woods. Outside, as Ivy double-checked her pager to make sure it was working, Francesca and Tara studied her.

Each walked on one side of her, put an arm around her.

She needed to reassure them somehow. But what confidence could she offer? What she'd told Cullen was true. Unless something changed, Matthew would hound him until one of them died.

"It's sibling rivalry. Matthew's mother died when he was twelve or so, and his father remarried. When Cullen came along, the judge was crazy about him, the way people are about babies. He's always favored him, I guess."

"It sounds as though Matthew needs counseling," Tara said.

"I think the chances of anyone talking him into that are slim." Although Ivy had told Tara about her long-ago affair with Matthew, she hadn't confided that Matthew was Gabriela's natural father. She wouldn't now, either. Today had convinced her that Matthew would never tell. Nor would Shelby. Only this total sense of allegiance, of shared love for Gabriela, could erase her doubts about keeping something so important from her daughter. Everyone cared about Gabriela. As far as each one of them was concerned, Cullen was her father.

Ivy knew in her heart that unburdening herself of this secret would only relieve her own conscience, not help her daughter. She would be a keeper of the secret, too. She would adopt with heart and soul the knowledge that Cullen and Cullen alone was Gabriela's father.

And no one would ever hurt Gabriela with the truth.

"I think he and Cullen are going to have to work

it out together. To actually talk to each other about this. Cullen looks innocent, but he's not. I think he has his own ways of getting to Matthew.''

"He has some legitimate gripes," Tara said quietly.

"Of course." Ivy flushed, remembering what she had done years ago. *And the judge caught us together, and when I fell down the stairs, he...* Who could guess what he'd done? No one would ever know.

She wasn't going to talk about that. There was no point.

"How is Shelby doing?" Gabriela had told them about the baby.

"Physically she's recovering from the miscarriage. She's badly bruised, but no serious injuries. She's really depressed, though. At least no one suggested putting her on the maternity floor.''

They'd all seen it before with miscarriages. Part of caring for a mother who miscarried or had a stillbirth was making absolutely sure that didn't happen.

Ivy took a deep breath, and so did Tara and Francesca. They held each other, leaned on each other. They would open no presents till tomorrow, and perhaps by then some of the pall of this day would have lifted.

"I'M SORRY, GABRIELA. I shouldn't have let your uncle do that," Cullen said.

Her eyes were miserable.

"You know, he was upset about Shelby and the baby."

"Why pick on you? What did you do?"

I've raised his only child.

"It has to do with Grandpa, I think. Matthew had a hard time when his mom died."

Gabriela frowned and resumed tearing up lettuce for the salad. "He tried to kill you."

"No. He didn't want to kill me."

"What *did* he want?"

"You got me." What did Matthew ever want? Did he want a different past? A different future?

He wants Daddy's love. He had it, but Matthew probably didn't believe that.

A memory flashed in his mind. *Cully gets everything.*

Had his father said that to Matthew? It was possible. Matthew had looked depressed when he came down the stairs.

He remembered what Ivy had said, that he and Matthew needed to work things out. She was right, but how could he do it without his brother's help?

"I'm sorry I didn't hit him back, Gabriela. I wish you hadn't seen any of that. I didn't want to fight him, but I have an obligation to you and your mom. It won't go that way again."

Gabriela met his eyes, and he sensed her measuring the weight of his promise.

He smiled, though it hurt his face.

She said, "You need to put that poultice back on. Go sit down. I'll ask if I need you."

Cullen felt worse than ever. For her and for Ivy, he would try to talk to Matthew.

CHAPTER ELEVEN

"YOU'RE KIDDING!" Gabriela stared at the ballet tickets in her hands. "We're going to New York? And we're going to see two ballets?"

"And visit two dance schools," Ivy added, smiling.

Her scream of delight set Tara and Francesca laughing, while Gabriela embraced each parent in turn.

"February. It's a million years away," Gabriela moaned. She collapsed on the couch.

The ballet tickets were the last gift to be opened. Tara had given Gabriela a friendship bracelet. Francesca had given her a pendant similar to the ones she and Ivy and Tara wore, not of a birthing woman, but of an ancient female figure. Ivy had given Francesca the wedding-ring quilt she'd bought from Emma Workman; for Tara she'd made a quilted wall hanging, designing the pattern—images of birth—herself.

Cullen had been the hardest to plan a gift for. What they shared seemed beyond ordinary gifts. He seemed to have the things he needed and he'd claimed not to want anything in particular. Finally, she'd settled on a good pair of binoculars. She treasured her gifts from him and Gabriela.

"Cullen and I need to go over to Coalgood briefly and exchange gifts with his family. Do you want to come, Gabriela?"

"I'd rather stay here."

Tara and Francesca cast looks of concern at Ivy and at Cullen, with his black eye and bruised face.

He said, "No fights today." In fact, Christmas was a good day for healing, for trying to mend his relationship with his brother.

"CULLEN, WHAT HAPPENED to your face?" Mitzi didn't wait for an answer. "It was Matthew, wasn't it?"

"I'm fine."

His mother frowned. Ivy watched the two of them, wondering about Mitzi's thoughts, wondering if she, too, felt helpless in the midst of her son's and her stepson's behavior.

Mitzi was arranging cookies on a platter. Everyone at Coalgood had opened presents this morning, but Ivy and Cullen still had gifts for everyone and gifts to open and others to take home to Gabriela.

"Can I help you, Mitzi?" Ivy asked.

"No, thank you."

Her mother-in-law's distance hurt, but Ivy understood. She was probably a prisoner of pain over the judge's illness. *I wish she would talk to me.* But it seemed as though it wasn't to be.

She tried again. "How is the judge?"

Mitzi shook her head. "I can't get over what happened yesterday."

What happened ten years ago, too.

"I had a miscarriage before Zeya was born."

The revelation surprised Ivy.

"It was so devastating. I wish I could do something for Shelby. She's so sweet, and there's just nothing to do."

Cullen kissed his mother, then Ivy, and excused himself, probably to go find Matthew.

Mitzi seemed to be almost talking to herself. "You know, when I had that miscarriage, my mother gave me a beautiful lace handkerchief that her mother had given her. I'd really like to give that to Shelby, but she's not a lace kind of person."

"I think she'd treasure it."

"Do you?" Mitzi glanced at Ivy but hid her own thoughts, whatever they were. "Then I think I will. Perhaps tonight."

IVY TOOK SHELBY'S Christmas gift up to her room. "I brought you something, Shelby."

Shelby was in bed upstairs. The room was filled with flowers from Matthew—even its own Christmas tree. Shelby had said he'd hardly left the room since they'd come home from the hospital, but now he'd gone out to leave Ivy and Shelby alone together.

Ivy handed her a soft, gift-wrapped package.

"Oh, Ivy, thank you."

She'd shed some tears when Ivy first embraced her, but now her eyes were clear. She opened the blue tissue paper and unfolded the garment inside. It was a white cotton sweatshirt painted with a picture of a dragon toasting a marshmallow with his fiery breath.

"It's beautiful." Shelby smiled. "He's cute, and I love him."

Ivy felt something tugging at her, some reason she'd ordered the sweatshirt for Shelby. She couldn't pinpoint it.

They hugged again, and Ivy contemplated that this woman had forgiven her for her past. *I'm so lucky.*

"Is there anything I can do? Are you still bleeding?"

"No, it's stopped. I'm just afraid this was an omen. That we'll never have a baby."

I fell down the stairs, too, or else the judge pushed me.

Suddenly, she remembered. She'd lost a baby. Cullen's? Matthew's? She didn't want to tell Shelby about the stairs. But she said, "When I hit my head, I lost a baby, too. It wasn't the same. I didn't know who I was. I didn't know..." Whose baby it was. She still didn't. "Who my family was, where I'd come from. But I mourned the loss. And Cullen really had trouble with it when I told him." She met Shelby's eyes. "But, Shelby, take it as a good sign that you became pregnant."

"I had an abortion when I was eighteen."

That was new information. "Any problems from it?" Shelby would have found out at the fertility clinic.

"No. But I can't help thinking this is some kind

of retribution. At the time, I felt I had no other choice. As I got older, I realized I did.''

She was crying again, and Ivy held her, wishing a baby for her and Matthew. She'd had many clients who'd had abortions. Emotions nearly always surfaced with pregnancy and birth, and usually the entire process helped with healing, with the stigma and silence and pain surrounding the issue. ''You're a wonderful mother, Shelby. You took such good care of yourself through these early weeks. You were wonderful to your child.''

Shelby continued to cry. ''What about the baby I aborted? Was I a mother then?''

''What do you think? That's what matters.''

''I suppose I wasn't ready to be.'' She took slow breaths. ''Someone told me that in France, a midwife is called a *sage-femme,* a wise woman. You've shown me why, Ivy.''

Ivy shook her head. She tried to find the best course of action in any situation, but sometimes her choices had unexpected consequences. If birth had begun to teach her anything, it was to try not to shape the future but instead face the present.

She found it the hardest lesson of all.

Tom was with the judge, and Cullen caught Matthew emerging from his and Shelby's room. ''Hi. How are you?''

He shrugged, avoiding Cullen's eyes.

''I'd like to talk.''

Matthew looked at him. ''All right.''

"Want to go for a drive?"

"I need to stay here. For Shelby."

They sat on the couch in the rec room. Cullen hadn't planned to say anything in particular, except a general suggestion that he'd like a better relationship with Matthew. "So. I'm tired of fighting."

"You don't fight."

"I do. In other ways. I ignore you. I act like nothing's wrong when you've totally pissed me off. That's my way of fighting."

Matthew remained silent, but only for a moment. "He says he's giving you everything. Which is what he's always done."

Cullen didn't smile. "He has Alzheimer's. It's not true."

"He says to me, 'Cully gets everything.' He wants you to have everything."

"He doesn't know what he's saying. And by the way, we need to convince Mother that he belongs in a nursing home."

Matthew said nothing.

The conversation was going nowhere. Whatever made Matthew behave the way he did wasn't something Cullen could fix. He stood up, made a last try. "I just wanted to say that I'd like to replace the sibling rivalry with a real relationship." *Even though you slept with my wife, and I'll never forget it and maybe never forgive you.*

Matthew didn't reply.

"Do you want to talk to Mother about the nursing home, or shall I?"

"George will be back tomorrow."

I don't live in this house. All of them do. Cullen backed away from the subject. "It's up to you."

IVY DROVE FRANCESCA and Tara to the airport the following day, and that evening Gabriela brought up the idea of snow camping. "We could do it tomorrow night."

Ivy had discussed her suggestion with Cullen, and now he left them alone up in the loft to talk about it.

Sitting on the tester bed with Gabriela, Ivy asked, "What kinds of things would you like to do?"

"Well, if we had two tents, I could pitch mine a little ways from yours."

"How about a long way from mine? No one should come around. This is our property."

"Okay."

"How would you feel about keeping a journal of that time? Just for yourself, not to share with anyone else. You could think about being a woman and explore your real feelings and the kind of person you want to be."

"Okay. I'd like that."

"Can you think of anything else?"

"Well, I've decided I probably have time even with ballet and school. I want to learn more about midwifery. Could you teach me to be your assistant?"

Ivy considered. "I'm happy to teach you anything I know about midwifery, but being an apprentice implies a commitment. You're just twelve, and I think you have plenty of commitments just now. How about if we call you a midwifery student? And I'll think of some ideas to start you off."

"Thanks! So we can do it tomorrow night?"

"Let's plan to."

GABRIELA HUGGED her father. "I guess we're going." He smiled, eyes shining at hers, and the expression warmed her. He thought she was the greatest. She said, "You're the best dad."

"You're the best kid. Young woman," he added and hugged her back. "Have fun with your mom. Let me take your pictures before you go, and then I'll take some more when you come home."

Gabriela liked the idea. Would she seem different when she returned?

Cullen took some photos of them in their winter gear, each wearing a mountaineering pack, and then they left. How differently Gabriela behaved since Ivy had come back. Less…childish. Most of the time. Erratic emotions were to be expected, but he saw her growing, and he liked the idea that she was interested in midwifery as well as ballet. He just hoped she'd never abandon her own gifts, her own hopes, her own dreams.

Ivy had told him a hundred times that Gabriela needed to feel sure in her identity.

When he considered the past, he saw that part of Gina's trouble might have been that she'd never felt that certainty. Her grandmother had been pretty controlling and of a completely different generation, and she hadn't been willing or able to give Gina the things Gina had wanted.

Closing the door, suddenly alone in the empty cabin, he offered up a wish for his child. That she know her true self and love that self.

Hello,

Here I am in the woods in my tent. I'm not going outside unless I absolutely have to pee. It's quiet. Whenever I hear anything, it's creepy. But I want to make that feeling of quiet when I dance. People who are really good, it's more than just good technique. When I see someone great, I fall apart inside and then when it's over I'm back together and I'm better. I want to do that to people.

This midwifery thing is kind of weird. It's like I want to know how to do it, but what I really want is to DANCE. God, I'm going to dance! I'm really good. I know I am. This is what I was born to do in life. I was *born* a dancer.

A woman. A woman *dancer*. That is me. But it would be cool to be a dancer who could also help deliver a baby if I had to. That would be a cool thing to know how to do. Mom gave me a special book for writing down thoughts about midwifery and writing down things I learn that I want to remember. I'll save my midwifery thoughts for that.

Now, as for Brad. Okay, I'm over him. I'm

glad we're just friends, especially since I might meet someone really cool this summer. Someone who *dances*.

Oh, god, I had a great idea. I'm going to go dance in the snow! Right now, in the dark, under the trees. See ya.

THE FOLLOWING AFTERNOON at four, Cullen, Ivy and Gabriela arrived at Rhonda Davy's house for a second prenatal appointment.

When Cullen saw the shack, he drew a slow breath. This place had a ways to go. But at least there was some junk lying around, things he could use to keep the wind out. He'd have to get creative with insulation. Fix the stove...

As they walked to the door, he paused to kick snow off mysterious shapes in the yard to see what lay beneath.

Ivy knocked on the door, and a woman who looked about twenty-four opened it. "Oh, hi."

They all went in.

"I brought my family. Gabriela said she'd watch your little ones again. Hi, Jessica." Ivy picked up the toddler. "Remember me?"

Gabriela scooped up the other one. "You look like a little chimney sweep, Justin."

Cullen hid a smile, thinking how Gabriela mimicked Ivy in some things and how she ran from any similarity to her in others.

"I wanted Cullen to take a look at your stove and water," Ivy was saying.

"Oh," Rhonda said. "Chad's going to get around to that stuff."

Chad was nowhere in sight; only the signs of his presence were there. Liquor bottles, for instance. Ivy was going to have to talk to him about his duty to his partner. It might do no good. On the other hand, she might be able to get through to him by pointing out that hey, this baby was his, and Rhonda was going to need some help. He had a responsibility to his family now.

"Great," she told Rhonda. "In the meantime, I need Cullen to start working on it because I can't in good conscience assist at a birth without making sure everything's as good as it can be for the baby and the mom. Agreed?"

Rhonda nodded.

Ivy glimpsed an ashtray nearby. They'd had this talk the week before. "Have you stopped smoking?" Obviously not. Chad chewed rather than smoked. Another habit with grim consequences—but at least not a source of secondhand smoke.

Rhonda shrugged.

"Look, you're hurting your baby when you smoke." She was hurting herself, too, but Rhonda had plainly said she really didn't care. "This is not an okay thing. I need an absolute promise that you're going to quit. For the baby and for you."

"I ran out of cigarettes today."

"Good. Don't buy any more."

Cullen was checking out the stove. Ivy knew he'd have questions about the water, too, but now was the time to talk about the baby, to build a good rapport with Rhonda. The shack was separated into two areas by a curtain. Behind the curtain was the area where Rhonda and Chad slept.

"Let's...go back there and see how you're doing."

"Oh, Chad's back there."

Sleeping? Ivy schooled her features. "I think you should wake him up."

"I'll try." She went behind the curtain, and Ivy heard her say, "Chad, you have to get up. The midwife's here."

Ivy couldn't make out his reply and moved away, to give them privacy. "What are you playing with, Jessica?"

IT WAS A SILENT RIDE HOME until Gabriela said, "I think Chad should get a job."

Cullen headed the car out of the unplowed hollow. "It's possible he can't."

"Well, he should at least do some work around the house instead of getting drunk all the time."

Ivy held her silence for a while. "Sometimes people need help to get over bad habits." Chad had not been receptive to that idea. In fact, he'd basically ignored her suggestions except to say, "Yeah, I'm gonna give her a hand."

I can't stand this. How can I help these people?

She'd learned early as a midwife that the best way she could affect a family dynamic was by providing a good experience during pregnancy, birth and postpartum. But men like Chad were a real problem—as

were women like Rhonda, who chose them. Except…
Ivy turned in her seat to look at Gabriela.

"Tara once told me a fairy tale about a dragon who'd been thrown out a window by the midwife right after he was born. He looked like a snake, you see. He grew up to be a dragon and married a succession of women and devoured every one. But then, a woman, even knowing he'd eaten his other brides, asked to marry him."

"Good grief," Gabriela commented.

"She convinced him to remove his skin one layer at a time. Every time she asked, he said no one had ever asked him to do that before. Finally, when he'd peeled off all his skin, she could see how damaged he was, and she scrubbed him clean and healed him, and he stood up and was a handsome and good man."

Gabriela did not seem to react.

Cullen said, "That's beautiful."

Ivy thought of Matthew. If any woman was capable of convincing him to peel off his skin, it was Shelby. She'd have to remember to tell Shelby that story.

That's why I ordered the dragon sweatshirt!

The thought filled her with hope.

Gabriela kept her thoughts to herself. *I would not want to peel the skin off some drunk.*

But she remembered what her mother had told her. That she was no better or worse than anyone else.

She supposed that applied to Chad, too.

In the back seat of the Saab, she rolled her eyes. And considered what she would've been like if someone had thrown her out the window when she was born.

CHAPTER TWELVE

"DADDY'S MISSING." It was Zeya. Cullen had come home early the day after New Year's to find Ivy and Gabriela out, probably visiting Devon or Rhonda or another woman who had phoned Ivy for an appointment.

"Where's George?"

"Day off. Matthew was watching him, and when Daddy took a nap, Matthew went to his and Shelby's room. Daddy woke up and wandered off."

Cullen considered saying he wasn't going to look, thereby increasing the odds that his father wouldn't be found. He rejected the idea. "Is he walking or driving?"

"Walking, and it's snowing. Matthew's gone looking for him. Will you come and help?"

"Yes." His father would be found by the time he reached Coalgood, but why not go? "See you soon."

MATTHEW WAS WALKING down the riverbank beside the bridge. Cullen pulled the Camaro to the roadside and jogged after him through the new snow, following his and their father's descent down the bank. Matthew was already halfway down, the judge nowhere in sight.

Cullen reached his brother and saw the other set of footprints on the shore, heading downstream and under the bridge.

Matthew said, "I'll find him. Go home, Cully."

"He's strong. If he starts arguing, it'll be better if there are two of us."

"I can handle it."

Cullen followed his slow progress. There was little shore to walk on down here, just the icy river.

They saw the judge. Farther downstream, he had stepped onto the river ice.

"Daddy!" Cullen yelled.

The judge did not turn.

Cullen wanted to run, to stop him, but Matthew was in his way, taking such slow steps.

The judge started across the river.

Cullen dodged around his brother, then slipped down ahead of him to river level. "Daddy!"

The ice cracked beneath the judge. His expression surprised, he plunged into the frigid water.

Cullen ran to the place where he'd fallen, Matthew behind him, skirting the shore, crowding him until Cullen fell. He picked himself up and stepped out onto the ice.

"Help!" the judge shouted.

"I'm coming. Stay still." Cullen flattened his body on the ice, reaching for his father's thin arms in the flimsy fabric of his shirt. *No coat, Daddy?*

He felt hands on his ankles, his brother holding him.

"Let me go farther, Matthew."

No reply.

Matthew was holding him back, out of reach of his father.

Cullen kicked free and the ice beneath his chest caved in, the water creeping into his coat. He was going through. "Grab me, Daddy!"

The icy water froze him.

The judge's next cry for help was inarticulate. The current pulled him, and Cullen tried to grab him, but the current was sucking at him, too. *I'm dying. We're both going to die here.* An ice monster, the cold, was sucking him down, cracking the ice. His father went under, and Cullen tried to grab him, losing his own purchase. Only holes in the water. Ice and nothing. *Daddy!*

"Cullen, keep still! I'm going to get you." Matthew yanked off his sheepskin-lined leather bomber jacket. He stretched out on the ice, held one sleeve of his coat and flung the other toward Cullen.

Cullen's mouth was open in a scream unspoken. *Daddy!*

His icy hands clutched the leather. It hurt.

"I'm going to move back, and more of this ice is going to break. Don't let go," Matthew warned.

Cullen held on to the jacket. *You killed him. You wouldn't let me reach him.*

Tears stung his eyes and froze on this cheeks.

The ice cracked. He was going under, going the way of the river. The leather jacket pulled him up. Ice cut him. *Daddy!*

The shore. He stumbled through snow, his legs crumpling, useless.

Beyond cold. Couldn't think.

Matthew hugging him, pushing him, dragging him up the bank. Searching his pockets for keys.

Shivering, Cullen tried to look to the river.

We have to get Daddy.

Crying, he saw Matthew's eyes, wet, too. *I have to go back to find him.* He tried. Matthew was hugging him, holding his arms down.

"He's gone. He wanted to die, Cullen. He asked me never to prevent it, and he asked you that, too. I could do it, and you couldn't. We know the one he loved best. Someday ask who loved *him* more."

Cullen was shivering too hard to find a word, let alone utter it.

Matthew had the keys to the Camaro. He shoved Cullen into the passenger side, came around and got behind the wheel.

Cullen couldn't think. Everything was too sharp. Cold. No, nothing.

The judge sliding under.

Coalgood.

Matthew was bringing him up to the house. Into the foyer.

"Matthew, don't drip on the—" Mitzi's silence was sudden and absolute. "Where's Daddy? Where's Daddy?"

"In the river. I'm sorry." Matthew was peeling Cullen's clothes off, dropping them on the way to the living room. "More logs on the fire. We have to warm him slowly. Get him a blanket."

His mother moved. "Zeya!"

BLANKETS COVERED HIM.

He shivered uncontrollably and could not even drink the hot tea his sister held to his mouth. *Everyone, go out.* He had to talk to Matthew.

Matthew, holding him back by his ankles.

Matthew, keeping him from the judge.

In any case, the judge might have gone down.

Together, we could have reached him.

They could both have died.

"What happened?" Shelby had come in.

Mother left the room.

Zeya said it. "Daddy's gone." She had been crying.

Cullen's chest was tight, and his heart... *Daddy!* Daddy slipping under, like in a dream where he was helpless to do anything.

Had Matthew wanted to goad him, to say he'd been the stronger of the two of them, letting the judge die? It hadn't felt that way.

What would have happened if I hadn't come?

Matthew walking so slowly along the bank.

"What happened?" Shelby repeated.

Matthew had answered that question for Mitzi. He answered it for his wife. "He tried to cross the river, and the ice cracked under him. Cullen tried to reach him, and the ice broke under him, too."

At this point, Cullen wondered, should he say that

Matthew had held him back, tried to prevent him from reaching the judge?

The front door opened, and he heard Ivy's and Gabriela's voices.

They must have gotten the message from Ivy's answering service.

Warmer now.

Her arms surrounded him. "Has anyone taken his temperature?"

"No. I didn't think of it," Matthew said.

"Let's get him upstairs to a bathtub. And bring me a thermometer."

GRANDPA WAS DEAD.

People were talking with the sheriff about how to get the body out of the river and the fact that it probably wouldn't come up until spring, far downstream.

Grandma had said she hoped they never found him.

All the words repeated themselves in Gabriela's mind.

Uncle Matthew had rescued her dad.

But no Grandpa anymore, saying weird things and pushing people down stairs. She knew she should be sad, but she wasn't. Not exactly.

She left the kitchen, where she'd gone to get away from everyone, and returned to the living room. The police were just leaving, and her dad was sitting on the couch with her mom. He'd put on some clothes of Uncle Tom's. Scout wandered into the hall before Gabriela could go into the living room.

"Gabriela." She beckoned. "Come here." Gabriela followed her into the dining room, where Scout shut the doors and asked, "Where's Grandpa?"

Gabriela sat down in one of the chairs that Lily always lined up against the wall. "In the river. He's dead."

"My mother says people bury dead people in the ground. Or sometimes they burn them."

"It's called cremation. They can't feel anything because they're dead."

"When will Grandpa get out of the river?"

"They don't know. His body should float up to the surface sometime, like in the spring."

"Will he be buried then?"

"I don't know. It's up to Grandma. He might never come up. Then he'd sort of be buried in the river."

Scout said, "I like that. He can live with the fishes."

Gabriela tried to imagine what bodies looked like after they'd been in the water a long time. Horrible, she bet. She hoped she never saw a dead body.

"Gabriela." It was her mother, calling for her in the hall.

"We're in here."

Before Gabriela could open the doors to the dining room, Scout said, "You know what we talked about? Don't tell."

"Okay."

THE JUDGE WAS DEAD.

Driving home, Ivy concentrated on the road, yet the thought returned again and again. The judge was dead, and with him the secret of whatever had happened after she hit her head.

But no, that secret was gone the moment she was injured, the same as all the secrets of her past. She would never know what had made Gina Naggy tick. If this had been some other kind of memory disorder she would've had the option of therapy to discover what had happened to her. She could have learned about her childhood, about how her mother's death had made her feel. Maybe these things could have told her how she'd come to betray Cullen.

But her fall down the staircase had ended those possibilities.

Maybe it was the judge who had done that.

I want it back. I want to know who I was, and I'll never know. It'll always be like reading a history book about the life of Julius Caesar. Historians can say what he did, but they can never say who he was.

No one would ever know who Gina had been.

Cullen could tell her some things but not enough to complete the picture.

I can't stand it. I can't stand it. I want my memory back.

"CULLEN."

Cullen broke his stare at the shadows on the wall. He'd thought she'd gone to sleep. He rolled over and rested his head against her.

Odd, how he'd cried so easily at the river.

Now he was numb. Numb except for when he'd made love to Ivy.

He thought, *He hurt my wife or let her be hurt.* It was worse than what Matthew had done.

But the father...his father was gone.

He spoke against Ivy's skin. "He asked me to let him die. Before he got so sick, he said he could wander off, and I could lead him into a mine shaft or the river. He asked Matthew the same thing. I thought about it—but I wouldn't have done it. When I lay down on the ice, Matthew grabbed my ankles and wouldn't let me reach him. So I kicked away. The ice broke, and I went in, and he went under. It was like a dream where something needs to be done and you can't do it."

Ivy absorbed it. He'd never told her what the judge had asked.

"When he talked to me about it, I kept wondering why he didn't end his own life instead of asking his children to do it."

Ivy tried to suppress her own desires of regaining her memory. She longed to tell Cullen, *The judge was a coward.*

But she found herself whispering, "I wonder if doctors could do something, something to help me regain my memory." But she knew the answer, the hopeless answer. She sighed. "No. I know they can't."

"Are you sure?"

"Yes. I'm sorry I brought it up." She hugged him. He'd lost his father.

In the darkness, in the quiet of his breath, Ivy heard

something outside. Footsteps in the snow? Someone knocked at the door.

"Devon." She jumped out of bed.

SHE WAKENED GABRIELA, and her daughter blinked, half-asleep, only waking as a child wakes. "Devon's baby is coming." Rowdy, Devon's boyfriend who had knocked at the door, had returned to the Workmans' place.

Gabriela opened her eyes wider. The baby was going to be born. "Can I come?"

"Of course."

Cullen was behind them in the doorway. "What about me? They might want photos."

"Come along, and I'll try to read how they feel about your being there."

IVY SCRUBBED in the Workmans' kitchen, demonstrating sterile technique to Gabriela and asking her to scrub, as well. Behind her, Devon told Cullen that he could take photos if he wanted. She didn't care either way. Rowdy said, "We can probably buy a few."

In the bedroom, Ivy listened to the baby's heart, timed contractions and checked how far along Devon's labor was. Four centimeters dilated.

"Why don't you get up and walk around, Devon?"

Devon assumed a method of standing up during each contraction, then resting between contractions, either on the couch in the living room or on her bed.

Gabriela stayed in the background but performed each task her mother set out for her.

Devon was walking the hall between the living room and the bedroom when her water broke. Seeing the huge gush of water, Gabriela felt her own heart pounding. She'd heard Tara and Francesca talking about "birth energy." Was this it, this feeling that everything in the whole house was alive?

While Emma mopped up the water, Devon returned to the bedroom. Gabriela followed her, alone, and Devon said, "I don't think I can do this. I don't think I can have this baby at home."

What should she say? What would her mother want her to say?

"You're doing great."

Another contraction shook through Devon as Ivy came in, followed by the others.

Devon said, "Everyone go out except you—" she pointed at Gabriela, then at Ivy "—and you."

Ivy gave the others a look that said, *You heard her.* Emma, Cullen and Rowdy filed out of the bedroom.

Devon settled on the bed to rest between contractions. She made no apology and gave no explanation for telling the others to leave. Neither Ivy nor Gabriela expected one.

"I want to listen to the baby's heart during the next contraction, and between contractions I'm going to check you again." When she examined Devon, the baby's head was crowning. "Devon, the baby's going to be born very soon. Can you pant like this?" She demonstrated.

Devon panted through the next contraction.

"Can the others come back in?" Ivy asked when it was through.

"Yes."

"Still want pictures?" Gabriela asked. She sure wouldn't.

"Right after."

"Now, here—you can feel your baby's head, Devon." Ivy guided the young hand over the velvety softness. The baby's scalp was healthy and pink, her heart tones just what they should be.

Gabriela went out to the living room. "Come quick."

When she returned to the bedroom, her mother asked, "Gabriela, do you want to touch the baby?"

That thing pushing out of Devon was the baby. Tentatively, Gabriela reached forward and touched the velvety head.

"Rowdy?"

He touched the baby, too.

"You can push now, Devon, slow and steady. That's right. Rowdy, put your hands here." The head was born, no cord around the neck. The rest of the body followed easily with the next contraction, slithering into waiting hands. Rowdy's. *Cullen caught Gabriela like this.* "Up onto Mom's stomach."

She felt Cullen somewhere behind her, and her eyes watered.

The emotion over her Gabriela's birth, the birth she would never remember, distracted her. She erased it to focus on Devon and her baby. To be a midwife. To be the woman she was at her best.

IVY WAS SUPPORTING DEVON as the placenta slid into a stainless-steel bowl in a rush of blood. Rowdy held his baby daughter, wrapped in a soft receiving blanket.

Moving around the room, keeping clear of Ivy, Cullen experienced the next moments through the viewfinder.

This is a life-or-death job you've got, Ivy.

No. More than a job.

You stay calm. I've never seen anyone more calm in a crisis.

Gabriela was touching the baby's foot. "She's so sweet."

Cullen remembered Gabriela's birth, that as she was born he'd remembered she was Matthew's child and yet sometimes he'd forgotten.

Grandmother Emma said, "Oh, Devon, she's just precious. You did so well."

The shutter clicked. It had caught Ivy, her woman's hand beneath the newborn's head.

He imagined his father pushing her down the stairs, then picking her up and putting her in the car to leave her somewhere.

His father was dead.

He lowered the camera very slowly.

CULLEN FOLLOWED IVY when she took Alison Angelina Workman to the kitchen to give the baby her first bath. He ran the water in the sink, tested it. She did, too.

He held the towel for the baby, and she put the wet newborn in his arms. She sang to her. "Oh, can ye sew cushions, and can ye sew sheets? And can ye sing balaloo when the bairn greets?"

Ivy dried Alison's soft little head. Cullen's hands looked so big next to the baby. *I wish I could remember him with Gabriela.* The anger at the stolen memories left her impotent. She stopped her song. "Let me take her back to Devon."

Tomorrow, she'd begin her postpartum visits, to make sure mother and baby were settling in as they should. There would be many visits.

She's so young.

But Ivy had learned long ago to support, rather than judge, a mother's choices. Whatever they were, they were the mom's.

As Ivy took the baby back to Devon and Rowdy, Emma joined Cullen in the kitchen. "How much will the photos be?" she asked. "We probably can't afford many, but I'd like a couple."

"I'll give you a set. No charge. Thanks for letting me be here. If you tell me what you want in the birth announcement, we can run a photo in the paper, too."

"Oh, thank you!"

It was 5:00 a.m. when he and Gabriela and Ivy went out to the car to head home.

Driving up the snowy road, Cullen listened to his wife and daughter.

"What did you think?" Ivy asked Gabriela.

"It was cool!"

Cullen's mind was stuck not on birth but on death and on the unchangeables, the things he could not say to his father now. What would he have done had his father been well when Cullen learned about Ivy's fall down the stairs? A crime had been committed.

You loved me. You called me your favorite.

Yet who had ever really stopped Matthew from tormenting him?

No one.

"We just can't do a thing with him." They'd said that all the time.

No one had suggested counseling.

No one had looked in the mirror.

Mirror, mirror, on the wall, who made my child act this way?

And his father had turned on Ivy, not Matthew. No, on Gina.

At the cabin, he said, "I'll be inside in a while."

Ivy asked, "Are you all right?"

"Sure." *The lies we all tell, that everything's fine when we're on the edge. It's called control.*

He walked in the snow through the trees and startled a deer. He often wished he could move like an animal, but that was denied humans, especially indoor humans. Where was the judge now? In the river, part of the river. Did he leave a soul behind to talk to his children?

Cullen thought not.

He kicked a tree. He kicked it again and again.

He did not cry.

WHEN HE RETURNED to the cabin two hours later, the phone was ringing. He picked it up. "Cullen, this is Shelby. I know it's early, but will you come over? Matthew went out in the middle of the night. He's down by the river and won't come back."

Cullen hadn't slept, but Shelby's words compelled him to go.

Instead of waking Ivy or Gabriela, he left them a note, then set out in the Camaro for the stretch of river near the bridge.

Matthew had walked.

Cullen found the footprints leading from Coalgood.

He followed them down the bank and thought for a moment that he would find Matthew and his father, alive. His father would not go out on the ice; he'd come home with Matthew and Cullen.

The footprints led over the path he and Matthew had walked, and he saw Shelby's footprints, too. She must have followed him down here when she discovered him missing.

Cullen saw his brother ahead. He wore the leather jacket that he'd used to save Cullen's life. He wore a blue stocking cap.

There was something different about him, something vulnerable, and Cullen tried to imagine what Matthew must have been like when he was small. He couldn't. But he could imagine his own mother dying when he was twelve, and it was a child's worst nightmare.

Matthew stood by the river looking at the ice, now

crusted over the water again, and Cullen saw that he must have been walking around to keep warm.

"Hi, Matthew."

Matthew looked at him.

His brother had saved Cullen's life at the risk of his own.

Would thanking him now make any difference in what Matthew was feeling? What *was* he feeling?

Cullen said, "Will you come home?"

Matthew seemed thoughtful. "You know, I should've asked him if he loved me, and maybe he would have said it."

"He loved you. He never protected me from you. He never blamed you for sleeping with Gina. He couldn't. You were his son, and he loved you."

"I don't think so. I wasn't what he wanted. I never *acted* the way he wanted. You were affectionate, and he could be affectionate to you. He never liked me. I was never who he wanted me to be. He never loved me. I think I see that, now."

Cullen didn't know what to say. "Your wife wants you to come home. She loves you."

Matthew blinked. "Where is she?"

"At Coalgood. She called me and asked me to bring you home. I think she wants to show you her love. Daddy must have been screwed up. I don't understand the things he did."

Matthew peered up the bank.

"Let's go home," Cullen repeated. They climbed the bank together. "You saved my life the other day. Thank you."

Matthew didn't answer.

When they reached Coalgood, Shelby opened the door and reached for Matthew, hugging him. "Come upstairs," she said.

Matthew held her as they climbed the stairs, and she was supporting him.

THE MEMORIAL SERVICE was held at a church in Guyandotte. Ivy didn't want to attend but knew she must, to support Cullen's family in their grief. She and Gabriela filed into a pew with Cullen beside Tom and Zeya; Scout was with a baby-sitter.

Another judge delivered the eulogy, praising Sam Till's integrity on the bench, his dedication as a family man. Every eye in the family's row was dry.

Outside, afterward, Cullen asked Matthew, "How are you?"

Zeya joined them. "The hypocrisy quotient is pretty high. What do you say we go acknowledge the judge's death our own way, just the three of us."

Cullen looked at Matthew and knew his brother was thinking the same thing. That they'd both seen the judge slip beneath the ice in the river.

But Cullen said, "What do you have in mind?"

"Let's write him letters and cut a hole in the ice and send them down the river."

Cullen considered. "I'm game."

"Me, too," Matthew agreed.

They set the launch date for the letters for that evening, and they all went to Coalgood.

Dear Daddy,
   Why didn't you love me?

Dear Daddy,
   I'm going to miss you so much. You were
the best dad.

Dear Daddy,
   You hurt my wife, or maybe you didn't hurt
her but just didn't help her when she was hurt.
I wish I knew what you did, and I resent finding
out so late that you're not the person I thought
you were.
   I wish I didn't love you. I wish I didn't at all.

TWO WEEKS AFTER his father's death, Cullen came
home from work to find Gabriela practicing ballet and
Ivy searching every corner of the house.

"What are you looking for?"

"Someone must have kept a journal. Gina or her
grandmother."

"Neither of you took much interest in writing,
though you read midwifery books."

"Maybe there's something. There has to be something."

Helpless, he let her search. The search had a frantic
quality at odds with his usually calm Ivy. "Why is it
so important to find it?" He crouched beside her as
she peered into some cabinets in the back corner of
the kitchen. He knew what was in every cabinet in
the house.

"I have to know who I was. I have to know what they did to me."

"What who did to you?"

"My grandmother. My mother before she died. I have to know why I slept with a married man and betrayed you."

Ivy seemed unaware of Gabriela's presence in the house, but Cullen was not. He glanced toward the door of the dance room. It was open, and music was still playing.

"Remember Gabriela's here," he said softly.

Frantic, Ivy hardly heard him. No journals. No books. Her grandmother's herbal and midwifery notes Ivy had already seen. Nothing personal in there. Did she have no feelings to record? Had she sublimated her feelings to that degree?

Cullen said, "Let's go up in the loft. Come on."

His eyes said she wouldn't find anything, no diaries, nothing to give her a clue to her past, to the person she'd really been.

Upstairs, they lay on the bed.

"I need to know who I was. I need some memory to tell me why I did the things I did."

"There's more I can tell you. I can tell you about every encounter I remember with you."

"But it'll be through *your* eyes. I want it through my eyes. And it will never happen." Tears came in a shaky flood, admitting the death of self. "I'm gone. I'm gone forever."

"You were born in that hospital in Boulder, all right?"

"It's not true. You've said yourself that I have the same gestures as her, some of the same speech patterns. I've never felt so weak in my life." She laughed through her tears. "In my memory."

"You know, what analysts do is put you in touch with your feelings, not necessarily your memory. You might be able to know the feelings of being Gina."

Ivy froze, breath suspended. He was right, of course.

"You have to be careful, though."

"Why?"

"You might not like what you discover."

She frowned. "It would take a damned good therapist. I don't know if I could find one in Guyandotte." And she had clients, a practice. What kind of impact would this have on them?

But I have to know.

"You're creative. Maybe you should do some reading, order some good books through the mail. You could make a quilt that's about your feelings. Don't *think* about it. Just try to feel."

She and Shelby and Gabriela hadn't finished their quilt. *I need to get Shelby working on it again.*

Her thoughts backtracked to Cullen's idea for accessing her emotional memory to try to get in touch with who Gina had been. She liked it. And she would give it a try. "I'm going to do that, Cullen. The quilt. And the books. I'll ask Tara if she knows of any. She's done a lot of therapy-type things."

Cullen remembered Tara's incredible vibrance and

vitality. He doubted Tara had it all worked out, and he liked Ivy the way she was. But if she needed to find Gina, he needed to let her.

Even if he didn't like the result.

CHAPTER THIRTEEN

THE NEXT TIME SHELBY came over to work on the quilt, Gabriela was gone, working privately with Tracy Kennedy, and Cullen was photographing a wedding.

While the two women sat in the living room stitching squares, Ivy asked how Matthew was.

"Different. Really depressed. Fortunately, all he has to do on the Atlanta project at this point is occasional consulting."

"You know, I thought of a folk story I wanted to tell you, but first I wanted to tell you something else. It's about the day you lost the baby."

Shelby waited.

"He loves you so much. I saw that."

Shelby nodded.

"And when he was beating up Cullen, Gabriela was watching, and he called her 'your daughter.' He could have hurt Cullen by speaking the truth then. But I don't think he'd ever hurt Gabriela."

"I know. He says Cullen's a good father. It may be hard to believe, but he loves Cullen. You know, he was expected to take care of both him and Zeya a good bit when he was a teenager. I think that's part of his resentment toward Cullen."

"I can understand that. He'd just lost his own mother, and he was expected to mother someone else." Ivy paused. "So let me tell you this story." And she told Shelby the story of the dragon who ate his brides.

When she was through, Shelby smiled. "That's really nice. Very true, too. I think some of Matthew's skins are coming off now. I love that dragon."

Ivy hoped Shelby and Matthew were trying to conceive again.

She wanted a real friendship with Shelby, not just a situation where she helped her friend and behaved as though she herself never needed help. "So, I've started this quilt and I'm reading these books." She began to tell Shelby about her self-therapy. "It's strange. I'm getting so agitated and impatient. It's like something's wrong, like there's something attacking me and I can't see it. I've got three clients now, all due later in the year, and that's all I can handle until I work this out. But I really need to know who I was."

"You might not like it, Gina." Shelby caught herself and laughed. "Ivy."

"Well, Tara subscribes to the wounded-child theory, that we all behave the way we do because of the way our parents and caregivers treated us."

"I agree with her. But you know, Ivy, your life seems pretty happy, and you're not engaging in Gina's old *behavior*. Maybe you should let it rest."

"I would if I could. But I am *obsessed* by it. I dream I'm looking for people—my grandmother, my mother and Gina. I dream I'm going to where they are, and whenever I get there I learn they've all died. I'm *obsessed* by it, ever since the judge died."

"Why since then?"

It needed to be said. To Shelby, because of what he'd done on Christmas Eve.

"Cullen and I think he may have pushed me down the stairs. And I lost a baby, too."

Shelby's eyes changed. She whispered, "I want to kill him, and he's already dead."

"I feel that way, too."

"Matthew needs my sympathy. Cullen needs yours. And *I hate him.* It doesn't help to tell myself he was sick. The price was too high. And he did the same thing to you."

"He told Cullen that I fell. But he never sought medical care for me. He must have driven me somewhere—God knows where—and left me."

"I wish I'd been there to push him under the ice. Matthew let him die, and I was glad. I was only sorry for him that he had to do it. And sorry that he saw it as an act of love toward his father instead of revenge for what the judge had done to me."

Ivy didn't argue with Shelby's feelings. They were feelings, and you couldn't argue with them. She hesitated. "Has Matthew told anyone besides you?"

"No, and he doesn't intend to. He says Cullen would have fallen through the ice trying to go farther out, to reach the judge."

Cullen had kicked away, and he *had* fallen through. Matthew's assessment could be correct.

"You know, there's a house for sale around the island from Coalgood. Matthew and I looked at it the other day. I asked him if he was serious about moving, and he said he wouldn't mind. He said he always sees Coalgood now as the house the judge wanted to give Cullen."

Ivy squeezed her eyes shut. How hard for Matthew. Cullen didn't even want Coalgood. He'd invested himself in the cabin, for Gabriela and for Gina.

Why had he loved Gina?

Ivy wished she could discover what had been lovable about Gina, what worth he'd found in taking credit for her unplanned pregnancy. That was a question she could put to him and had, but his answers never quite satisfied her. "There was something about you. I liked the way you felt about the baby. I liked the things you spent your time doing—gardening, growing herbs, midwifery."

When Shelby went home, Ivy turned to her own quilt. The nervousness came back. So far, she'd sewn some kind of road. But now she cut out a figure to appliqué to the sheet she was using as backing. A small blond figure.

Lost, so lost.

I hate me. I hate me.

A scream built inside her.

Cullen came in. She glanced up. "Ivy, are you all right?"

She shuddered.

He looked at her quilt and sat beside her to hug

her. She tried looking in his eyes and could not see him as a helpful human.

She backed away, tried to back away from the feelings.

She folded up the quilt.

"Do you think you were sexually abused?" he asked quietly.

"I don't know. I don't think so. I like making love with you."

"How does the quilt make you feel?"

"Deserted. I don't want to talk about it." She stood, trying to remember what day it was. Saturday.

Any appointments? No.

"I think I'll go for a walk."

"Want company?"

It was growing dark. She wanted to walk alone in the darkness and feel those emotions, those simple fears—that a bear might attack her, that something might get her. Because at the moment, it was all she could feel.

Cullen embraced her and helped her dress warmly. In those moments, she was Gina to him. There had been something broken about Gina, something that had made her do the things she'd done, and he wanted to help her heal. Wanted to heal the woman who'd gotten pregnant at twenty by his married brother.

"How long will you be?"

"I don't know. I just want to walk. Don't worry."

He would. He would worry until she returned, but he had to accept her need for solitude. Her need to search inside herself for who she'd been and who she was.

HE WENT TO PICK UP Gabriela at the ballet studio.

Tracy said, "I'm so glad you're going to look at dance schools in New York. Even if it's just for the summer."

Gabriela was excited about the trip to New York. They were going the following weekend.

His mind still on Ivy, he hardly responded to Tracy.

On the way home, Gabriela chatted about ballet and an audition that summer at whichever school she chose.

He listened as best he could, but when they reached the cabin and went inside, he saw that Ivy's coat and hat were still gone. "Your mom's out for a walk. I think I'll go find her."

He took a flashlight and a thermos of warm tea and told himself she'd be all right.

SHE WAS—physically anyhow. "Thanks for the tea. I'm cold."

"See anything interesting?"

"A deer. I followed its trail for a while. Tara says deer can lead you to magical places. So I followed it."

"What did you find?"

She didn't answer. She just shivered and drank some more tea.

"Want to see a professional?"

She shook her head. "I like going forth alone. Or with you."

He embraced her. "I'm always here."

ZEYA WAS GETTING MARRIED again, and Mitzi was taking her to buy a wedding dress. Ivy went along and saw Mitzi smiling over Zeya's choices, frowning at others, giving advice. Ivy was on the outside. Not a sister, not a daughter.

She woke slowly, and Cullen hugged her from behind, snuggled her close in safety. She could feel that he wanted to make love, but she didn't. In fact, she thought she couldn't bear it.

She shivered, trying to stop thinking.

"Why did you finish your workout early?" he asked.

"I couldn't concentrate."

"Ivy, I have some misgivings about what you're doing."

"Me, too."

"What did you feel working on the quilt?"

"Loss. It hurts."

"Do you know what you lost?"

"I think," she admitted, "it's who. Not what." And the tears came, tears for the mother who had died when she was five.

CULLEN AND GABRIELA accompanied her to her next prenatal with Rhonda Davy. Rhonda was five months pregnant. Her baby should arrive before Gabriela went away to study ballet for the summer.

Ivy noticed some change in Chad. When she came for prenatal visits, he at least feigned interest in the baby and caring for Rhonda. Ivy told herself repeatedly, *It is not my job to heal him or to send him away.* She'd never seen evidence that he abused any of the children. She'd never seen him play with them, either. But he was the baby's father.

She'd spoken to Mata Iyer about the situation, and Mata had said, "It's hard to know what to do. Sometimes a hands-off approach seems as useful as anything."

Ivy had begun teaching Gabriela to assess the baby's lie; Gabriela practiced the skill on Rhonda while the children stood near, watching.

When they returned home, the phone was ringing, and Ivy picked it up. It was Tara.

"Guess what?"

"What."

"Alex sold his house and the Victorian to an *obstetrician.*"

Ivy sank into a chair at the kitchen table. "Tell me everything."

"Well, Mom's stopped her home-birth practice, and I'm going up there in the fall. I've agreed to stay at Maternity House until then."

"How does Mom feel about your coming to Precipice?"

"She keeps telling me not to do it, but I've told her it's a free country, and nothing's to stop me from renting a trailer in Precipice. Living with her would probably drive me nuts anyway."

Ivy carefully withheld comment. Tara's voice grounded her, the same way the presence of her family did.

She told Tara about the quilt and the search for her identity.

"Are you doing okay?" Tara asked. "Do you need me? If you do, I'll tell them I have to go. I can give them two weeks later on."

"I think I'm fine. I've found the crux of it—losing my mother."

"Maybe you should put her and your grandmother in your quilt. Start rebuilding your past from the roots up. Use it as a way to celebrate your survival…your strength.'

Ivy drew a deep breath. "Tara—I love you."

THEY LEFT FRIDAY for New York; they were going to spend four days there. In Charleston, Gabriela had bought a dance magazine with reviews of the shows they were going to see. One was classical—Stravinsky's *Firebird*—the other was a performance by the Joffrey Ballet.

She'd also brought a book about ballet schools that profiled the two schools they'd be visiting. Neither of them had boarding options, but they were going to visit an aunt of Cullen's in the city who had expressed interest in Gabriela's staying with her for the summer.

Once they landed, Cullen got a taxi to take them to their hotel. The first ballet was Saturday night, the second a Sunday matinee performance.

In their two-room suite that night, after Gabriela

had gone to sleep on the foldout sofa and while Cullen was down the hall getting ice, Ivy went into their bedroom and took out the quilt to work on it. Using her recollections of photographs of her mother, she began an image of a woman giving birth to a child, to her.

With every stitch, she knew Tara's suggestion had been the right one. Cullen recorded memories with his camera. She would trace her life with this quilt. Not just the grief and sorrow but goodness, too.

When Cullen returned, he sat with her, watching her quilt and finally picking up a needle and thread to quilt with her. "Do you think you've found Gina?" he asked.

She nodded. "Not the Gina I hoped to find. And I guess I'll never completely understand why she—I— did the things she did, what drove her. But I realize I'm going to have to accept the Gina I've found."

THEY WALKED THE STREETS of Manhattan, saw ballets, visited ballet schools and met his aunt.

When they returned home, Gabriela had selected her dance school, and they'd made arrangements for her to stay with Cullen's aunt for the summer—if she was selected in the audition. Auditions for the summer program would be held the week after they returned home in major cities around the country. They would have to spend a week in Atlanta while she went to audition classes.

The following week, Cullen and Ivy drove her to

Atlanta, where they would stay in a historic hotel and visit historic sites when Gabriela wasn't in classes.

THE AUDITION CLASS was huge. Gabriela had never been in a room with so many other dancers, except during the audition for *Nutcracker,* and this felt like an even bigger deal. A girl about her age named Amy said, ''There's a whole room full of us. They'll probably choose, like, three.''

Gabriela had been warned of that, but seeing how many other dancers wanted to participate in the summer program was different from just hearing about it.

After class each day, she stayed behind practicing while her parents watched and talked together, until someone came to close up the school for the night.

The audition came at last.

Gabriela tried to quiet the butterflies in her stomach. She hadn't felt this nervous since she was Clara in *The Nutcracker* in Charleston. What if she totally flubbed the audition? What if the technique she'd learned from Tracy in Guyandotte wasn't good enough?

The ballet master was Russian, and he'd been picking on Gabriela at every single audition class. It was easy to see he thought she was the worst student in the class, the least likely to make it into the school.

What if she failed in front of her mom and dad? *I'll die. I'll die. I'll never go to ballet class again.*

A thought comforted her. If she wasn't good enough to be a ballet dancer, she could still be a midwife.

But I want to be a dancer. And I'm going to be.
She went out to show what she could do.

As GABRIELA FINISHED the exercises, everyone in the
room applauded. *Is it my imagination,* Ivy wondered,
or are people clapping more loudly for her? Many of
the children had been excellent, but Gabriela... *She's
so lovely when she moves.*

They would receive the news by mail, but Ivy had
a strong feeling that Gabriela had done well. If only
the ballet master's face was easier to read...

Afterward, as the three of them went out to the car
together to drive home, Cullen asked his daughter,
"How do you think you did?"

Gabriela bit her lip. "I'm not sure. I tried to remember everything he said, but some things were
hard."

"In any case, we're proud of you," Ivy told her.
"That was a hard thing to do, and you looked it right
in the face and did it."

IN THE FOLLOWING WEEKS, Gabriela resumed accom-
panying Ivy to prenatal appointments. She lived to
find out if anything had come in the mail that day.

Ivy resumed work on the quilt, incorporating both
facts of her heritage and new, blossoming moments
of her life. She included Tara and Francesca as well
as Cullen and Gabriela, the Rockies as well as the
Appalachians. She felt herself—and Gina—beginning
to heal. And Cullen sat beside her and helped with

his man's fingers, appliquéing the cabin, their home, to the fabric.

Ivy, Shelby and Gabriela had finished piecing the other quilt and had put it on a frame when Shelby announced, "So. I'm pregnant again."

It was March, and Gabriela immediately asked, "If I get to go to New York, will I be back for the birth?"

"When are you due, Shelby?"

"Late October."

Gabriela gave a thumbs-up.

Later, when Ivy walked her out to the car, Shelby revealed, "Matthew's started talking to someone, a therapist. A guy in Charleston."

"Great!"

"I'm pretty happy about it." Shelby hugged her. "And you're doing okay?"

Ivy nodded. "Everything's wonderful. I'm putting in a garden."

"How's your own quilt coming?"

"Better than I could have dreamed. I'm beginning to know myself. I didn't know how badly I needed to."

Shelby smiled into her eyes. "I'm sure I'll like it."

The remark brought Ivy some peace. Gina, with her pain and her problems, was part of her. And thanks to Cullen and Gabriela, she'd become whole.

GABRIELA HAD NO TROUBLE keeping the names of the herbs straight in her mind. As she and her mother walked in the woods collecting them, she tried to absorb everything Ivy said about when certain herbs should be picked.

Later today, they were going to Rhonda's. Gabriela's dad had helped Rhonda and Chad with their water problems, and he'd fixed their stove. The kids seemed a little cleaner lately. Her dad had taken some photos of them with their mom and given them to Rhonda.

She heard a camera shutter, and Ivy turned around. "What are you doing here?"

Smiling, Cullen pushed through the weeds. "An appointment canceled, and I thought I'd come home and find my family."

"We're about done." Ivy lifted her face for his kiss. "Gabriela and I need to take these home and hang them to dry."

"I'll carry those, Gabriela," he offered, reaching for the sack brimming with cut herbs.

"Can I go home and start practicing, Mom?" *Darn. If only that letter would come. I'm going crazy.*

"Sure. Go on. Your dad can help me."

As she left, running over the grass, Cullen said, "It's going to be a long summer without her."

"You're telling me."

"But a good chance for you and me to spend more time together."

"Yes."

"Matthew came by the studio today."

Ivy knew this was significant. "What did he have to say? Anything?"

"Yes. He said he was sorry for sleeping with my wife."

Ivy consulted his face. She knew this remained a sore subject for Cullen—and probably always would.

She was right. His eyes had taken on a cold look, the unforgiving look. "I asked him if you two used birth control. He said you used some natural method. Which was what you did with me."

The baby could have been Matthew's. Or Cullen's.

"I'm sorry." How long would she have to apologize for this? When would he forgive?

She took a shallow breath. "I have some news for you."

"Yes?"

"I'd planned to tell you at a happier moment."

He waited, facing her in the tall weeds beneath the trees.

Come on, Cullen. Please. Forgive and forget. "I'm pregnant."

His mouth opened and shut. His eyes changed slightly, softening some.

He took her hand to walk home.

"Can you forgive me, Cullen? Really forgive me?"

"I'm working on it. In some ways, it was easier before your quilt. Now...you've become more Gina to me, as well." *And you're part of me, and I can't help it.*

"Is there anything, anything in the world, that I can do to make up for it?"

"Ivy, you know there's not. You can't make up for

it. But I love you, which you know, and you love me, and we should both try not to forget that.''

"What if—'' She stopped him on the trail they were following. "What if we got married again? Renewed our vows? We could do it alone or with your family. Do you think it would help?''

He considered. She'd healed some of Gina's wounds. And he and Matthew had settled some of their differences. Matthew and Shelby were having a child of their own. He and Ivy were having a child.

"How about…'' he suggested uncertainly, "a double ceremony?''

"With Matthew and Shelby? Will Zeya and Tom feel left out?''

"I think Zeya will understand what's going on.''

"I'd love that, Cullen. Shelby is a sister to me the way Tara is.''

"Let's wait a little while,'' he cautioned. "I need to sort some things out.''

Ivy understood and felt some misgivings. He was saying he wanted to forgive her completely but didn't know how.

"WHEN SHOULD WE TELL Gabriela?'' he asked her that night.

"I'm not sure. Soon.'' Ivy frowned. "She'll need time to accept the idea. Who knows what she'll feel about the baby? She was deprived of me for crucial years of her life, and she'll have to see me care for a younger sibling and be there all the time for that child.''

"She'll get used to it. I couldn't love her more than I do."

Cullen realized how hard he sounded and knew that his bitterness toward Matthew was tied to the child Ivy now carried.

I've got to get rid of those feelings.

He closed his eyes. "You're right about Gabriela. I vote on telling her sooner rather than later."

"Let's wait at least a week or so. It's very early yet."

She could lose the baby. He didn't even want to think about that. Anger washed through him, anger at himself.

Why couldn't he just feel love for his family, including the new baby inside Ivy? Why couldn't he be the one to pull them all together? *I have to get to that point. I have to get rid of this anger somehow.*

He told Ivy, "A week or so sounds fine."

THE FOLLOWING SUNDAY, while Ivy and Shelby and Gabriela worked on their quilt, Cullen hiked by himself back into the woods, enjoying the spring, feeling the onset of summer with its bugs and humidity. The bugs were already bad, but he wanted to return to a place where he'd seen a fox the other day.

He wanted to be alone to think about what Ivy had said.

To think about the nature of true forgiveness.

Thoughts of Matthew and Gina had faded entirely for a while. But Matthew had brought them back, and the notion that the child she'd been carrying could just as well have been his brother's, the fact that the possibility was very real, might drive him mad.

It occurred to him sometimes that his father had known, too—and that he'd pushed Gina down the stairs because of it.

By now, he'd seen enough of Ivy's emotional memory through the quilt that he could sympathize with what Gina must have suffered.

But it doesn't lessen her blame.

I married her. I agreed to become her child's father.

And she had betrayed him.

All he could come up with was the fact that he had a choice. He could hold on to this and let it make them both unhappy. Or he could rid himself of it.

But how to do that?

With a symbol?

What would symbolize Gina's betrayal?

He gazed down at his camera, and he knew.

CHAPTER FOURTEEN

HE'D SELECTED the wedding photo at random, barely glancing at it before tucking it in his shirt pocket to take to the river, the river where his father had died. Now he stood by the water, watching the tadpoles and the fish swimming in a slow eddy, and removed the photograph from his pocket.

He looked at it and saw his own young face, his love for Gina, and her smile back at him, a smile he'd interpreted in different ways—as trusting, as loving, even as manufactured for onlookers. He still couldn't guess what she'd really felt at that moment, but he couldn't quite believe shc'd married him planning to continue sleeping with Matthew.

Their hands were joined, and he knew what he'd felt. He was going to marry the woman he most loved, the woman he most desired. They were going to have the baby at home....

He swallowed.

He'd planned to drop the photo in the river, to throw out the old marriage, the bad marriage, with its betrayal and pain.

He could not.

It was the same marriage he had today.

And he loved it.

He placed the photo back in his pocket and walked up the bank to go home.

GABRIELA FELT HER MOUTH falling open. Of course. Her mother and father *could* have another baby. It just never crossed her mind that they would. Her mind leaped to Rhonda's children, to Scout, to all the children who had annoyed her at one time or another. "Am I going to have to take care of it?"

Her mother laughed. "Of course not. It's not your baby."

"Phew." Gabriela released a sigh and looked somewhere between the two of them. She didn't even want to *think* about her parents doing what was required to make a baby.

Her mother was watching her in a penetrating way. "How do you feel?"

Well, you could have consulted me. But it didn't seem like the kind of thing parents did. She shrugged. "It's your headache."

Her dad said, "But we're a family. You're going to have a sister or brother."

Gabriela tried to imagine it. A baby in the house, and her mother would nurse it. She had the most interesting idea. What if *she* could help at the birth? "Can I help when the baby's being born?"

"All you want. I think I might try to arrange for Tara to come out here if she can, or for us to go there."

"The baby should be born here." Gabriela glanced around the living room. "All the babies in our family are born in this cabin. We don't want her—or him—to be born in Colorado.''

Ivy smiled, relieved by her reaction. "Okay. If everything looks like it's going well, maybe we'll do it like we did with you. But you have to keep in mind I'm not twenty years old anymore.''

A thought needled Gabriela. What if the baby was a girl and grew up to want to be a midwife? Would her mother love the baby more? Especially now that she was going away to school…

Her father sat beside her on the couch and put his arm around her shoulders to hug her. "Gabby. We're not going to love you any less. No one could replace you.''

She felt silly then. What was she, six? "I'm not jealous.''

Her mother said, "It's okay if you are. Or pissed off or anything else. Just know how much we love you.''

Gabriela smiled. "I think I do.''

Her dad had stopped hugging her and taken her mother's hand. "So the other thing…" And he told her about the renewing of their vows.

GABRIELA'S LETTER CAME the next day.

Ivy stopped at Cullen's studio on the way to pick up Gabriela after school. "It's here.''

"Did you hold it up to the light?''

She laughed. "Of course. But I couldn't read anything. I guess Gabriela will have to tell us. Want to come with me?''

He shook his head. "Better not. In case she didn't get in."

"Good thought." Ivy kissed him. "If it's good news, we'll come by and tell you."

WHEN HER MOTHER HANDED her the envelope in the car, Gabriela trembled. "It's no big deal," she said. "If I didn't make it, I can still do other things. Maybe I can get into another summer program or something."

"We're proud of you in any case." Ivy waited a moment to see if Gabriela would open the envelope.

A second later, she did. Her face lit up, and she couldn't prevent a small shriek. "They gave me a scholarship!"

She started to cry, and Ivy hugged her tight.

CULLEN, IVY, MATTHEW and Shelby set the renewal of vows for May Day, and Shelby and Ivy shopped together for their dresses, with Gabriela along to give her frank opinion. They'd decided to have the ceremony at the state park. They'd say their vows to each other with Tom standing in as minister. They were already married after all.

On May Day, the whole family gathered in the park. Cullen remembered the last time he'd been there with his father, when snow was on the ground.

As they prepared to begin, Gabriela straightened her mother's ivory cotton skirt and chemise, then the flowers on her head. "I want to tell you something," she said. "Not that it really matters. I just thought you might like to know."

"What, Gabriela?"

Her mother's smile was so beautiful. *Should I bring it up? Well, why not?* "Tracy's getting married."

Ivy carefully concealed her flicker of annoyance at the mention of the name and concentrated on the news. She was truly happy for Tracy. It couldn't be easy to find the person you wanted to marry in such a small town. "That's great. I'm so pleased."

"He sells real estate, I think, or something boring like that."

Ivy laughed. "Obviously, she doesn't think so."

She glanced toward the area on the grass where Shelby and Matthew were holding hands, gazing into each other's eyes, and then she saw Cullen, waiting for her.

"Okay." She kissed her daughter. "Here we go."

"DO YOU, IVY, TAKE CULLEN to be your husband, to have and to hold, for richer for poorer, for better for worse, in sickness and in health, as long as you both shall live?"

Her eyes met his, giving a promise that she would always remember, and that her heart had remembered from long ago. "I do."

As Cullen repeated his vows, his eyes were on hers, and she knew he'd finally forgiven her, that the past was behind them and they were ready to move forward together. And she heard the healing and com-

mitment in Matthew's and Shelby's voices, too, as
they repeated their vows to each other.

As each couple kissed, Mitzi, Gabriela, Zeya and
Scout cheered, and Ivy and Shelby turned, as planned,
and scattered handfuls of flower petals all over the
family.

Mitzi embraced each of the brides in turn, and for
the first time Ivy thought she saw real warmth in her
mother-in-law's eyes. She said softly, "I'm so glad
you came back. Cullen and Gabriela needed you so
much."

"Thank you." Ivy hugged her. "And I'm glad to
be home."

Her purse, which Gabriela was holding, emitted a
series of beeps.

Everyone turned toward the sound of the pager, and
Ivy said, "Sorry," and hurriedly checked it.

The answering service.

"I'll bet you anything," she told her daughter,
"that Miss Rhonda is in labor."

IVY HAD A FEELING this would be a long labor and
hoped it wouldn't be. Rhonda's previous labors had
been long, she was uncomfortable with physical ex-
ams and she'd been a victim of sexual abuse; she'd
told Ivy that. One of her other children had been delivered by paramedics, the other in the emergency
room.

The message had been left with the answering service by Chad. He'd said Rhonda had started having
cramps early that morning, before it was light.

Since Rhonda had no phone, Ivy changed into the spare clothes she always kept in the car and Cullen drove her to the house, promising to return with Gabriela after they'd both changed their clothes.

Ivy found Rhonda pacing the front room. She wore a green cotton sundress. Chad was holding one of the children and yelling at the other one to be quiet, Mom was having a baby.

Ivy picked up Justin and held him as she asked Rhonda, "How are you feeling?"

"I feel like I'm halfway there. It's getting intense."

Halfway? Ivy watched the next contraction, timed it. "Justin, let me put you down so I can see how your mommy's doing, and then I'll hold you again, all right?"

IT WAS 9:00 p.m. Progress through the first stage had been slow, and Gabriela had swept the little dwelling, played with the two children and gotten them both to sleep.

In the curtained-off bedroom, Rhonda repeated, "I really don't want to be touched." No one was trying to touch her.

If Rhonda and Chad had been a different kind of couple, Ivy might have suggested they kiss and cuddle in the privacy of the bedroom. She said, "Well, I'm sure Chad won't try to touch you if you go for a walk with him. And if you need someone's hand to hold, he'll be there."

Her eyes distrustful—of her surroundings, of Chad, of Ivy—Rhonda slowly climbed off the bed. "Okay."

Ivy was glad to see Chad help her on with her sweater and kneel down to tie her shoes. Rhonda actually reached out and stroked his hair, then cast another glance at Ivy.

They all left the bedroom, and in the middle of the living room, Rhonda had another contraction. She looked exhausted, and though Rhonda had kept her liquids up, she hadn't been able to sleep. "When you get back," Ivy said, "if you've had a little more progress, we might try rupturing the membranes."

Rhonda nodded, and the couple went out.

Cullen rose from where he'd been sitting with Gabriela and approached Ivy. "How's the midwife holding out?"

"All right." In reality, she was feeling some of the exhaustion of early pregnancy. "You know, I think I'll nap until they come back. When you hear them, will you wake me?"

"Sure."

BY THREE IN THE MORNING, Rhonda was ready to push. She sat back in her bed with Chad holding her, while Ivy supported the baby's head, making sure it wasn't born so quickly that Rhonda would tear.

When the head was born, Ivy discovered the cord around the baby's neck, explained the situation to Rhonda and asked her to pant. "Rhonda, I'm going to loosen the cord and try to slip it over his shoulder. I can keep it loose enough for him to be born safely, and then we'll unwrap it." A few moments later, she

said, "Okay, Rhonda, you can push now. You're doing great."

As the baby was born, Ivy guided it into a sort of
somersault, to keep his head close against Rhonda and
not tighten the cord. Gabriela watched its wet pink
body come into the world as she'd watched Devon's
baby being born. *How could I ever have thought birth
was gross?* she wondered. It was totally amazing!
"He's so cute."

Her mother unwound the cord and said, "Oh, look
at you, you sweet little boy." Gently, Ivy placed the
baby on Rhonda's stomach.

Chad twisted around to see the baby's face. "Look
at him. Oh, wow!"

Rhonda touched her new son. "He's beautiful. Dylan. Dylan Jason Davy."

"You did so well, Rhonda," Ivy said, watching
carefully for vaginal bleeding, for signs the placenta
was coming.

Cullen asked, "Would you like some photos?"

"We can't buy 'em." Rhonda didn't lift her head.

"I give them away to new moms and dads."

"Thanks," Chad said, posing beside Rhonda with
a big grin. "Thanks a lot."

ON THE WAY HOME, Ivy said, "So now I have a res-
ident photographer."

"I think every couple should get the chance to have
photos of their newborn and whatever photos of the
birth they want."

Ivy briefly covered his gearshift hand and smiled tiredly at the man to whom she'd renewed her vows.

In the back seat, Gabriela said, "That was the cutest baby I ever saw."

Her dad said, "Oh, I've seen one I think was cuter."

"Mom?"

"Yes?"

"Do you think by the time our baby is born, I could catch it?"

"I think that's very possible. Barring any big problems, you can certainly help."

Gabriela shivered with excitement. In her heart, she knew how it would be, and she couldn't wait.

AFTER GABRIELA HAD GONE to bed, Ivy and Cullen made quiet love up in the loft. Later, holding her, Cullen said, "Renewing our vows was a good idea. You know, I went to the river to throw out one of our old wedding photos, like I was going to throw out the first years of our marriage, and I couldn't do it. I have no regrets, Ivy. Not one. I loved you then, and I love you now."

These words, more than anything yet, brought her a feeling of peace with herself. With her past, with her present, with her future as his wife and Gabriela's mother and the mother of the baby inside her.

"That makes two of us," she said. "With no regrets."

CHAPTER FIFTEEN

GABRIELA'S THIRTEENTH birthday fell two weeks before she left for New York. She would stay with her great-aunt Chloe, her grandmother's sister, and early in July her parents would come stay in the city for a week to spend time with her.

They'd decided to have her birthday party at home, and Tara drove up from Texas; Francesca wasn't able to come with so many clients due. After dinner, they all sat in the sunroom listening to the sound of insects outside, and Gabriela opened her presents, choosing Tara's first. Before unwrapping the purple tissue paper, Gabriela read the handmade card that said, "To the coolest girl I know. Love, Tara." She opened the package and drew out a hand-painted T-shirt bearing the legend "Mountain Midwifery" and pictures of many of the herbs she'd picked with her mother. "Look—nettles! And a raspberry bush!"

Tara said, "You can advertise your mom's business and tell people about midwifery if you want. It's big, so you can wear it over your dance clothes or to bed or whatever."

"I love it!" She did, too. She helped her mom so much she was part of Mountain Midwifery anyhow.

The next package, from her parents, contained

some CDs she wanted. Then her dad gave her a framed picture of him and her mom. The last package was from her mom, and it was pretty heavy.

Her mother sat beside her on the wood-frame couch in the sunroom as Gabriela untied the ribbons on the yellow tissue-paper package. Her mother had tucked dried flowers into the ribbon, and Gabriela couldn't help smiling at her. Her mom was so special.

She removed the tissue paper carefully and opened the box. "Oh, wow!" On top were new copies of *Spiritual Midwifery* and *Heart and Hands*. Beneath was her great-grandmother's midwifery book, with handwritten notes on different types of deliveries.

She grabbed her mom and hugged her. "I love you. This is the best present ever."

LATE THAT NIGHT, after her family members from Coalgood had stopped by with more gifts for Gabriela, Tara and Ivy sat curled up in the sunroom to talk.

"So, how's Mom doing with the new landlord?"

"He's given her notice that after December, when her lease expires, he'll be renting the Victorian to skiers on a weekly basis."

"*What?* That beautiful house? He's out of his mind."

"Mom says he wants the money. It's making her sick, you can tell. For the time being, she's even stopped arguing with me about my coming back there."

That had been a real sticking point between the two

of them. Francesca was for law and order; Tara believed in a woman's right to have her babies wherever and with whatever attendant she wished. And Francesca had voiced to Ivy her concern that Tara's arrival in Precipice could hurt her own reputation; Tara was a well-trained and experienced midwife, but she wasn't licensed to attend births in Colorado. Only certified nurse-midwives were.

"Well, can you really find a place to live? Will *she* be able to find another place to live?"

"She's looking already, but it's too early. And she can't afford to buy a house in Precipice. Who can?"

"No kidding." Ivy changed the subject tentatively. "So, I don't suppose you've met any interesting men in Sagrado?"

Tara laughed and shook her head. "You think I *want* a man?"

"Still hurting over Danny?"

"It doesn't hurt anymore."

"Even that he and Solange are having a baby?"

Tara made a face. "That has a tendency to evoke disgust in me, I have to admit. But I mostly get angry. No, I don't feel hurt."

Ivy wondered if Tara had ever given in to her feelings of hurt about Danny. She'd never shown them to Ivy. "I think the move to Precipice might be a good thing for you."

"Sure, I can meet someone rich and drive a Hummer and build my own birth clinic."

Ivy giggled at the picture Tara painted, and Tara laughed, too.

"Not," she concluded.

"We'll see," Ivy teased. "Or maybe it'll be the landlord-OB/GYN."

"Never."

"What if he's like Michel Odent?" Ivy named the French physician who'd long been an advocate for natural births and water births.

Tara kissed the air. "Well, *that* would change everything. But it's hardly what I expect from the greedy low-life scum who's kicking Mom out of her home."

AT THE FIRST boarding call, which included children traveling alone, Ivy and Cullen hugged Gabriela and walked with her to the airline representative who would be responsible for her until Aunt Chloe met her at the airport in New York.

After introducing Gabriela to the attendant and exchanging the paperwork, Ivy hugged her once more. "I love you. You can call us any time you want, any hour of the day or night."

Gabriela's smile said she was unlikely to call them at all.

Her dad hugged her next. "I'll miss you."

"I'll miss you, too. Both of you."

It was time to part. Gabriela carried her tote bag slung over her shoulder. She looked older and more self-assured than thirteen.

When she'd disappeared from sight, Ivy said, "We should watch the plane take off."

"Yes."

As they stood beside a window, arms around each other, and watched the plane finally move away from the gate, Ivy said, "You know, I never think of her as Matthew's and my child. Never. I sometimes completely forget that she's not your biological child."

Sometimes, rarely, Cullen forgot, too. He said, "I couldn't love her more. She's wonderful." He turned Ivy to face him. "And speaking of people I couldn't love more..."

"I hurt you, Cullen. I'll never forget that fact."

"But I forgive you." His eyes were on hers. "Completely and forever."

They turned to the window and watched the plane lift into the sky, carrying Gabriela to her dreams.

EPILOGUE

October

"SHELBY, YOU'RE DOING beautifully."

Ivy held Shelby's eyes through the next contraction while Matthew supported his wife as she sat on a beanbag chair and leaned back against him. Gabriela knelt beside her mother, and a camera shutter clicked.

"Gabriela, put your hands here." Ivy showed her how to push gently against the baby's head to slow the delivery. "Shelby, you can push. Try to do it in a long breath. Push with your breath. We want the head to come out slow and easy."

Between contractions, Ivy placed hot compresses on Shelby's perineum.

When the baby's head was born, Gabriela checked to make certain the cord wasn't around the neck. The baby's head rotated toward Shelby's right thigh, and as the shoulders came through, the infant opened its mouth in a yawn or a silent cry. There was the click of a camera.

The infant had been born into Gabriela's arms, and she carefully brought his slippery body up onto Shelby's stomach. She felt a sense of holiness. After a summer spent dancing, this was a different world, and she felt it tugging her in, pulling at her. *Oh, God, beautiful baby, beautiful birth.*

"A boy," Matthew said. "Look at him, Shelby."

A peacefulness settled on the two parents and their child, and Gabriela half leaned against her mother while Cullen photographed the new family and Ivy twisted around to see the baby's face again.

Behind his wife and daughter, Cullen lowered the camera and met his brother's eyes, and they were open and warm and filled with love for those around him.

Turn the page for an excerpt from
Margot Early's second book in the
Midwives miniseries—

TALKING ABOUT MY BABY

Watch for it next year!

PROLOGUE

Maternity House
Sagrado, Texas

DECEIT COULD BE BOTH survival and a way of life, and so it was for the girl who called herself Julia, who had come across the river to have her baby in the clinic, the Maternity House, on the United States side of the river. Tara Marcus knew this about Julia soon after meeting her. The lies were a survival mechanism, and there was no point in arguing with survival.

"I saw the owl," Julia said. "It flew over the river as we were crossing. I am going to die. Having the baby will kill me. I know it."

Spanish had become automatic to Tara; she understood it as readily as English, and she followed the teenager's words effortlessly.

"An owl came to me the day my mother died, too," Julia continued. "But this one was for me."

The border taught respect for superstition. If Julia *had* seen an owl, Tara would have worried; owls portended death. But there was something about Julia's eyes.... Living the way Julia probably lived on the other side of the river made a person lie; it was better to invent a fiction, even a name. Truth had no purpose down there, while lies did; they increased the odds that the person who told them would live to see the next morning.

Now, even glowing in the first stage of labor, Julia's eyes were desperate, and they did not distinguish lie from truth. Every word from this woman's mouth could be a lie, perhaps even into transition, perhaps through the birth of her child.

She wasn't afraid, either.

Tara held her hand because it would have been natural for a girl this young, maybe sixteen, to be afraid—but where Julia had come from was so much worse.

"Promise me," Julia said. "Promise me that if I die you will take my baby and raise it. Swear on your mother's grave."

"My mother isn't dead."

"On your father's grave."

Tara grinned. "He's around, too—and so will you be." She sobered. "Julia, there are adoption services. Are you worried you won't be able to care for your baby?"

"I would never give my baby to someone else! Not unless I am dead! *I* will take care of my baby. This baby's father is a diplomat. He is descended from Pancho Villa. My mother…my mother's family was very wealthy in Mexico City."

"Relax," Tara murmured. She smoothed Julia's hair. "I'm on your side."

The touch electrified Julia. Eyes round and dark,

she clutched Tara's fingers, tightly enough to make the bones crunch. "Then promise! Swear you will keep my baby."

"I'm divorced. No man. Always broke. Midwives make no money."

"You're *rich*."

You'll lose this argument, Tara. Where she comes from, you're filthy rich, like all Americans. Just drop it. She grabbed a blood-pressure cuff and fitted it around the expectant girl's arm. There had been no protein in her urine, but Tara checked for edema anyway. Julia's hair looked dry and dirty, without luster.

"Promise, please, that you will care for my baby."

I have to get away from the border. And she was going, just in time. The desensitization was happening. Another midwife at the clinic had told her, "You give and give and give, and then suddenly it's gone." It wasn't gone yet, but...

But I look in this girl's eyes and see only deceit and not her fear.

Only pointless lies instead of survival lies.

"Okay. Okay, I promise."

"Swear." She glowed, powerful already in labor. "Swear on the names of your mother and father."

"I swear on the name of my mother, Francesca Walcott, and my father, Charlie Marcus, that I will care for your child in the event of your death." The words sent a chill over Tara.

Especially because Julia still squinted at her with a look of dissatisfaction.

TARA STAYED at the birth center for forty-eight hours, catching sleep when she could in the sleeping nook off the staff room. She attended eight births; four of the mothers had arrived with pre-eclampsia. These were not the uncomplicated births that her mother, Francesca, saw in her midwifery practice in Colorado. Even working in rural West Virginia, Tara's sister, Ivy, had the opportunity to give prenatal counseling.

But when women crossed the Rio Grande and arrived at the birth center to have their babies, they were often visiting the United States for the first time. They had risked their lives to cross so that their children would be born in the U.S.—and become citizens.

Like Julia.

Julia had left the clinic that evening, with her baby daughter, Laura Estrella. She had departed without telling anyone, as though afraid she'd be held to pay for the services she'd received.

You couldn't wonder where she'd gone or if she and her child would be safe.

The sky was starry, and as she walked to her car, a rusty dark green Safari station wagon bought from a local rancher, Tara could make out the lights of the border-patrol stations just a mile away—as well as the neon from the bars in town. In Colorado, it would be cold now. But October on the border—balmy.

Her car was as she'd left it last, when she came out the day before to throw soiled clothes in the back seat. Bats fluttered near the parking-lot lights. One winged close to her ear as she casually checked the station wagon and got in.

Music... Rock and roll to take her home.

Jackson Browne. *I love you, Jackson.* Her fantasy man. She sang with him as she reversed out of her space, ready to head back to the trailer. Her heart pounded the lonely rhythm of her nonworking hours.

I wish the best for Danny and Solange and little Kai. I do not resent their love for each other. I do not resent that they have a baby.

It was two years since he'd told her. It didn't help that he and Solange hadn't consummated their desire for each other at the time, that they hadn't physically betrayed her. Sometimes she wished they had. Instead, they both expected her to appreciate their self-restraint.

Now they were living in Hawaii with their new baby.

The road to the trailer court was dark and poor and unpaved, and as she reached the turn, a low-rider spun out of the drive, spitting dust in the night. It backfired, and a cat meowed.

No, not a cat. Not a meow.

The short hairs under Tara's ponytail lifted.

She should pull over.

The baby cried again.

The baby was in her car.

And she didn't have to look over her shoulder at the back seat to know whose baby it was.

HARLEQUIN SUPERROMANCE®

DEBORAH'S SON

by award-winning author
Rebecca Winters

Deborah's pregnant. The man she loves—the baby's
father—doesn't know. He's withdrawn from her for reasons
she doesn't understand. But she has to tell him. *Wants* to tell
him. She wants them to be a family.

Available in October
wherever Harlequin books are sold.

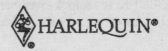

HARLEQUIN®

Look us up on-line at: http://www.romance.net

HSR9ML

SEXY, POWERFUL MEN NEED
EXTRAORDINARY WOMEN WHEN THEY'RE

Destined for Love

Take a walk on the wild side this October
when three bestselling authors weave wondrous stories
about heroines who use their extraspecial abilities to
achieve the magic and wonder of love!

HATFIELD AND McCOY
by HEATHER GRAHAM POZZESSERE

LIGHTNING STRIKES
by KATHLEEN KORBEL

MYSTERY LOVER
by ANNETTE BROADRICK

Available October 1998
wherever Harlequin and Silhouette books are sold.

HARLEQUIN®
Makes any time special ™

Silhouette®

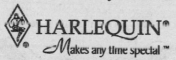

HARLEQUIN SUPERROMANCE®

FINDERS, KEEPERS

is a detective agency that specializes in finding lost lovers, friends, family, etc...

If Noah had been adventurous enough to discover the world and himself, he could be adventurous enough to visit an agency that specialized in finding lost lovers. But meeting Maggie Tyrell, proprietor, was an adventure in itself. However, Maggie wouldn't be deterred from the task at hand—even if Noah wanted her to call off the search. *Even if it meant her heart would break...*

Found: One Wife

**Harlequin Superromance (#809)
October 1998**

by Judith Arnold

Available wherever Harlequin books are sold.

◆ HARLEQUIN®

MEN at WORK

All work and no play?
Not these men!

July 1998
MACKENZIE'S LADY by Dallas Schulze

Undercover agent Mackenzie Donahue's
lazy smile and deep blue eyes were his best
weapons. But after rescuing—and kissing!—
damsel in distress Holly Reynolds, how could
he betray her by spying on her brother?

August 1998
MISS LIZ'S PASSION by Sherryl Woods

Todd Lewis could put up a building with ease,
but quailed at the sight of a classroom! Still,
Liz Gentry, his son's teacher, was no battle-ax,
and soon Todd started planning some
extracurricular activities of his own....

September 1998
A CLASSIC ENCOUNTER
by Emilie Richards

Doctor Chris Matthews was intelligent, sexy
and *very* good with his hands—which made
him all the more dangerous to single mom
Lizette St. Hilaire. So how long could she
resist Chris's special brand of TLC?

Available at your favorite retail outlet!

MEN AT WORK™

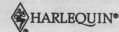 

Look us up on-line at: http://www.romance.net

PMAW2

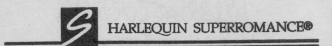

COMING NEXT MONTH

#806 A MAN CALLED JESSE • K.N. Casper
Love That Man!
Jesse Amorado is a proud man determined to preserve his community—the barrio in Coyote Springs, Texas. Developer Winslow Carr has other plans for the area: tearing it down. Winslow's daughter, Tori, is now a partner in the firm and is an even greater threat to Jesse's peace of mind. Because Tori makes him think of other kinds of partnerships—the kind that last for life.

#807 A FATHER'S VOW • Peg Sutherland
Hope Springs
Will Travers left Hope Springs almost ten years ago. Accused of a crime he didn't commit, he tried to make a life for himself in another city. But now he's faced with raising his son on his own, and he realizes there's no better place to do that than his hometown. Even if it means facing his accuser, Libby Jeffries—the only person who can help him make enough sense of the past to give his son a future.

#808 DEBORAH'S SON • Rebecca Winters
9 Months Later
Deborah loves only one man—a man she expected to marry. But Ted Taylor rejected her for reasons she doesn't understand. Hard as it is on her pride and her heart, she *has* to see him again, has to tell him she's pregnant with his son.

A deeply emotional story by the author of *Until There Was You.*

#809 FOUND: ONE WIFE • Judith Arnold
Finders, Keepers
Noah had been adventurous enough to discover the world—so he could certainly be adventurous enough to visit an agency that specialized in finding lost loves. But meeting Maggie Tyrell, proprietor, was an adventure in itself. Noah soon discovered he was less interested in finding the woman he *thought* he'd loved than in finding out more about the fiery self-styled love detective!